FOOLISH games

A CARTWRIGHT
BROTHER ROMANCE

lilliana ANDERSON

INTERNATIONALLY BESTSELLING AUSTRALIAN AUTHOR

FOOLISH GAMES

CARTWRIGHT BROTHERS, BOOK 3

LILLIANA ANDERSON

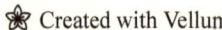

For the fools who love a good time

Whenever I think about the experience of writing this book, I think about that joke, 'I just flew in from out of town and boy, are my arms tired.' It's not that I had to do a lot of travelling during the course of this book, it's just that I had terrible muscle pain from the hours I spent at my computer, deleting then rewriting, deleting then rewriting.

I scrapped over half of this book—twice! Why? Because Ronnie was a really difficult character to write, and if her words didn't sound authentic to her, I didn't want them in the book. But, we got there in the end. Early readers have been telling me that Foolish Games is their favourite Cartwright book yet.

It's funny, it's intense, it's *sexy*. And it's also bitter-sweet because it marks the halfway point of our Fool Series journey. Two more fools to go. I think we're all going to miss them.

Take heart, we get to enjoy the journey together. And what a journey it is.

I hope you enjoy, *Foolish Games.*

CHAPTER ONE
MACGYVER IS FULL OF SHIT

"BUM A SMOKE?"

Maree squinted in my direction as she leaned against the building, one arm across her middle, the other angled toward her mouth, menthol cigarette hanging loose between her fingers.

"Hey Ronnie," she said, reaching into her pocket to pull out the gold packet with a green band around the bottom. She handed it to me. "Want one?" Her voice was so raspy, the kind of sound only those with a serious nicotine habit developed after years of abusing their lungs. It was kinda sexy if I was being honest.

"You ever thought about being a phone sex operator, Maree?" I asked, placing the cigarette between my lips. I lit up and inhaled while she gave me a sidelong glance that said, *"You've got to be kidding me."*

"I'm serious." I laughed, the fresh cool feeling of the menthol coating my mouth as the receptors in my brain fired up. I didn't generally smoke menthols, but beggars couldn't be choosers as my mother always said. "You'd be great at it."

"Why would I want to talk to some random guy while he jerked off in my ear? That would be the worst job ever."

"Worse than waiting tables wedding after wedding while drunkards grab your arse and call you 'sweetheart'?"

She bounced her shoulders on her wiry frame as she sucked her cigarette down to the butt. "I'm far too old for any guy to grab my arse, drunk or sober," she said, smoke popping out of her thin lips with each word. "And this job is OK. It pays the bills while Daz is still finding his feet."

"*Still* nothing?" I asked, watching her stub the butt with the toe of her black dress shoe.

"Nah. That ex of yours pissed off and still no one will work with Daz. This going straight stuff is for the birds, I tell ya. If I ever find the guys with the Ute, I'll have their balls and make myself a nice necklace out of them."

Laughing through my nose at the mental image of a testicle necklace, I nodded in agreement. We'd both seen some hard times over the past year. And I put the blame for that squarely at the feet of a certain group of brothers. Life was much better before they came along. Sure, *I* was the one who took *their* car. But *they* took it back, and it should have ended there—they didn't need to ruin our lives over it too.

"Why don't *you* do phone sex if you need the money?" she asked, flicking her faded blonde hair out of her eyes.

"Because I don't have a sexy rasp to my voice like you do."

That made her grin. "You could do that video sex then. You know the ones where they pay you to touch yourself?

I'd do that if I was still twenty-seven and had great tits like you. Reckon I'd rake it in. Sex sells you know."

"Nah. I don't have a computer."

"What happened to the one you had?"

"Those dickheads stole it from me when they took their Ute back." Although, to be fair, I'd stolen it originally when some kid decided to use the restroom in a coffee shop and just left it there on the table. I walked past and *yoink,* I tucked it under my arm like it belonged to me. Too easy. I had a habit of taking things left unattended, and a sweet-looking MacBook was too hard to pass up. Still, I was pissed that it was gone. I had to watch Netflix on my phone now.

Glancing at her watch, Maree gave me another shrug. "Sucks to be you, hey? I guess you're stuck here working with me. *Sweetheart.*" Her mouth kicked up at the side just before she slapped me on the side of the thigh.

"Fuck you, old lady," I teased, smiling because despite our twenty-year age difference, she was probably my favourite person. She was also my boss, and didn't look like an old lady at all. She just looked like someone who didn't sleep much, smoked, and drank a lot.

She laughed at my dig and opened the side door. "Better finish up. They'll start arriving for the reception in about ten minutes. Don't want the guests to find us out here smoking. Anyone bitches, I might lose my job, and I doubt anyone else would put up with *your* slacker attitude and criminal history."

Showing her my half-finished cigarette, I smiled as I flipped her my middle finger. She laughed.

"I won't be much longer."

She nodded. "See you inside."

Taking my time with the cigarette, I looked out at the parking lot. There were a couple dozen cars in it, mostly belonging to employees. Pretty soon, it would be full of random vehicles, all belonging to the friends and family of the happy couple.

Happy couples. They made me want to vomit. I'd seen so many of them in the several months I'd worked here. They gazed into each other's eyes, and linked arms to do that stupid champagne-drinking thing. So sweet it made me sick. I was never going to get married. So far, every guy I'd ever dated had been nothing but a disappointment. In high school, I dated guys my own age, and they just turned out to be morons who wanted sex to crow about. Then I started dating older guys, because I hoped they'd be more mature, and maybe they would, I don't know, be stable enough to take care of me somehow. But that was a bust. *I* ended up feeling like the moron in that situation. Now I just focused on keeping my own shit together. It was better when I quit thinking about anyone else. No one counted on me, and in turn, I didn't count on anyone else either. It was easier that way. I was fine. Whatever fine was supposed to be…

Finishing my cigarette, I dropped it on the ground and stubbed it out where Maree had. Then I kicked both butts into the garden and turned to head inside. Just as I opened the door, the flash of sun against a windscreen drew my attention. *And here they come.*

Normally, I'd go straight in and give everyone a heads-up, but this time, I stood and watched. Familiarity kept me rooted in place as a Ute, a burnt-orange colour with grey accents, pulled into a parking spot. *Holy shit. It's him.*

A little under a year ago, I was dating a guy named

Johno. He wasn't much into the whole nine-to-five gig, but he was really good at stealing cars. I wasn't too bad at it either. Working with Maree's husband, Dazza, we were making bank, taking a car once a month and selling it off. It was a sweet life. We were happy. But then I spotted an opportunity to get my hands on *that* particular car—a Holden Ute that was less than twelve months old. The owner left his keys in plain sight while he taught some girl how to surf. He basically begged me to take his ride. So, I did. Next thing I knew, there were two dudes and a chick breaking into our house to steal the Ute back.

They took it, my computer, and my Beats. Then they tied me up, beat Johno until he passed out, and made it pretty clear they'd kill us if we ever crossed them again. After that, we couldn't sell food to the starving.

And now, after becoming the reason my life was in the toilet, the Ute guy was parked maybe fifteen metres away from me. Maree would have a fit when I told her he was here. She'd also need to get her testicle-cutting knife ready.

My jaw ached from clenching my teeth so hard. But I couldn't tear my gaze away waiting for the driver's door to open. I couldn't breathe, my heart beating so hard it hurt my ears. Then he was outside, larger than life, the monster under my bed, looking just like a man. He was taller than I remembered, his huge body unfolding itself as he straightened and looked around with a dimpled smile, pulling sunglasses from eyes so blue I could see them from here. So carefree. His dark brown hair had grown—before it was cropped close to his head, but now it was short at the sides and longer on top, styled so it looked like he'd run his hands through it and it just stayed like that. *I hate people who look so effortlessly good.* He wore a suit that moulded to his body like it was made of liquid, showcasing some crazy big muscles.

He was hot. *Ridiculously* hot.

I hated him even more.

Anger flared inside my chest. So what if he was good-, no, *great*-looking? He messed with my life and he needed to pay for that…somehow. But, what was I going to do? I could go over there and kick a dent into the side of his stupid car right in front of him. Or, I could spit in his food, fill his glass with toilet water, trip him so he fell into the wedding cake. There were so many choices. But damaging his car felt the most cathartic. I really wanted to kick that thing.

Clenching my fists at my side, I set my shoulders and started marching in his direction. I didn't care about him seeing me. I didn't care about losing my job. I only cared about vengeance. I barely made it five steps when more cars turned up, and I froze where I stood. People started getting out; a couple of guys who looked related to the first. Older brothers, I guessed. I'd seen one of them at the beach during an altercation with Ute guy. But the other one I'd never seen before. He held open his car door and helped an overweight blonde woman out. Then they all stood together and spoke before they stopped and looked at the Ute as the passenger door opened. I thought it was going to be the woman I'd seen Ute guy with on a couple of occasions, but it wasn't a woman at all, it was another man—another brother—and he looked *exactly the freaking same as the first guy.* Twins. The arsehole had a twin brother.

Double the hotness.

Shut up, brain.

"What are you still doing out here?" Maree's voice snapped me out of my vengeful thoughts.

"Um…" I started, trying to decide what to tell her. She didn't know these guys by sight. Did I tell her who they were now, or wait until the end of shift? While I was willing to risk my own job by kicking the crap out of the Ute, I didn't want to risk hers too. She had a mortgage to pay. "I was, um…"

"Whoa," she said, looking in the same direction as me. "Is that the bridal party? They look like those guys on the stripper cruises. Stupid hot." She placed her hand on her chest like she might swoon.

"Yeah," I said simply.

"Ha! Look at *you*. You're speechless over them. Bet you wouldn't mind one of them grabbing your arse and calling you sweetheart," she crowed, nudging me in the arm with her elbow and giving me a lewd smile.

Giving her an awkward laugh, I shook my head and turned away from the parking lot. It took some effort to uncurl my fists, crescent marks from my nails stinging my palms. "Let's just get back in there, hey?" I suggested, deciding it was best to wait. Doing something now, telling her who they were, it would just do more damage to us. And we'd already suffered enough.

C…

Pressing my fingers against the length of my key, I forced the point through the copper-coloured paint. It took a bit of effort—that paint protection stuff wasn't easy to get through—but I was making headway. The letter was looking nice and bold, carved into the driver's door.

Turned out I couldn't wait. On top of being fond of five-finger discounts, I also had impulse control problems. Sue me. Seeing them inside, knowing the car was here, I had no choice but to satisfy my itch.

To my credit, I waited for my break and made sure the coast was clear before I came out. The only person who knew I was here was me. I took great delight in messing with these guys when they weren't aware of it.

U…

Ten bucks to guess what I was writing. It was fitting. The guy was definitely a cunt. He and his family obviously had a shitload of money based on the cars they drove and the size of this wedding reception. From what I heard inside, it wasn't even the first wedding. This was a vow renewal after the couple had been married for *a year.* I mean, who the fuck did that? Worse was the fact that the couple in question were the other two that had stolen the Ute back from Johno and me. Alesha and Sam Cartwright. And after the speeches, I learned that the twins were called Kristian and Abbot—although, I had no idea who was who, because they had the same hair and the same outfit on because they were groomsmen—and the other two brothers were Nate and Toby. The woman I'd seen get out of the car was Holland, and she was the matron of honour. I wasn't sure if I should hate her by association, but decided it was best to just have a blanket loathing for all people with the Cartwright surname. Seemed a safe bet to me.

Serving dinner wasn't a lot of fun. I had to work the back table and keep my head down so none of them recognised me. I had to keep trading jobs with someone every time I was required to do something that involved going near the bridal party. Freaking nightmare.

Those people seemed to have everything anyone could ever want. The happiness displayed between Alesha and Sam was like acid at the base of my throat. Kristian and Abbot were those classic boy's boys—you know those guys in a group who are the life of the party everyone loves to be around? That was them. They had the attitude of men who didn't have a care in the world, everything was a joke, everything was a good time. It didn't seem fair. They had everything and I had nothing. They took far more from me than I ever took from them. *It isn't fair.*

I pressed my key harder against the door, hitting metal. You couldn't tell me that they didn't have insurance for this thing, that they couldn't have just reported it stolen like every other person would and left us the hell alone. It would have been win-win: they'd get another new car and Johno and I would have still been OK. I'd still have a roof over my head and none of this would even be a problem.

"Stupid rich pricks," I muttered, working on the lower part of the U then pushing the key upward to finish it off. I could hear the music playing inside, the dance floor filled with semi-drunk guests reliving their youth while dancing to Vanilla Ice. They'd move on to Salt-N-Pepa soon. It was always the same. My head ached.

Almost ready to start on the N, I blew away the paint dust to check on the U's boldness. I wanted this guy to drive around town letting everyone know exactly what he was without anyone having to squint.

A throat cleared behind my right shoulder, and I froze.

Crap.

Slowly, I turned my head and looked up, up, until I found myself locking eyes with one of the brothers. He looked like he was late thirties, early forties with bright blue eyes and super neat hair. *Toby*. He'd given the shortest speech and been the quietest out of the Cartwright bunch. I'd noted the look of discomfort on his face a few times throughout the night. Maybe the grass wasn't so green on *his* side of the fence.

He tilted his head inquisitively and folded his arms across his big chest, leaning on the BMW sedan parked next to the Ute.

I palmed my keys and stood bolt upright, hiding them behind my back. "Can you believe this?" I said in a rush. "I'm shocked, to be honest. This is a classy establishment and this kind of thing isn't common here. I'm just taking photos to show management so we can get the owner compensated."

Toby lifted his brow so I knew he wasn't buying a single word of what I was selling. *Well, it was worth a try.*

"You were taking photos?" he asked. "With your keys?"

"There's a tiny camera inside them. For close-ups," I squeaked, and I swore the corner of his mouth twitched.

I should run.

Run, you idiot!

Turning on my heel, I took off—well, that *was* the plan. Instead, I took a single step, probably only a half step if I'm honest, before he caught me by the arm and pulled me to his side.

"I think you need to come with me."

"I'd rather *make* you come first." I wasn't above

offering sexual favours to get myself out of a sticky situation.

He quirked a brow. "You couldn't handle me."

"Is that a challenge?"

"It's a fact, little girl."

I tried to tug my arm free, but his grip was like a vice. "I'm not a little girl."

"Is that why you're acting out like one?" He started towards the function centre doors, pulling me along with him.

"I wasn't acting out. I was simply advertising a fact." I ran along beside him, knowing from experience not to bother fighting. It wouldn't get me anywhere. When I first came in contact with this family, I'd tried to fight against the groom—Sam—and he'd simply held me under his arm while I kicked and punched and twisted until I gave up and just hung in place. You know how *The Rock* is this massive dude and everyone around him looked like children by comparison? That was basically how the Cartwrights were too—a family of Rocks. I was like a hobbit next to them. Minus the hairy feet, thank God.

"A fact?" He met my eyes. "What'd Kristian do? Fuck you and forget to call?"

I scoffed. "I would *never*." OK, so the twin I was after was Kristian. At least that was cleared up. Although, I still had to work out how to tell them apart.

"Then why is he a cunt? That's what you were writing, correct?" I opened my mouth to respond just as recognition lit up his eyes. "Wait. I know you. You're the girl with the colourful language…the one from the beach. You stole Kris's car, right?"

"And he stole it back."

"So you should be even."

"It's not that simple. He took more than just the car."

"Because you took his money." I may have stolen his wallet too.

"He still took more."

"You're playing a dangerous game, girl." The muscle in his jaw ticked as he pulled me inside the function centre then looked around. "What's in there?" He pointed at a door near reception.

"Linens."

He pulled me towards it then pushed me inside.

"Oh, kinky," I said as the light flicked on. "I thought you said you were too much for me."

"I need you to come to the foyer, second door to the right of reception." At first I thought he was talking to me, but then I saw his phone pressed to his ear. "We've got a problem."

I shrugged. "I've been called worse things in my life."

He pointed a finger at me. "Stay."

I barked.

He rolled his eyes and left the room. Normally, I'd wait a couple of minutes and leave, but I had a feeling he was on the other side of the door waiting for whomever he called.

Pressing my ear to the door, my suspicion was confirmed when I heard Toby relaying the details of our meeting to someone, the words 'your car' telling me it was Kristian, AKA my nemesis.

"Are you fucking serious?"

"Kris!" Then a sigh.

"What's his problem?" A new voice entered the conversation and Toby relayed the information again.

"Oh shit." The other guy chuckled. "Not his precious Ute."

"He's out there having an aneurysm over it now."

"I should film it so we can laugh later."

"Don't." I heard a thwack, like someone just got hit in the arm or something.

"Fine. What'd you do with the girl?"

"She's in there."

My heart leapt into my throat, and I jumped away from the door so I wouldn't be caught eavesdropping. I leaned against the shelving casually just as the other twin, Abbot, opened the door.

"Fuck you," I said when I met his eyes. He laughed and shut the door. I rushed back over and pressed my ear to it again.

"She seems like a sweetheart. What are we gonna do about her?"

"That's up to Kris."

"What's up to Kris?" Another voice. Great. Seemed we were having a family reunion over this. Things were explained again.

"That chick's like a cockroach; can't get rid of her."

Thanks, arsehole.

"Don't be stupid, brother." I heard the warning in one of the brother's voices just before there was a scuffle of feet and a growl that said, "Get out of my fucking way." I had about half a second to get out of the way myself before the door burst open and a very angry-looking twin burst through, nostrils flared.

"You are gonna pay," he said, his voice eerily calm as he shoved the door closed and flipped the lock, his brothers urging him to calm down from the other side.

Oh shit. What are you supposed to say before you die? Bless me, Father, for I have sinned? Is that it? Or was that just what you were supposed to say before bed. *Fuck.* I had no clue. I was going to die and go to hell because I didn't pay attention during scripture at school.

Stalking towards me as I skittered backwards, Kristian's eyes narrowed, the redness of anger crawling up his neck.

Oh God.

My back hit the shelving and I gulped. This was the end. He was big enough to snap me like a twig. At least it would be over fast. And really, I'd had a good run. Twenty-seven years of being a less-than-ideal human being, my greatest accomplishment was managing to stay out of prison the whole time. There wouldn't be a great hole left by my absence, not a lot of people mourning my loss—Maree would be upset, but that would pass. It would be OK. Nothing was really tying me to this world.

"Just do it," I forced out, my eyes locked on his blue but dark and stormy ones, my chest heaving as I tried to keep my cool.

He was so close, his hands holding the shelving above my shoulders, caging me in with his thick arms. I could smell his cologne, his skin, the champagne they'd been drinking, a hint of the meal we'd served.

"Are you stupid?" he asked, his voice far calmer than I expected from the aggressive vibe I was getting from him.

I shook my head, but then I said, "Stupid, or stubborn. Take your pick."

He stared and studied my expression. I held my breath.

"The flat tyres, the syphoned tank, they were you too, right?"

I looked away and kept my mouth shut, but yeah, they were me. I fucked with his car every chance I got.

He slammed his hand on the metal shelving, causing me to jump. "Answer!"

I didn't. I just clenched my jaw and met his dark glare. He brought his face so close to mine I could barely focus.

"I'm gonna make you wish you left town." He hit the shelf again then withdrew from me completely, stalking out of the room muttering something about me being lucky I was a girl. *Was I?*

The door opened and slammed shut then all of the air rushed out of my lungs while my blood roared through my ears. Holy fuck, I was so sure he was going to hurt me then.

Breathe, Ronnie. Breathe.

Pulling the elastic from my hair, I ran my hands through the wavy blonde locks and stared at the closed door. I had to figure a way out of this. Sitting in here like a duck wasn't going to work. But how was I supposed to get out with them blocking the door? It was an internal room with no windows. The only way was up. Escaping through the ceiling always worked on TV.

Looking up, there was a fluorescent light and an air conditioning vent set inside sectioned panels. If I used the shelves as a ladder, I might be able to climb between this room and the office next door. It was definitely worth a try.

Working quickly, I pulled the linens from the shelf and set them on the floor, clearing the shelf space then testing it for durability. It was that beige-coloured aluminium shelving that was practical but never pretty. It wobbled a little, but I was fairly sure it would hold my weight—I was five foot six and less than fifty kilos, so there wasn't a lot of me.

Placing my foot on the lowest shelf, I pushed up through my thigh, hefting myself toward the ceiling. *This is going to work. I'll be free in no time.* I smiled, feeling pleased with my ingenuity. MacGyver had nothing on me.

Just as I reached the top, I lifted my arm above my head, pressing my fingers against the panel, expecting it to lift. Except it didn't lift at all. "Come on," I hissed, placing my knee on the very top shelf so I had better leverage. I used my shoulder and back to push more weight against the panel. It resisted, then all at once, it relented with a crack.

"Whoa! *Shit!*"

The shelving tipped back, taking me down with it. I braced myself for the pain, knowing that the concrete floor was going to slam against my body no matter what I did. *I'm going to die.*

I hit the ground with a whack and a loud clang, the air whooshing from my lungs on impact. "MacGyver is full of shit," I muttered. Then my world went black.

THIS IS the way the world ends.
This is the way the world ends.
Not with a bang but a whimper.

I HAD NEVER BEEN MUCH of a student. But that quote always stuck in my head. My English teacher had been crazy passionate and spent a whole lesson talking about the truth and power behind such meaningful words. I guessed it resonated with me on some level, because it was my first conscious thought in a situation where I knew my life, as I'd come to know it, was over. I'd gotten myself into some serious shit this time.

"Is she breathing?"

"I think so." Male voices.

"Where's Leesh? She's good with this stuff."

"She's entertaining the guests with Holland. We can't *all* disappear." The last voice was female.

"What are we going to do with her?" That was another male.

"Kill her." Same female. "I'm not having our family threatened again because some girl doesn't know her place."

Wait, what? Who are they talking about? I cracked my eyes and blurry figures came into view. It took a moment for me to figure out why I was on the floor in the linen closet, but when I looked up and saw the hole in the ceiling, my memory cleared. *Fuck.*

"No." The word came out as a growl. "Scratching up a car doesn't deserve the death penalty. Get your head on straight." I recognised that guy. What was his name again? He didn't want a blowjob...Toby! Toby. I agreed with Toby.

The woman spoke again, and I was pretty sure she was their mother, she had a similar look but was obviously older than the men. "This girl has gotten in the way too many times now. She's a problem."

"You're being insane," Nate said, his arms folded across his broad chest. "Just let her go. We'll make her leave town and the problem is solved."

"As if that's gonna stop her," one of the twins put in. "She's got some lady boner for my Ute." Kristian. "You know, I've had to fix *four* flat tyres over the last six months. *Four.* That can't be a coincidence."

"So get a different Ute," the other twin, Abbot, fired back. "Problem solved."

Shit. I wish life was that easy for all of us.

"I shouldn't have to. She can fucking pay to fix it then leave it the hell alone."

"She's never going to fix it, brother," the tallest one, Sam, said. "Look at her. She's a mess."

"Gee, thanks," I mumbled, pushing up on my elbows to try and sit. My head hurt so bad.

"She's probably got a concussion," the mother said without an ounce of feeling in her voice.

Toby knelt down beside me. "Can you sit?"

I struggled and he helped me up. "Everything hurts."

"Take a deep breath. Is your chest hurting?" I did as he asked and shook my head.

"I think I'm just bruised."

Placing his hands on either side of my face, he looked intently into my eyes. It was kinda unsettling, and I snatched my head away. "What are you doing, creep?"

"Checking to see if you have a concussion. Your pupils are a bit messed up."

"What does that mean?"

"Concussion," the twins said in unison, something told me they had first-hand experience.

"We can't leave her like this," Toby pointed out.

"That's not our problem," the mother said. "She's the idiot who climbed the bloody shelving."

"We should at least make sure she gets home to that boyfriend of hers. What was his name again?" Sam said.

"Johno," Kristian told him, glaring in my direction. *He remembers his name?*

"Johno and I are history. Broke up months ago," I said.

"Lucky Johno," Kristian scoffed.

"Fuck you," I spat. "You don't know anything about me."

He crouched down in front of me, levelling me with his intense blue eyes. I could smell him again, woodsy, manly. *Why are my nipples hard?* "I know you're a piece-of-shit thief who doesn't know what she's doing or *who* she's taking from."

"Well, who the hell are *you*, the newest member of the backstreet boy mob?"

He smiled in a way that was kinda scary before he licked his lips. "I'm the guy who owns your arse."

I scoffed. "Excuse me?"

"Don't you fuckin' dare," Abbot said, shaking his head. "We've just finished with this kind of shit." Maybe as twins they could read each other's minds.

Kristian glanced at his twin and smiled before looking back at me. "You heard me right. You belong to me. Until I decide your debt to me is paid, you're my slave."

"Fuck you," I returned.

He looked me up and down then grimaced before meeting my eyes. "I'm not that desperate."

I glared at him, not sure what the heck to think, or what I was in for. *Should I scream?* That would be pointless. *Should I be scared?* Probably. It was pretty obvious that the Cartwrights weren't the good guys in this situation. I wasn't really sure what that made me. The lesser of two evils?

"Oh for fuck's sake." Our staring competition was interrupted when the mother threw her hands up in the air. "There's a party going on out there and we're ignoring it for this *nuisance*. Do whatever you want with her, Kristian. She's your responsibility so keep her in line. Samuel, Nathaniel, I'm sure your wives are wondering where you are. We're done here." Turning away with a dramatic twist that caused the skirt of her dress to flare, the mother left the room with *Samuel* and *Nathaniel* following her.

"Make sure you sort this shit out," Nate said as a parting note. I noticed Toby clench his jaw and roll his eyes a little. There was definitely tension there.

"Come on," Toby said, his voice gentle as he put an arm around my waist and helped me stand. Pain sliced through my leg and I gasped in shock.

"I think I've twisted my knee."

"Can you stand?"

I nodded. "It just surprised me." I tested my ability to hold my weight then transferred most of it to my other leg.

"Maybe we should get you an X-ray."

"No. I'm fine." The last thing I wanted was to spend all night in emergency when this was more than likely a sprain, or maybe just a jar.

He studied my expression then nodded. "I'll get you home then."

"No," I practically yelled while at the same time Kristian took a hold of my arm.

"You're not taking her anywhere," he argued. "She owes me a new paint job, among other things. The girl is mine."

"Am I the only one who feels like bursting into song right now?" Abbot said, ignored by everyone but me.

Toby kept his eyes on Kristian, his expression creased in a way that showed concern and distaste. "You're walking into the darkness, brother. Once you go down this road, there's no coming back."

Kristian set his jaw then scooped me up in his arms like I was a bag of feathers. "Fuck you, Toby. I'm not gonna rape the girl. What the hell kind of person do you think I am? I'm gonna make her mow lawns and shit until she pays me back. You're so doom and gloom these days."

Wait. What? Mow lawns? Who the hell were these people? I was completely lost.

"Come on, Abbot, we'll take her out to the surf shack, take turns watching her so she doesn't get away or die from a swollen brain or something."

"Wait, you can't take me. I'm supposed to be working." Maree would have a fit when she realised I was gone.

"Don't worry about it," Kristian said. "Tobes'll take care of it."

With that, he carried me out the door, into the parking lot, and over to the desecrated Ute. Abbot followed us, Toby stayed behind. The party kept raging unaware.

"Are you seriously kidnapping me to make me mow lawns?" I asked when Kristian put me in the back seat and clipped me into the seatbelt like I was a child. Although I didn't complain over that. I was actually feeling a little ill and pressed my hand to my stomach.

"Yep," he said simply.

"That's all?"

He met my eyes. "Do you want me to do more?"

"What? No. I just...I don't know, you gave the impression that... Your whole family acted like..." I couldn't really explain. I swore they were all on the same page, and that I was about to punished in any number of ways that bad guys usually punished women. *What the hell is going on?*

"Yeah. I know what you thought, and when you quit messing with us, maybe we'll quit messing with you."

"None of this makes any sense," I whispered. Maybe it was the concussion causing this to feel crazy.

"It doesn't need to," Abbot said, jumping into the

passenger's seat. "All you need to know is that we're in charge and you do as we say."

A sudden wave of nausea rolled through me. "Oh God, I'm gonna be sick."

"Not in the car!" Kristian said, even though it was already too late. It happened before I could stop it. The seat was covered in it.

Abbot coughed and wound down his window. "Following instructions is already a bust."

"Fucking hell," Kristian said before he headed to the back of the Ute and lifted the tray cover. He returned with a towel.

"I'm really sorry," I said, feeling better for puking, but shitty for getting it everywhere.

"It's the concussion," he said as he cleaned it up. I tried to help but he pushed my hands away. "You think you can manage to hold it in for twenty minutes?" The absence of emotion in his voice made me feel even worse. I nodded.

"Good," he said, throwing the towel on the ground behind him. "Because now you owe me a towel *and* you need to clean the car. Looks like we're off to a great start, slave." If I had anything left in my stomach, I might have puked at that. Instead, I was left with a sour taste in my mouth as we drove toward *who the fuck knew what*....

CHAPTER THREE
ALL THE SPACE IN THE ROOM

"MAKE HER LIE DOWN. She's no good to you dead." Abbot and Kristian were arguing while I thanked my lucky stars Kristian's Ute had a leather interior—it made the clean up so much easier. We'd arrived at the quaint little beach house about fifteen minutes before. I'd been immediately shown to the cleaning products and instructed to remove all traces of my mishap. It was hard to do when I kept trying not to puke again.

"When she's finished with the Ute. I don't want it to stink," Kristian replied as he stood and watched me with his arms across his chest. Abbot shook his head.

"Look at her, mate. She's pale as fuck. Let her do it tomorrow."

"I'm almost done," I called out, wiping over the leather to dry it before spraying some deodoriser in the cabin. Then I opened the window a crack to let the fresh air in and closed it up.

"See? She's tougher than you think," Kristian said, walking over to me and taking hold of my upper arm.

It wasn't rough, but it wasn't gentle either. He walked me into the house. "There's a bathroom in there. Get cleaned up and you can sleep on the couch."

"Should I sleep in my clothes?" I pulled at the uniform white button-up I was wearing from work. There was a small stain on the front from my earlier puking incident. It needed to be washed.

"Take a shirt from the second drawer down. We'll get your shit tomorrow."

I baulked. I really didn't want him taking me to 'get my shit'. He didn't need to see where I lived.

"The shirt is fine. Thanks."

"I'm right here listening," he reminded me. "Leave the doors open."

Nodding, I went into what appeared to be the main bedroom, soft blue walls with yellow windowpanes. There was a surfboard with medals hanging off it on the wall and your typical pine bedroom furniture. I wasn't sure if this was Kristian's bedroom or just somewhere he stayed, because it didn't have a lot of personal stuff in it and the drawers he'd directed me to didn't have more than a few items of clothes inside. But it was nice, the kind of house a beach lover would dream of.

Taking my newly acquired shirt into the bathroom, I set it on the towel rack then went to the sink and turned on the tap. I would have preferred a shower, but since I had to leave the doors open, I figured some water and toothpaste would have to do.

When I rinsed out my mouth, I pulled my hair away from my neck and looked in the mirror. I was pale all over and my hazel eyes were sunken. No wonder Abbot was insisting I lie down.

When I stripped off my clothes, I tried to listen for any movement or voices so I'd know how close they were. But all I could hear was the muted sound of a television. Still, to be safe, I dropped the T-shirt over my head and removed my bra through the sleeves so I couldn't be caught half naked. I would have left it on, but I could never sleep with underwire poking into me.

Moving back into the room, I stared longingly at the bed. It had been a long time since I'd been on one, my living situation had been…unusual these past months, and the temptation was simply too much to bear. I walked over and sat down.

"Simple luxury," I whispered as the soft down pressed beneath my thighs. *They won't miss me if I lie here for a few minutes.* Lifting my legs, I lowered myself onto the big pillows and folded my arms across my chest, sighing happily to myself as the bed hugged me like the memory of a better time, a better life. "This feels so good." I revelled in the softness as the aches in my body drifted away, telling myself I was going to go back out there in a minute.

"Just one more minute," I murmured.

A BED. Soft and warm. I wasn't hot. I wasn't cold. Like Goldilocks, I was just right.

I also wasn't alone. *Oh shit! I fell asleep.*

"Where do you think you're goin?" a sleepy voice asked from beside me, his head buried in the pillow, his arm draped across my waist.

Was he spooning me all night?

"Unless you want me to piss the bed, I'm going to the toilet."

He sat up and rubbed his face, looking at me with sleepy eyes. "Go on then." His voice sounded like gravel as he nodded toward the bathroom door.

Swinging my legs out of the bed, I stood carefully, my body aching even more than it did last night, my knee especially. With a limp, I made it to the small en-suite bathroom.

"Leave the door open."

"Seriously?" I said. "The window in here is tiny."

"So are you, doll. And I have zero trust where you're concerned."

"Is that why you hugged me in your sleep all night?"

"That's why I *held you in place* all night. A man needs to sleep without worrying about escaping car thieves."

"That seems like a ridiculous reason, especially since I was supposed to be on the couch."

He shrugged. "You were passed out with a concussion. I didn't know when you'd wake up from it, and I was tired."

"But there's two of you. You could have taken turns or better yet, tie me to the bed so I couldn't escape. Have you never watched a kidnapping movie?"

"You saying you'd rather I tied you to the bed?"

"I'm saying I'd rather you didn't hug me."

His mouth quirked into a grin as he leaned back, holding himself up on his forearms. The angle gave me a perfect view of his shirtless chest, and flexed abs.

Holy heaven and hell, he has the body of a god.

My mouth went dry and I struggled to swallow.

"Just go and pee. I'm not gonna look."

Stepping into the tiny bathroom, I sighed then plopped down on the toilet to do my thing. He couldn't see much more than my legs, but still, it took a moment to get the stream going. Peeing in front of one of my least liked acquaintances sucked.

"So, which one are you anyway?" I called out, hoping conversation would make this a little easier.

"Which one what?"

"Which twin."

"You can't tell already?"

"You look exactly the same to me. Same face, same height, same smile, and same hair."

He laughed. "Yeah. The hair was to tease Alesha, our sister-in-law. It was her wedding yesterday. I used to shave my head and Abs used the have hair to his shoulders. We got the same do just before the wedding for a laugh."

"Did it work?"

"Kinda. She freaked out, but she could still tell us apart."

"How?" I appeared in the doorway after finishing and washing up.

He shrugged. "Mannerisms, I guess. She lived with us for a while, got to know us individually."

"So there's nothing about your looks that's different?"

"Of course there is. I have a freckle on my chin, right here." He lifted his chin up and pointed to the tiny brown fleck. "Abbot does not."

"Lucky I'm short enough to see beneath your chin."

"Lucky I don't care if you can tell us apart or not."

Inhaling slowly, I met his cool gaze, his mouth set in a straight line. I was going to have to be on my guard around him. He flipped from personable to teasing to indifferent quickly and effortlessly. That was fine, I'd handled more than my fair share of irrational men in my time. Johno wasn't all sunshine and roses, and the guy I was with before him got angry when he drank. I could manage Kristian Cartwright.

"How's this supposed to work anyhow?" I asked, folding my arms across my chest. The T-shirt I was wearing was so big it almost touched my knees. "I don't leave your sight until I've mowed enough lawns to cover the cost of your car door?"

He stood up and sniffed. "Something like that."

There was something about seeing a man as enormous as Kristian uncurling his body and straightening his shoulders. It was kind of like watching the Incredible Hulk emerge out of Bruce Banner's body. And judging by the bulge in Kristian's boxer briefs, like Hulk, this guy was big all over.

He sauntered past me, going straight for the toilet where he flopped his dick out and took a leak. He obviously had no shame, and I wasn't about to let him think he was making me uncomfortable. I stood there and looked straight at him as I spoke.

"And how long is that going to take? I have a job, you know? Responsibilities. I don't come from some silver spoon-giving family like you obviously do."

Placing the lid of the toilet down, he flushed then pointed at the closed lid. "Sit."

"Why?"

"Because I want to take a fuckin' shower and I need you where I can see you."

"Why can't Abbot watch me?"

"Because he isn't here. He left last night. Will be back when he's done surfing."

Surfing. I hadn't been in months. I didn't have a board anymore, because I had nowhere to store it. I missed the surf.

I sighed. My arms were still folded over my chest as I moved toward the toilet and sat on the lid. "This is harassment you know."

"And scratching the shit out of my car is vandalism; stealing it and spending my money is theft. Don't use the fucking law on me, doll. We both know we're way past that." He turned the shower on, holding his hand under the spray until steam started to rise and he was happy with the temperature. Then he stripped, completely naked, save for a few leather and twine straps around his wrist, then he got in.

I tried not to look. I really did. But I'd seen the bulge and I wanted to know if he was all balls, or whether his dick took up a chunk of that space too. I was pleased to report that he was *very* well proportioned.

"Take a picture. It'll last longer," he said as he started rubbing soap all over his body.

I crossed my legs, feeling warm in places I probably shouldn't.

"Can't blame a girl for looking, mate. You made me sit here."

He grinned at me through the glass then dipped his hair under the stream, soaping it up then rinsing himself off. The whole thing took about three minutes, but it felt more like half an hour of slow soapy seduction.

I think I need a shower now. A very cold one.

Kristian Cartwright might have been a jerk, but he was

an obscenely good-looking one. His whole family was, actually. It really didn't seem fair that they should all be blessed with such good looks, height, and wealth. It seemed greedy to a short, poor woman who was only decently attractive. They were probably all brilliantly smart too.

Shutting off the water, he ran his hands over his hair then down his arms and body like a squeegee, flicking water off before stepping out of the cubicle and grabbing a towel. As he dried off his hair, I watched the muscles in his arse flex and relax. It was mesmerising.

I forced myself to look away. "So, um, what time do we start this mowing thing?" It was so weird that he wanted me to mow lawns to pay him back.

Securing the towel around his waist he shrugged then walked out of the bathroom.

"Tomorrow."

"What are we supposed to do today?"

"I'll find something for you to do. This place needs a clean."

"So I'm a maid too?"

"You're whatever I want you to be."

"OK. Can I start with the laundry? My work uniform is a mess and I can't really wear this all day." I gestured to the stretched-out shirt.

"I'd rather you didn't wear that one at all. It's actually one of my favourite shirts, and you're messing it up by being inside it."

"You're a jerk," I shot back. "Here. Take your damn shirt." I reached for the hem and pulled it over my head. "I'd rather wear my puke clothes." I threw it at him then noticed how cool the air was against my skin. *Shit*. I didn't think that one through. Now I was standing in front of him wearing nothing but a tiny pair of purple panties.

His Adam's apple bobbed as his eyes took in my chest. One of my more redeeming qualities—*You have a great rack, sweetheart*—as well as my arse. Men were one or the other, and I happened to have a decent set of each.

"Take a picture. It'll last longer," I said, staring straight at him defiantly, my shoulders back. Two could play at this game.

Leaning down, he picked up the shirt and threw it back to me. "Put it back on," he commanded, his voice a little thicker. "It's yours now. You've already ruined it." Then he turned to the chest of drawers and started getting dressed himself, pulling on a pair of camouflage pants and a polo shirt that said 'Cartwright Garden Maintenance'.

"I thought we weren't mowing today."

"I changed my mind."

Unmoving, I wracked my brains for something else to say. I didn't know what I was trying to do or what I was trying to get out of this situation. I just knew I felt stuck and my instincts told me to fight.

"I said get dressed." He glared at me, his jaw ticking.

"Make me." *What the hell am I doing? I shouldn't be taunting a man twice my size!* But, I couldn't help myself.

He inhaled in a way that told me I was really starting to piss him off. His shoulders seemed to get broader and his eyes darker. It seemed his nostrils were flaring too.

"Put the fucking shirt on."

"No." This was half of my problem in life. I had huge issues with authority figures, and every time someone told me to do something, I dug my heels in and refused to budge. It didn't matter if I was right or wrong. I just didn't want to be told.

He stalked toward me, so fast that my eyes fluttered closed expecting some sort of impact. Instead, I felt the breeze of his body as it stopped in front of mine then crouched down, scooping the shirt off the floor. When he stood, his clothing grazed my nipples and I sucked in my breath. Then the shirt came down over my head.

"I said no," I argued, springing to action, pushing the fabric away again.

"Stop behaving like child," he growled, catching me around the waist and keeping the fabric in place.

"I'm not a child. You're just treating me like one."

"That's because you're *behaving* like one."

I bit him.

"Fuck." He jerked back and I threw the T-shirt back on the floor.

"I don't want your fucking shirt," I yelled.

"You're insane," he said, his eyes going wide before he came at me again, this time pushing me onto the bed and pinning me with his knees around my waist. I struggled and scratched, but he caught my hands and forced the shirt over my body. By the time he got it to my waist, we were both panting and out of breath with his hands pinning mine beside my shoulders.

"Get off me, jerk," I spat, twisting my hands beneath his.

He didn't move. He just kept staring at me, drinking me in, the fury in his eyes slowly fading and being replaced by something else: hunger. A heat seemed to build in the air between us, crackling with electricity, growing thicker with each ragged breath. My heart thumped solidly. This was far too intimate. And to add to the insanity, my mind dared him to lean closer and do more than just pin me.

"Kris!" The front door slammed and he jerked back, blinking a couple of times like he was coming out of a trance. I sat up and shook the moment from my head, scowling. *I don't want him. He's nothing but a jerk, same as all the others.*

"In here," he said. Holding his hand out to help me up.

I slapped it away and stood up on my own, pulling the shirt in place and walking straight past him into the bathroom. He didn't stop me this time. He knew what it would have looked like if Abbot saw the state we were in.

"Where is she?" Abbot asked, his voice coming from the bedroom now.

"Bathroom."

I turned on the tap and splashed cool water on my face before cupping my hand under it and taking a drink.

"She give you any trouble?"

I heard him blow out his breath. "Nah. None at all."

"Good. I've got some food in the kitchen. Tobes said he's comin' by with some shit for her."

"Sure," Kristian said, sounding a little detached from the conversation.

"Come on then."

"Give me a sec."

"Why? Did I interrupt you fucking?"

I heard a thud then a chuckle mixed with the word, "Ow."

"Sorry, I didn't realise she was so special."

"Fuck off, Abs. She's not," Kristian said, and for some

reason that declaration caused a slight pang in my gut. "I just need a fucking minute."

There was quiet for a moment then Abbot's footsteps receded until I was sure he left the room. Once the sound of a chair scraping reached my ears, I turned around, ready to go back into the bedroom and put my dirty uniform back on so I wasn't wearing this fucking shirt anymore. Of course, Kristian was standing in the doorway of the bathroom, his giant body taking up all the space in the room.

"I shouldn't have done that to you," he said, his voice surprisingly gentle.

I folded my arms across my middle and met his eyes. "I don't have a fucking clue what you're talking about. As far as I'm concerned, nothing happened." The other half of my problem was that I was too proud. I didn't want a single thing from anyone—not even an apology. My mother used to call me 'Blue' because I was always fighting over something, even when there was nothing to fight about.

Kristian stood up straight then nodded slowly, a curious look in his eyes. "Can I trust you to make it to the kitchen without climbing out the window or into the ceiling?"

I shrugged one shoulder and stuck out my chin. "I guess. I wouldn't get far on my sore knee anyway."

Nodding slowly, he withdrew from the room, and suddenly I could breathe again. I didn't know why or even how, but somehow, Kristian Cartwright stole all the oxygen and space in the world. And I didn't like that. Not one bit.

CHAPTER FOUR
NOTHING TO LOSE AND EVERYTHING TO GAIN

"THOUGHT you could use a change of clothes." Toby arrived after breakfast with a backpack and a duffel bag. *My* backpack and duffel bag.

"How did you get these?" I demanded in a harsh whisper. If he had my things, he'd seen where I lived. *No one* knew where I lived.

"I lifted your keys, then your boss was kind enough to let me collect your things from your locker. I also moved your car somewhere safe and got you some clothes."

"Why would Maree hand my things over to a complete stranger?"

He smiled. "Because I said please."

She was always a sucker for a guy with good manners. A polite gesture was that woman's kryptonite. And the fact she'd been perving on them all night would have helped him out too.

"So you know."

He nodded once. "Based on your reaction, I take it you don't want either of them to know?" He inclined his head towards Kristian and Abbot who were transferring gardening equipment from a shed to the tray of the Ute. Abbot was complaining about working when they were supposed to take the day off.

"No one knows, and I want to keep it that way," I said, folding my arms across my chest.

"Especially since this arrangement with my brother is more of a lifeline than a punishment to you, right?"

I lifted my chin. "It's no lifeline. I can take care of myself."

"You're living in an old hatchback. How is that taking care of yourself?"

"Why do you even care?"

"I don't. But if you want me to keep your secrets, I want a little information." Toby kept his voice low. "Why are you living in your car?"

I tightened my arms across my chest and released my breath through my nose. "Remember that day on the beach when Kristian told us we couldn't surf there anymore?"

"I recall something along those lines."

Not long after the Cartwrights made Johno, Dazza, and me *personas non grata* to anyone we traded with, we'd run into them while surfing. Kristian and I had traded a few heated words while Dazza and Johno took off with their tails between their legs. I was so pissed that I laid into Johno the moment we got home. *Fucking pussy.* The end result was us breaking up, and me leaving with nowhere to go.

"Well, that's when Johno and I broke up. I was pissed at him for not standing up to you lot, and he kicked me out. All I had was whatever I could pack and my shitbox car."

"So you decided to live in it?"

"Not right away. Stayed in a couple of motels, an Airbnb or two while I tried to find a place. I even tried to get a room in a share house. But it didn't work out, and the longer I went without a physical address, the harder things got. Then I ran out of money, and now you're up to date on my shitty life."

"You didn't have any relatives to go to?"

I looked away, frowning. "Nowhere I'm welcome."

"Surely your family wouldn't turn you away if they knew you were living in your car."

I scoffed in response. He'd obviously never encountered the maternally challenged woman who gave birth to me. And my father? Who the fuck knew where that guy was. He'd split not long after I was born. I wouldn't know him if I passed him on the street.

"How do you even shower?"

"My God. Why are you so interested? The gym, the beach. Some guy's house if I pick up."

"You aren't scared out there on your own?"

"Of what? It's not like I'm sleeping out in the open."

"It's not exactly safe for a young girl like you."

"I'm twenty-seven. I'm not a girl."

He looked me up and down carefully. "You're a girl."

I reached out and snatched my bags from his hands. "And you're a condescending arsehole."

One side of his mouth quirked up as I turned and went inside to change, limping a little because of my sore knee.

The moment the screen door shut behind me, I heard Kristian yell to Toby that he wasn't to let me out of his sight.

Controlling jerk. They were all treating me like a toddler. Or more accurately, a prisoner.

Although Toby was right. I hadn't hit rock-bottom, but this *was* like a lifeline for me. He probably had no idea how hard it was to be living pay cheque to pay cheque, hoping that one day I'd get ahead. Kristian was a pigheaded jerk, but I had a place to stay, a bed to sleep in, running water, and a kitchen *with* food. A *temporary* lifeline, but a lifeline all the same. Who cared if I had to mow lawns and clean for a while to keep it? I was going to enjoy being here as best I could.

"I'm just gonna take a shower and get changed," I said over my shoulder when I heard Toby enter the house. Kristian had called it a *beach shack* last night because it was literally on the beach. You walked out the front and within a few metres your feet were hitting sand. I couldn't even imagine how much a place like this was worth. It wasn't beautiful architecture or anything, just a basic two-bedroom, one-living-area fibro place with pale blue siding. But the location was amazing—the smell of the sea, the sounds of the waves. It was every surfer's dream.

When I was done showering, I pulled on what I thought would be suitable to mow lawns in—a pair of leggings and a T-shirt, plus put a baseball cap on my head. I didn't have any sort of work boots, so I just wore my runners. They were falling apart, but they did the trick.

"You going to be OK working with that knee?" Toby gestured to the way I was limping around the kitchen, looking for a bottle to fill with water for the day. It was already feeling warm.

"I'll be fine," I muttered, finding what I was after in a cupboard beneath the stove. "Best to get this over with as soon as possible. You guys want me gone as much as I don't want to be here, I'm sure." After filling the bottle from the tap, I took a sip before screwing the lid on.

When I looked up, Toby's expression told me he didn't believe me. But I wasn't going to let him know he had me pegged, and that sleeping in my car every night scared the shit out of me. Last night was the first time I'd actually slept the whole night in months—even if the pervert had kept me close to him for *security*...

I cleared my throat. "Where is my car, anyway?"

"Safe," he responded.

"Safe where?"

He just smiled.

"What if I need more of my stuff?"

"That won't be a problem. I'll bring all your stuff here."

"What about my purse? My phone?"

"Got someone you need to call?"

"Maybe. Just because I'm homeless doesn't mean no one gives a shit about me." Actually, that's exactly what it meant. "Besides, I can't just not show up for work. I'll get the sack."

Toby dug into his pocket and pulled out an old iPhone 5c with a blue case and a cracked screen. It was mine. "Let's see." He tapped at the screen and squinted a little through the cracks. Then he started to read. "'Hey Maree. I hate to do this, but I need some time off'."

My mouth fell open. "You messaged my boss?" I tried to grab my phone from his hand but he evaded me by holding it above my head and kept reading.

"'Are you OK?' she asked. 'I heard you had a fall last night'. You replied, 'I'm fine. But I need some time off.

Family stuff.' Then she said, 'No probs. Let me know when you're—spelt U R—ready to come back.' She's *super* understanding."

"Give me my phone," I said, teeth clenched.

"You should be thanking me for handling your shit for you." He handed me my phone and I grabbed it before he fully let go.

Tears burned behind my eyes, and I didn't know why. I guess I just hated that he was all up in my business where *no one* belonged. "Why would I thank any of you for anything?"

"Because your life just got a whole lot better." He looked around the shack while he said it.

"Fuck you, Toby. You know *nothing* about me."

A smug expression flitted across his face before he went for my jugular. "Veronica Sutton. You've floated from shitty relationship to shitty relationship since your tits grew in. You didn't finish school because you decided partying was more fun and quit showing up. You've worked every crappy job there is, drawing the line at becoming a stripper or a hooker, but you have no problem stealing to make ends meet. You're the product of a broken home. Your father was barely in the picture and your mother didn't know what to do with you since she was basically a kid herself. You're the kind of person who bounces through life, doing nothing constructive while looking for the next person who'll let you sponge off them. All because being a productive member of society makes you want to claw your skin right off your face. This situation right here, is a dream come fucking true for you."

"Fuck you." My hand flew up and was caught mid-air,

inches before it collided with his face. I snatched it back to my side and balled my fist, my nails digging into my palm.

"It's my job to know who those knuckleheads are hanging out with. And I'm *very good* at what I do." He smiled.

God, I wanted to slap that smile away. I felt…violated. I had no idea how, but *somehow*, this man had discovered everything I tried to keep secret—even the things I hid from myself. I wasn't proud of how I'd lived my life. I'd messed up more than I did well, and I was trying to be better. I really was. But when you always seemed to be down on your luck, it was a little hard to pull yourself out of it.

"What are you planning to do with all that information?" I asked, my eyes cast down to the floor, my voice quiet. I had no bloody clue who these people were. I could see what they were presenting to the world, but the way they spoke and the power they seemed to exude told me that nothing was what it seemed from the outside looking in. They were hiding something huge. I knew it. And now I seemed to be smack in the middle of it.

He released a sigh. "Well, I was thinking about taking it to the papers, but they'd think it wasn't newsworthy. I could write a book, but that would probably be boring as fuck and a waste of my time. A skywriter would be crazy expensive…"

When I looked up, I found a cheeky glint in his eyes. Despite myself, I laughed. Perhaps out of relief, perhaps because Toby had actually been kind of OK to me. He was a dick, but he was a nice one.

"So you can relax," he continued. "I won't cause you any trouble as long as you don't cause us any trouble. And if you play your cards right, we might even help you get back on your feet. Do we have a deal?" He held out his hand.

A deal. The irony wasn't lost on me. I had nothing to offer here, and no one who cared enough to figure out I was in trouble. They could quite easily get rid of me and never have to face questions. Yet somehow Toby made it sound like I had a choice, that being compliant was my bargaining chip. I didn't think it was, but still, his words had piqued my interest. *If you play your cards right, we might even help you get back on your feet.* I didn't know how he'd make that happen, but that dangling carrot called *hope* was something I hadn't seen in a very long time.

"Yeah. We have a deal," I said, slipping my hand in his and shaking on it, because at the end of the day, I had nothing to lose and everything to gain.

CHAPTER FIVE
SEARCHING FOR MEANING

"SO, how much did I make today?" I asked from the back of the Ute as we idled at the curb to keep the air conditioning going while Abbot 'dropped off some paperwork' to where, I had no clue. My skin felt like it was covered in salt and grime from weeding three different gardens in the day's heat, so I was glad for the reprieve.

Kristian glanced at me, his eyes doing a quick up and down before they met mine. "I'm not payin' you, doll. You're working off a debt."

I closed my eyes. *Lord, give me strength.* "I'm aware of that. How much did I pay off my debt?"

He shrugged and turned back to face the front of the cab. "Haven't worked it out yet."

A quiet fell between us and I looked out the window, watching a few people walk by. It'd been like this all day. Kristian and Abbot didn't really speak to me unless they were telling me what to do. If this was the way this whole indentured slave thing was going to work it was going to get old real quick.

"Do you smoke?" I asked, needing the nicotine as much as I needed to break the silence.

"Nope," he responded, the end of the word popping between his full lips. "Abbot does. They're in the glove box."

Taking that as an OK for me to grab one, I leaned over the seat, arse in the air so I could reach. After a moment of digging, I found the packet and shook one out, sticking it in my mouth before returning to my seat. He watched me out the corner of his eye the entire time.

"Want me to smoke it outside?" I asked before lighting up.

"Just crack the window. Abbot smokes in here all the time."

I did as I was told then flicked my thumb over the plastic lighter. "This thing isn't working," I said, checking that it still had fluid inside.

Kristian reached over the seat and took it from my fingers, tapping it against his palm before rolling the flint and producing a flame. He held it while I lit up. "The smell doesn't bother you?" I asked, sitting back so I could exhale out the window.

"Not particularly. I'm used to it. Jasmine smokes too."

"Jasmine's your girlfriend?"

He looked at me as though I just kicked his dog. "She's my mother."

"Oh, the woman who wanted me killed?"

His mouth curved slightly as he looked at his phone. "She doesn't like inconveniences."

"That's what I am, is it?"

He looked at me and grinned. "Yeah. You're a fuckin' huge one."

"Then why are you smiling?"

He didn't answer, just directed his attention to where Abbot could be seen approaching with a bag of food and three Cokes in his hands.

"Sustenance," Abbot said as he slid into the car. He handed out the drinks and sandwiches before his eyes noted the cigarette burning between my fingers.

"I told her she could have it," Kristian said.

Abbot shrugged. "Whatever, mate." Then he turned back to me. "Didn't know what you liked so got you chicken and salad."

"It's fine. Thanks." Finishing the cigarette, I flicked it out the window. "And thanks for the smoke. I don't have a big habit."

"It's cool. I don't mind sharing."

We ate in quiet for a moment then Abbot spoke around his food. "Ran into Nadine and Karen out there."

"Oh yeah?" Kristian asked, more focused on his food than the conversation.

"They seemed keen to party. Told them to stop by the shack Friday night."

Kristian wiped his hand across his face and shook his head. "Call 'em and tell them no. I'm not in the fuckin' mood this week."

Abbot's eyebrows almost met his hairline. "It's *Nadine* and fucking *Karen*. Are you seriously saying no to that?" He gestured near his chest to point out that at least one of the girls had great tits. I hid my smile behind my sandwich and pretended I wasn't listening.

"It'd be weird."

"Why? Because of her?" Abbot jerked his head towards me.

Kristian gave him a look that said, "Um, yeah."

"You can party with whoever you want. I won't get in the way," I said, ignoring the strange feeling, heavy at the bottom of my gut.

"Another time," Kristian said, like it was the end of the matter.

Abbot pouted. "You used to be fun."

"Yeah? And you used to be cool, but now you're just this creepy old guy hitting on young girls."

"Mate, I'm your fucking mirror. If I'm creepy, so are you. And those girls are at least twenty."

"And you're not." Finishing the last of his sandwich, Kristian started the engine. "Mate, I'm *not* in the fucking mood to party."

The confusion on Abbot's face was kind of hilarious. He obviously wasn't used to his twin not wanting to get it on with a couple of hotties. I wondered if they ever did that whole kinky twin thing where they fucked the same girl—or did that just happen in porn?

"Listen, if I'm cramping your style I can make myself scarce. I'm sure you guys have your needs."

"Fuck. I'm just not interested, OK?" Kristian snapped, pulling into traffic.

Abbot and I exchanged glances, and I shrugged. The guy obviously didn't want to party.

"Why don't you drop me off at Jazz's?" Abbot said.

"Throwing a tantrum 'cause I won't help you get your dick wet?"

"No. My car is still there. I'll shower and call the girls, let them know we'll hang out some other time. I'll just meet you at the shack later."

"Fine."

After we dropped him off outside a massive white rendered house, Kristian met my eyes in the rear-view mirror and said, "I'm not your chauffeur."

I took that to mean that he wanted me to sit up front. I climbed over the back of the seat then clipped myself in. "Happy?" I asked, pulling the baseball cap from my head and shaking my hair out.

He grinned. "You really don't like me, do you?"

I couldn't help but smile back. "What's to like?" I teased.

Shaking his head, he chuckled then turned the Ute around in the driveway and headed back out.

"Your brother seems pretty disappointed that you didn't want to party with those girls," I said after a while.

"He'll get over it."

"I hope it wasn't because of me."

He sighed. "I'm just tired of fucking around."

"The soul of every guy who ever lived just screamed in agony over that sentence."

He laughed. "It's not all it's cracked up to be."

"I don't know," I said, picking out a piece of grass that was caught in the fabric of my leggings. "I think keeping things casual has its benefits. If you aren't hoping for anything you can't get upset when it doesn't work out."

"Yeah, well it gets old. I mean, I see how Sam and Nate are, married and settled, and they're so fucking happy about it. Sam's wife is really cool. She's the sweetest thing you ever met in your life, all wide-eyed and innocent but with this crazy fight in her."

"She's the one who kicked Johno in the nuts?"

He chuckled fondly. "Yeah. That's her, the bride from last night."

"Sounds like you have a crush on her."

"Nah. It's not like that. She's like the sister I never had. The whole dynamic of our family has changed drastically over the last year. We've been through a lot together and she makes it all better. I guess I'm just changing my outlook."

"You want some meaning in your life," I stated.

"Yeah," he agreed, a frown creasing his brow. It seemed he hadn't thought about it like that before.

"I get it, man. We're all searching for meaning somewhere."

Taking a deep breath, he cleared his throat. "I guess. I don't even know why I'm telling you this shit."

I shrugged. "People always spill their guts to me. It's a gift. I've got an open face or something. It puts people at ease."

"Giving you the perfect opportunity to rob them, huh?"

Pressing my lips together, I looked out the window, not dignifying the jibe with a response. I didn't need to be reminded of who I was. I lived with that knowledge every day and didn't once pretend I was a good person.

BY THE TIME Friday rolled around, I'd mowed about twenty lawns, cooked multiple dinners, and cleaned their place from top to bottom—Cinderella had nothing on me. Honestly, it was exhausting. Not only was I working my arse off, but I was under constant watch. Even in my sleep I had someone beside me, reacting to my every move. The moments where Kristian or Abbot spoke to me kindly were few and far between. But I was eager for the conversation when it came. Call me lonely, call me intrigued, but I enjoyed those moments when it felt like they forgot to hate me. It made me forget to hate them for a moment too.

With Abbot needing to run some errands, it was just Kristian and me for dinner. I had no idea what a quiet Friday night usually entailed for these guys, but I hoped it involved a lot of sleeping. I could definitely go for that.

Despite my bone weariness, when we got back to the shack, my eyes drifted longingly towards the roiling surf. Perfect surf conditions.

"Would it be against the rules for me to go for a surf? Or at least a swim." The idea of hitting the water to cool down seemed like heaven.

"After we get this equipment cleaned and locked away, I'll take you down."

I didn't understand why we kept hosing down mower blades that kept getting filthy again, but I helped him get everything tidy and stored back in the shed.

"Surf or swim?" I asked as we entered the house.

"Surf," he said, grabbing a pair of board shorts from the top of the laundry basket that had been on the floor next to the couch since yesterday, waiting for me to fold it.

He walked through the house, stripping off his shirt, the muscles in his back rippling with his movement. Then he stopped at the laundry door and threw the shirt inside before removing his pants and adding them to the pile.

"Go on then," he said, glancing at me before he pulled his shorts on. "Get your suit on."

"I'm not supposed to leave your sight, remember?"

"Then leave the bedroom door open."

Brushing past him in the hall, I entered the bedroom and dug through my bag, finding my bikini and rashie. I stripped quickly and re-dressed, feeling his presence the entire time. He wasn't watching me, couldn't even see me from the hallway. But he was *there* all the same, his existence this oppressive being that crept into every space.

At least you have a roof over your head. Maybe he'd settle down in time, dial back his contempt for me, and give me space to breathe. He didn't seem entirely unreasonable, and I kept catching glimpses of a guy who loved fun in the way he interacted with his brother. Kristian and Abbot had wrestled and joked their way through the workweek, Kristian's serious side seeming reserved for his interactions with me. I didn't know if he had to remember that he disliked me, or if there was just something about *my* presence that pressed all his buttons the wrong way.

"Interesting tattoo. I keep meaning to ask you what it means," he said when I emerged from the room, my legs bare, but the rest of me covered in my surfing gear.

I looked at the script that surrounded my left thigh. "Oh, it's elvish or something. I got it from Pinterest."

"Isn't that the *One Ring to rule them all* from Lord of the Rings?"

"Same font, different words."

"What does it say?"

"We've all got light and dark inside us. What matters is the part we choose to act on."

His brows lifted a touch. "Deep."

I shrugged. I'd gotten it on a whim. At the time, I thought it would be a good reminder to stay on the straight and narrow, to better myself, but it seemed my dark side kept winning.

"You got any tats?"

He shook his head. "I don't really do identifying marks."

"Except the freckle on your chin."

His hand floated up and he pressed his fingers to the spot as his eyes narrowed slightly then he relaxed his entire stance with the release of his breath. "Boards are in the shed," he said, leading me outside.

CHAPTER SIX
YOU'LL NEVER BE DONE
WITH ME

KRISTIAN SAT in the middle of his board, his features a little harder to make out as the sun set behind him. "You're good."

My lips curved wider than they had in months. "I'm out of practice." The words came out in pants. "And out of breath."

He shrugged. "No matter how tired I am, I always have energy to surf."

I had to agree. The power of the ocean awakened a limitless energy inside me as well. Torquay's main beach wasn't as fun to surf as Bells or Jan Juc, but when it was at your doorstep, it certainly did the trick. I never wanted to return to dry land.

"Then why haven't you been surfing all week? It's not like you had to travel."

"Babysitting your arse." He flicked water at me.

"I'm not going anywhere, you know. You can relax a little." I wiped a hand over my face as water ran from my hair past my right eye. "I pay my debts."

He looked at me for a long moment, thinking God only knew what. But I felt weird under his scrutiny, so I turned my face towards the horizon and wondered how long it would take for me to evolve into a mermaid so I could survive out here.

I said as much to Kristian.

"You want to be a mermaid?"

"It'd be pretty cool. Sleeping on the ocean floor, catching fish in your teeth, riding waves all day for fun. The only things you'd have to worry about are the sharks."

"And box jelly fish."

"True."

"And fishing nets, killer whales, sea snakes, moray eels, blue-ringed octopus and let's not forget microplastics. Those are really fucking with the sea life."

"You're a ray of fucking sunshine, aren't you?" I said, my daydream crumpling into a nightmare before my eyes. "Way to stomp all over something really cool."

"I'm a realist."

"You don't like to imagine a life different to the one you have now?"

A frown creased his brow as he cocked his head slightly to the side. "Look around you, Ronnie. What more is there than this?"

I did exactly that, took in the beauty of our surroundings as I inhaled the sea air. "I guess the perspective is different when you live right on the beach," I said.

"You live in the same town."

Looking back to the horizon, I watched the disappearing glow as the sun slipped farther from sight, leaving pinks and purples in the sky. "We might live in the same town, but we don't have the same life."

It must be nice being at the top of the food chain, being able to do whatever you pleased without worrying about money, or even where you'd sleep that night.

"Why did you do it?" I asked through the silence.

"Do what?"

"Block us."

"Don't know what you're talkin' about."

"Sure you do. We took your car. You found us, took it back. Then suddenly we couldn't unload a single thing. That's quite a lot of power for someone who mows lawns for a living."

His mouth kicked up at the side. "Hungry?"

"That's not answering my question."

"There was a question?" It seemed he was being intentionally vague.

"Why did you do it?" I repeated.

With a sigh, he kicked his feet back and forth in the water. "Why does anyone do anything?"

"Because they can."

"Exactly. Why did you fuck with my Ute? Why did you steal it in the first place? Because you could."

"Wrong. I stole it because I needed money. Then I fucked with it because I hate you for ruining my life."

"*I* ruined your life?"

"You and your family."

"That's putting a lot of power at our feet, doll. You sure you didn't fuck it up all on your own? Don't think I didn't see the coke in your bedroom that day. I know *I* didn't put that there, but you used my money to pay for it, right?"

My jaw clenched. After taking Kristian's Ute, Johno and I found his wallet in the glovebox. There was cash in it, so we decided to celebrate and detoured past our dealer's place. Back then, it was the way we celebrated everything. I was never a full-blown addict, but I'd spent a lot of my life partying. I hated that he was using that against me. I also hated that he was probably right.

"I don't do that stuff anymore. But it's beside the point, your family—"

"Did you a favour," he boomed over the top of me. "That shit fucks *everyone* up. If we hadn't done what we did, you'd have kept going around, stealing shit to feed your habit, and you'd probably be in prison right now. Which incidentally, is exactly where that boyfriend of yours is."

Johno is in prison? I held my shock in the centre of my chest and kept my expression calm. "So you admit it," I said, my eyes locked on his.

To my surprise, he laughed, a rich rumbling sound that entered my ears and did things to my body that I'd rather not admit. I almost smiled watching him.

"How about we catch one more wave before we head in? I'm starved, and you have a meal to cook."

"Sure thing, boss," I said, saluting him. It was obvious our conversation was over, and I wasn't getting any more information. In a way, I got what I wanted anyway—they blocked us from working simply because they could, and somehow Kristian twisted it to sound like an act of benevolence. *Is Johno really in prison?* I hated to think that if we'd stayed together, I could be too.

Positioning for the next set, Kristian glanced my way then smiled in this way that lit up his eyes. The animosity we felt toward each other dropped away in the anticipation of catching a wave. We just smiled at each other.

"Race you to shore?" As he spoke, the twinkle in his eye told me he was really just a boy wrapped in a man's body. *A crazy-hot body.*

"And If I win?"

His grin widened. "I'll let you pee with the door closed."

It was an offer I couldn't refuse.

"You're on."

Then he took off, paddling with his powerful arms as the wave crested behind us.

I was only moments behind, launching myself forwards as the wave lifted me up, the water roaring behind me. I popped up, staying low until I felt steady enough to rise. Then I laughed, forgetting to be pissed off as I rode that thing all the way to the shore, only stopping when the sand wedged against the board.

"It's no good for the board to ride it into the sand," Kristian said as he came up behind me, carrying his board under his arm.

"You're just a sore loser. You probably get off on watching me pee," I teased, still smiling.

His eyes flicked between mine before the tiniest of frowns flitted across his brow. "I don't get off on you at all."

Wow. Consider my face slapped.

Once again, we were catapulted from light-hearted conversation into an uncomfortable silence as we returned to the shack. Kristian was a difficult man to be around. One minute he was barking orders, the next we were arguing, then just as fast we were laughing, only to slip back into the verbal snipes that were so well timed and precise, they cut me to my core and made me feel like the piece of shit I knew I was. Considering the short time we'd spent together, he knew how to push my buttons remarkably well.

"The fuck?" Kristian muttered as we got closer and music hummed in the air. At first it was a distant beat. Then it got louder and louder until we were close enough to see. A party. Right in front of the shack.

Kristian growled and shoved his board into my arms. "Motherfucking twins who don't listen." He stomped off, and I rushed to keep up.

"Krissy-boy!" Abbot stood from the plastic chair he was occupying around the firepit and welcomed his brother with open arms. I rested the boards against the house and stood back to observe.

A couple of girls were there—one with a necklace that said 'Karen' and the-one-with-the-tits-whose-name-I-couldn't-remember—as well as two other guys who had 'surf bum' written all over them. I was pretty sure I'd seen them around town at some point. Sitting around, drinking and surfing seemed to be their entire MO. *Nice life.*

"What are you doing?" Kristian demanded, the annoyance clear in his tone as he absorbed the small party on the front lawn.

"Enjoying life. Something you should also be doing, brother."

"Oh Em *Gee*. You guys are *brothers*?" The girl with the tits said with wide eyes. *She's clever, that one.* I hid my smile behind my hand. Kristian didn't even bother with a response.

"You're an arse." Kristian shoved Abbot in the chest. "I'm going inside. Keep it down out here." They only seemed to get louder.

Kristian swept past me and headed into the house. I followed dutifully behind, then accepted the beer he handed me once we made it to the kitchen. One thing I had to say was that he kept his 'slave' fed and watered well. I never had to sit and watch him or Abbot eat or drink without joining in.

"Can you believe him?" he lamented after downing almost half of his and slamming it onto the table. "We're thirty-three, and he still thinks he can act like a teenager, and that he gets the fucking final say because he's four fucking minutes older."

"And you expressly told him you didn't want a party too," I pointed out, keeping my voice calm as I agreed with him. Personally, I didn't care if there was a party or if we all sat around staring at the wall for hours on end. But since this guy was calling all the shots in my world, I was going to back him up and let him vent. It may have seemed calculating, but in my experience with men, they didn't want women to challenge their way of thinking. Once, I dated a guy for a few months who got real riled up whenever things didn't go his way. If I did anything that looked like I didn't agree with him, I'd cop it. So, I learned to listen and agree. Men just wanted someone to tell them they were right.

"Exactly. I couldn't have made it any fucking clearer. Just because it's a Friday night, doesn't mean we need to party. *Fuck.* It's like this merry-go-round that we've been on since we were seventeen." He picked up his beer and downed the rest of it before going to the fridge for another. "I want off."

"Off the merry-go-round?"

"*Yes.* I love a party as much as the next guy, but there has to come a time when it isn't all we do."

Listlessness seemed to be a curse for the wealthy, I supposed. I would love to get to a point in my life where I'd had too much fun.

"Have you always shared a house?"

Watching the level of his second bottle of beer get lower and lower, I moved around the kitchen and opened the pantry. He'd be onto his third in a moment. If he was going to drink that fast, he'd need food to soak it up.

"What are you doing?" he asked when I pulled out a pack of pasta and a jar of sauce.

"You said you were starving. I'm making dinner."

Necking his beer, he kicked out a chair and sat at the dining table that dominated the room. There wasn't much bench space, so I used the table to gather all my ingredients: chicken, bacon, cream cheese, mushrooms, spinach, along with what I'd already taken from the pantry.

He bounced his foot, the action causing the table he was leaning on to rock gently. "It was always easier," he said suddenly, looking out the front window to where Abbot was standing and talking animatedly with his arms going everywhere. He looked like he was having a great time. Someone hooted as a group of three new people showed up. Kristian released another groan and drank more beer.

"What was easier?" Trying to ignore the growing party, I put water on to boil then set a frying pan to heat while I chopped the bacon into small pieces then added it to the pan.

"Living with Abbot. Because of work. Because we

were always together. Because we never thought we'd settle down."

"That seems to be on your mind at the moment. Settling down."

He sat back and set his beer on the table, only about an inch of liquid left in it. "Don't get any ideas."

I held my hands up to say, "I wasn't" and started slicing chicken.

"It's probably because of the wedding. It's just got me thinking, I guess. I'm not desperate for a wife and kids or anything. I just…" He let out his breath, focusing his gaze outside again. "I want something to change. I want…*more*."

Now, *that* was something I understood.

Adding the chicken to the pan, I stirred it around until the pink turned white. "If you could magically change one thing in your life like that"—I clicked my fingers to go with my words—"what would it be?"

When I turned around, he needed to lift his eyes to meet mine. It looked like he was checking out my arse. I was still in my bikini and rash shirt.

"I'd have the giant C and U disappear from the side of my Ute." He held my gaze as he licked his lips before gulping down the last of his beer.

He wants me gone that badly?

I turned away from his gaze so he couldn't see my eyes and the distress his comment caused me. Having his Ute magically fixed would mean I'd be back sleeping in my car during that same click of the fingers. I didn't want that. Not yet.

"Interesting. That's the first thing I'd fix too," I lied, pouring the pasta into the now boiling water. "At least then

I could be done with you." Giving it a stir, I then dropped the last of the ingredients into the meat mixture and put on the lid before I turned the heat right down.

Kristian scoffed. "You'll never be done with me."

My eyes flicked to meet his. "What's that supposed to mean?" I snapped.

He looked away. "It means you're incapable of letting shit go."

"Jesus, you think you know me so well, don't you?"

His eyes connected with mine again. "Am I wrong?"

That was the shitty thing. He wasn't wrong at all. I was angry for what my life had become, and I blamed him and his family for it. There was no way I could let that go. In a way, I felt like they owed this living situation to me. They'd taken everything else as a result of their actions, so the least they could do was get me off the street. Toby had suggested as much earlier in the week, and all I had to do was stay out of trouble. Arguing with Kristian was probably the opposite of that. I knew I should keep my mouth shut and just do what I was told, but I couldn't help myself. All I knew was how to fight.

Moving about the kitchen, I cleaned up what I could then checked on the food. It needed at least ten minutes more to be ready.

"Am I allowed a shower?" I asked as I dried my hands on a tea towel.

"Go for it," he said with a flippant wave of his hand.

"And do I need an escort, or did I win full bathroom privileges out there?"

His eyes went to my face first, dropped to my chest, then made their way down to my bare toes before returning to my face. His Adam's apple bobbed then he shifted his focus to the empty beer bottle in front of him where his fingers were busy peeling off the label. *God, this guy burns hot and cold.* What was it they said about people picking at drink labels? That it was a sign of sexual frustration? Was that his problem? He needed to get laid? I didn't know him well enough to be sure, but I knew men, and most were a hell of a lot nicer after a good fuck.

There's a party outside with many willing participants, Kristian. Go play. Unless of course, his 'frustration' was directed at me... Could it be?

The entire label came off with a tear and he rolled the paper into a ball with his fingers. "It's fine. I'll keep an eye on the food." He cleared his throat then looked back over at me. I stood a little straighter, pushing out my chest as I watched his eyes drop down and heat. *Holy shit.* "That means go," he snapped, seeming to effortlessly slip back into the man who thought I was a nuisance.

What if I'm reading him wrong? No, I didn't think I was. We'd been sharing a bed for days, sharing a bathroom too. He'd seen my body. I'd seen his. Of course he was interested, he was a man, after all and I wasn't completely unattractive. I supposed what was impressive was his restraint. He had me in a position where he could do whatever he wanted to me, and he chose to hold back. Was there honour in my captor? A line he wouldn't cross?

Still, when I thought about it, I'd noticed him enough times this week to be fairly certain there was a part of Kristian who wanted *me*. A drop-dead gorgeous man—who could have any woman with a click of his fingers —*wanted* to watch me shower but couldn't trust himself in his determination to keep that façade of distaste he had going on. Was *that* it? If I was right, *that* Kristian was a man I could work with, a man I could convince to keep me around.

But was that who I was now? A whore? I'd sworn to myself that that would be the line *I* never crossed. But was tempting a man I disliked but found attractive in the *hope* he'd keep me around the same thing? Or was I just someone desperate to stay in the safety of a beach shack, even if it was with a man who'd probably kick me out the minute my debt was paid?

At the end of the day, I didn't think my reasoning mattered, my motivation was still the same—I wanted to give him a reason to keep me around.

Reaching down, I took a hold of the hem of my rashie and pulled it over my head, revealing the string bikini underneath. It was royal blue and brought out the green flecks in my hazel eyes. I watched the heat flare in his gaze, felt it lick over my body before I turned and walked away, a smile playing on my lips as my body reacted to him. This time, my reaction didn't piss me off. It opened the door to a world of possibilities. Kristian Cartwright wanted me, and maybe—just maybe—I could rock his world so hard he'd *never* want to let me go. Probability? Possibly zero. But I had to try. *Because I have nothing else to offer.*

CHAPTER SEVEN
I SHOULD HAVE GONE
TO BED

BY THE TIME I finished in the shower, the pasta was cooked and Kristian had already eaten. I found him outside sitting by the fire pit, the pull of the party obviously too much for him after all.

I had dressed myself in a pair of jeans shorts and a pink tie-dyed T-shirt—nothing too revealing because Kristian had made it clear that he wasn't interested in screwing around any more. Meaning, if I wanted to try to gain his trust, and a bit more time out of my car as my home, anything too sexy might turn him off. I was going to give him the fantasy he was searching for. *Even if it's only temporary.*

To the outsider, seeing what I was doing and knowing the thought process behind it probably seemed super conniving. But, put yourself in my shoes. I had no one to count on, nothing to help me but my wits and looks. Kristian Cartwright was my meal ticket, a place to rest my head. He was the kind of man I'd been searching for—he had his own business and home, so was therefore stable;

he knew what he wanted and was therefore driven. Sure, there was that whole crooked side to him I hadn't figured out yet, but I wasn't one to complain about a little criminal activity. If I was honest, it was part of what excited me about him. When I weighed everything up, he seemed to tick all the boxes. It certainly didn't hurt that he was gorgeous as fuck too.

Making myself a bowl of pasta, I sat inside and ate it, picking up a surf magazine and flipping through the pages while listening to the murmur of chatter outside. I wanted to go out there and be a part of the fun. But something told me the better option was to stay inside and wait until he came to me. Suddenly changing tack and being all about him would only give me away. So I waited.

I cleaned the kitchen. I curled up on the couch continuing to flick through more magazines. Surprisingly there was no porn, but that didn't mean much; they could just be hiding it or prefer videos over pictures. Anyway, about an hour had passed, and I was reading an article about Australian surfer, Stephanie Gilmore, when he came inside to get more beer.

"You don't need to spend all night alone in here," he said over the top of the fridge door. "You can come out."

I closed the magazine and set it to the side. "It's OK. I didn't want to overstep with your friends."

"You surf these beaches. I'm sure you know some of them too."

I looked outside then stretched my arms above my head, yawning. "Yeah, I probably do. But it's been a really long day—week, actually. I wouldn't mind going to bed early."

He grinned, the alcohol obviously making him a little

more personable. I had to admit that I liked it when he was like this, softer. "You reckon you can sleep through all that?" He nodded to the party outside. It was noisy, but after the conditions I'd been sleeping in over the last few months, I was fairly sure I could sleep through anything if it was in a bed.

"I'm pretty tired."

Moving closer, he held out his hand. "It'll take more than beating me to shore to earn the bed to yourself."

"You're really pulling the whole master and slave thing to get me to go to a party you didn't even want to happen?"

He pulled me to standing. "If I suffer, you suffer. Besides, it's Friday. We can sleep in tomorrow."

It was then I noticed a slight sheen to his eyes. "You don't look like you're suffering. You look like you're stoned."

He bounced a shoulder. "A little weed makes a shitty situation better. Come on, you're making the place look messy."

He picked up the beers he'd taken from the fridge and handed me one, leading me outside and introducing me to the group. He was right, I had seen a few of them before, but I'd never interacted with them. I'm not the best people person on the planet and tended to keep my distance.

Kristian shooed a couple of guys away then took a seat on a white wicker couch with a worn green cushion featuring a bamboo pattern. He gestured for me to join him, then he tapped his beer bottle against mine. "That's better. Wasn't so hard, was it?"

I grinned and tried not to shake my head as I took a sip

of beer. I loved that he thought he was doing me a favour by getting me to join in.

The conversation around the fire consisted of stories about big waves, shark sightings, party fables, and anything that could produce a laugh. Which wasn't hard when joints were getting passed around. I took a hit and held it in as I handed it to Kristian. His smile came easy and his fingers brushed against mine, eyes connected as he sucked the smoke into his lungs. Everything was going so well. It was the longest stretch of time we'd spent without arguing or snapping at each other. As my buzz made its way around my body, I started to think successfully seducing Kristian was a real possibility. Then the girl with the big tits dropped into Kristian's lap and asked for a hit, grabbing him on either side of the face and basically sucking the smoke directly from his lungs. My stomach bottomed out when he pulled back and licked his lips, a dimple-producing smirk on his face. *Fuck.* Next thing I knew, one of her friends slipped in the tiny gap between Kristian and me and wriggled her hips to make me move. It was a targeted attack, designed to get me out of the way so they could have Kristian to themselves. But I wasn't so easy to get rid of. I wedged myself in place, squished at the edge of the chair with the arm of it digging in my hip. Every time she laughed, she jostled her hips and squished me more. In return, I dug my elbow in her side. She glared at me. I smiled. Then she flicked her hair back and it copped me in the face. I caught Abbot watching me from the other side of the fire pit, amusement in his smile. He thought this was funny, which meant those girls were making me look like a fool. And I was nobody's fool.

The next time her hair flicked, I caught it in my hand

and yanked her head back. "Get the fuck off me, bitch. Or I'll get the clippers and give you a reverse Mohawk. I'm sure you'll look real cute with a nice bald strip."

She cried out in pain and made way more of a scene than she needed to. When I released her, she screeched that I was a psycho and stomped off, her friend went after her. The whole party went quiet, all eyes looking my way.

I cleared my throat and squared my shoulders as I glanced at Kristian then stood up. "Told you I should have gone to bed."

He said nothing and sat with a completely impassive expression. I'd blown it already. I knew that. There was no way he'd view me as the 'settle down' girl after this. I was too wild. Although, who was I trying to kid? He already knew that about me anyway. I was being a dumb-arse. *As if he'd ever really want what I have to offer.*

Deciding the party wasn't the best place for me, I headed for the house to go to bed. But not before I paused in front of Abbot and fixed him with a glare, not caring if I was out of line since I was sure they thought I was crazy anyway. "You know, Abbot, the next time your brother tells you he doesn't want a party, fucking listen to him. And don't go pretending you weren't being a dick by bringing this here when you could have done it somewhere else. We both know you just didn't give a fuck about what he wanted."

Abbot just smiled and took a drag of his cigarette, blowing the smoke out of his nose. I huffed out my breath and took off for the house, the party starting up again the moment I walked inside. Laughter carried into the house like a switch had been flipped.

Who needs those people anyway? I was never going to

fit in. Going with the flow was never really my style, so it was stupid of me to even consider turning myself into something I wasn't. The doting girlfriend was never my thing. I wouldn't have been able to pull it off.

Taking off my bra and jean shorts, I set them on top of my bag before I climbed into bed, my phone in my hand as I listened to the revelry outside. Lighting up my screen, I unlocked the phone then opened up the realestate.com app. Going through photos of pretty houses was one of my favourite things to do when I wanted to calm down. I knew it was a stupid pie-in-the-sky dream, but sometimes I needed to dream to hide from the shithole that was my life.

"Trying to call for help?" Kristian's voice startled me. Fumbling my phone, I grunted when it fell and hit me in the face.

"Motherfucker," I muttered, groping to pick it up while he chuckled at my misfortune.

"Sorry, doll. Didn't mean to startle you."

"What are you doing in here anyway? You should be out there swapping smoke with titty Barbie and her big-bottomed friend."

"Didn't like them much, hey?"

I slid my phone underneath my pillow. "They sat on me."

"Rude."

"You're telling me." I rolled onto my side and got comfortable. "You seemed to like them though," I added, knowing it made me sound jealous but being unable to keep my bloody mouth shut.

"It was just a bit of fun. Nothin' to it. Told them all to go home so I could get some sleep."

"That wouldn't have made Abbot very happy."

"He's got both girls to himself. Trust me, he's *very* happy."

"Oh God, so I'm going to have to be nice to them in the morning?"

"Nah. He took them somewhere else. The brunette is a little afraid of you."

"She shouldn't have squashed me."

With a chuckle, he headed into the bathroom and had a quick shower. I took the opportunity to slip my phone into my backpack before getting back into bed.

I was almost asleep when the bed depressed and his bare chest pressed against my back, his warm arm sliding around my waist. He let out a sigh. I almost did the same. I couldn't lie. Having his arm around me felt good.

"Are you going to spoon me under the pretence of holding me prisoner every night?"

"You ask too many questions. Go to sleep."

I was quiet for about two seconds.

"I shouldn't have yelled at Abbot." It wasn't an apology, just an admission of wrongdoing. I didn't do apologies.

"Abbot deserves to be yelled at. He's a shit."

"I probably shouldn't have threatened to shave that girl's head either."

His body rocked slightly from a chuckle. "Is that what you said? I couldn't hear over her freaking out."

"She kept flicking it in my face."

"Served her right then."

We fell quiet for a moment, my mind searching for something more to say. I was tired, but I wanted to keep talking, wanted to talk away the uneasy feeling twisting up my chest.

"I realised something tonight," I whispered.

"What's that?" he asked, his voice growing sleepy.

"I thought I hated you, but it turns out I don't."

A burst of air left his nose in silent amusement.

"I mean, I don't exactly *like* you, but I don't hate you either. Does that make sense?"

"Yeah. Now go to sleep. I stopped a party so you could."

"I thought you did that for you."

"Hmm. Turns out I don't hate you either."

CHAPTER EIGHT
TWO PEOPLE WHO DON'T HATE EACH OTHER

VOICES COMING from the other room woke me some time the next morning. I was alone in Kristian's bed, and even though it was obviously mid-morning, I still didn't want to get up. I was *so* comfy.

"Are you fucking her?"

My ears pricked at the question, the voice sounding like it came from Abbot. *He's obviously finished with his party girls.*

"I haven't touched her." That was Kristian.

"Then what's your deal? *Why* is she in your bed?"

I pressed up onto my elbows, listening. It was obvious they were talking about me.

Do they know how well sound carries in this house?

"Where else is she going to sleep?"

"The couch. Or, since I didn't sleep here last night, she could have taken your bed and you could have had mine, or vice versa."

"There is no way in hell I'd make *anyone* sleep in your

bed. I know what you get up to in that thing, and God only knows when you last changed your sheets."

"I see, so this is a hygiene thing?"

"Too right."

"A hygiene and a vengeance thing—because this is all about teaching her a lesson for fucking with your wheels, right?"

"It's about teaching her not to mess with what she doesn't understand."

"Cartwright pride, huh? You don't think we taught her that lesson when we blocked their ability to profit from stealing cars?"

"I think we taught her *boyfriend* a lesson. If she learned it, she wouldn't feel like she could call me a cunt via my car door."

There was a pause, coupled with the sound of tapping, like something was being placed on a hard surface. I sniffed the air. Toast and coffee. They were having breakfast. My stomach growled, but I couldn't exactly walk out there to join them because they'd know I'd been listening.

"And how long is this *lesson* of yours going to take?"

"I don't know. It'll cost a grand or two to fix the door, so a month?" It sounded like he was looking for confirmation from his brother.

"A *month*?" Abbot obviously didn't think having me around for that long was going to work for him.

"It's not cheap."

"You can't keep her here for a *month*."

"Why not? Nate and Sam *married* Holland and Alesha to stop them from being a problem. This is way less drastic."

"You can't seriously be comparing the two situations."

"Why not? Jazz wanted this one dead too."

"Because she's annoying. *Not* because she knows anything. You could cut this girl loose at any time, and you know it."

"Then how is my Ute gonna get paid for? I let her go, she'll never pay for it. She needs to stay and work off her debt."

"All this trouble for a couple grand. Jesus, *I'll* fucking pay for it. Hell, I'm pretty sure we could call in a favour and get it fixed for free if we wanted."

"I'm not giving my wheels to a chop shop. I'll never get it back."

Abbot laughed, but in a disbelieving way. "You're making excuses. Turn her loose, brother. If you're not even fucking her, there's no point in her being here. Unless, of course, you want her here… Do you like her, Kris? Is that what this is about?"

"It's not about that at all. It's the principle—"

"Then *turn her loose.* She's a liability to the business and you know it."

Fuck. My heart leapt into my throat, beating wildly as the pause drew out with no response. Then it came and the ground disappeared from under me.

"Fine."

No. No. No. Not yet. I knew this wasn't going to last, but I thought I'd have longer than a week. I pressed my hands to my eyes. *God, I'm such a loser. Even my kidnappers don't want me.*

A chair scraped and footsteps echoed down the hall, getting closer. Panicked, I flipped over to my stomach, my hair covering my face as I forced my breathing even, pretending to sleep while my mind raced. *What am I gonna do?*

The door opened then closed and I could feel his presence pressing in around me. Nothing happened for a moment. It seemed like he was just standing there watching me sleep. Then he let out a sigh and went into the bathroom. The shower turned on.

I don't want to sleep in my car tonight.

I sat up and looked around. I needed more time. Even a month was better than nothing. Maybe it would give me enough time to win them all over so Toby would follow through and help me find my feet like he said. I *needed* to stay.

With my heart beating like crazy, I got up and walked towards the bathroom. The door was ajar and when I pushed it farther open, I could see him in the shower, bracing himself against the tiles, his head bowed forward as the spray hit the back of his neck.

He was a fine specimen of a man. Tan and taut all over, muscles bulging, skin so smooth you wanted to lick it. It made what I was about to do so much easier.

I took a deep breath for courage, then I pulled my singlet over my head, quickly pushing my panties to the floor. *I can do this.*

As I reached for the shower screen, my hand shook, but I pushed through. *The worst thing that can happen is he kicks you out.* And from the sound of the earlier conversation, that was going to happen anyway. So I had absolutely nothing to lose.

Closing my eyes for a second, I pulled the screen open then stepped inside. Kristian froze, lifting his head from the spray as the cool air hit his skin.

"What are you doing?"

"I woke up and heard the shower on," I said in a soft murmur. "Thought you might like some company." Placing my hands on his back, I then slid them around his torso, pressing my body against his, skin to skin. His muscles quivered beneath my fingers, giving me the confidence to keep going. "I had a dream about you last night," I lied. "It was a lot like this. You were there. I was there, and you were"—I slid my hand lower, triumph and relief flooding my system when I found him—"hard." My hand barely managed to wrap around his girth. He was even bigger aroused than he was *au naturel.* It set my entire body on fire, imagining what it would be like to take something so big inside me, what it would be like to take him in my mouth. I hummed with pleasure as I slid my hand along his length and his breathing changed. My clit pulsed between my legs as my own excitement intensified, then his hand clamped down around mine, stopping me.

"This isn't why you're here," he said, his voice thick, strangled.

I pressed my lips against his back, running my tongue up his spine. "I know that. But this could be an added benefit. We're both adults. We have needs. It doesn't have to mean anything. Just"—I tightened my grip from beneath his hand, feeling his cock pulse against my palm—"two people who don't hate each other having a good time." He groaned and released his hold on me just a touch. When I moved my hand, he moved his with me, as if he could handle this more if we jacked him off together.

It was ridiculously hot. I hadn't realised how much I wanted him until I started touching him. Now I couldn't think of anything but. My body ached with need.

As we stroked his cock, his breathing increased and my insides tightened. I relieved some of the pressure by rubbing my breasts against his back, satisfying my need for friction.

"Fuck," he groaned, suddenly pulling my hands away and turning around, pinning me against the tiled wall by my wrists. "What are you trying to do to me?"

His erection pressed into my stomach and I rolled my body against it. "Nothing that you aren't doing to me."

"This isn't—"

"Why I'm here, I know," I whispered. "But it's what I want."

His heated eyes flickered then dropped to my mouth before returning to my gaze. He was fighting it.

"Don't you want it too?" I asked, rolling against him again. "It feels like you do."

He growled and then his mouth landed on mine, brutally taking control of the depth and angle of the kiss. I felt...consumed, the intensity of what was happening between us far bigger than I'd expected.

His hand slid down my side, pulling at my thigh then lifting me so I was wrapped around his waist, his cock resting firmly against my core as he pressed against me, his shaft gliding up and down through my juices, over my clit. It was the closest you could get to fucking without actual penetration. The friction sent me into a mind-numbing frenzy. I moaned into his mouth, whimpering and quivering, my sounds echoing off the walls as he kept moving, both of us getting lost in the sensation.

"Fuck me, Kristian. Oh God." I threw my head back, hitting it against the tiles as his movement increased and the pressure at my core reached bursting point. "Holy fuuuck!" I screamed, coming undone against his shaft, just as he twitched and his warm cum squirted between us, landing on my stomach and his.

"Shit," he hissed, dropping his head against my shoulder, his hot breath hitting me in the neck. "We shouldn't have done that."

"Why? That was the best non-fuck I've ever had," I gasped, a little shocked that someone who could be such a jerk could kiss me like that.

He laughed. "The wettest dry-hump on record?"

"Yeah. And it was…unexpectedly intense," I returned, fishing to see if he'd felt the explosive power of what we'd just done the same way I had.

His brow knitted as he nodded, his eyes searching mine. "Unexpectedly intense," he repeated.

I nodded, my body still wrapped around his.

"Fuck." I wondered what that expletive meant as he lowered me to the ground and helped me get cleaned up before shutting off the shower. He even wrapped the towel around me and secured it at my chest when we were finished.

"It's OK if you want me to go," I said as he secured the towel around his own hips. Something about his silence told me he was deep in thought, the discussion he'd had with Abbot was obviously weighing on his mind. "I don't want to be in the way."

"You heard us talking?"

I nodded. It was probably dumb to admit I'd overheard them talking. But Kristian was a smart guy, he'd figure it out on his own.

Letting out a sigh, he ran his hands through his dark

hair causing his muscles to flex. My insides jolted, and all I could think about was tasting every part of him.

"Fuck, you're good-looking," I whispered, unable to stop the words bursting out of my mouth.

The corner of his mouth quirked and he moved closer, hooking his finger underneath my chin. *Oh God, please kiss me.* "Two people who don't hate each other, huh?"

I smiled. "Yeah."

"OK," he said. Then he lowered his lips to mine and kissed me until I was a puddle of need at his feet.

"Kristian," I whispered, my hands resting against his chest.

"Hmmm?" He moved his mouth so he was sucking beneath my jaw.

"Please tell me you have condoms."

"I do."

"Good. Then get one and fuck me."

CHAPTER NINE
A PUDDLE OF LIQUID THAT
CAN'T EVEN SPEAK

"SO WHAT DO you guys normally do on the weekends?" I asked when I emerged from the bedroom, pulling my hair into a ponytail. I was wearing my jean shorts again with an orange fitted tank top that I tucked in at the waist. It was simple, but functional. Living in a car meant that I only had the bare minimum of clothing, so I made do with what I had.

"Depends," Abbot said, holding the remote in his hand and flicking through channels while he lounged on the sofa.

"On?" I asked, feeling a little uneasy with the tightness in his jaw as he focused on the TV. If the sound travelled both ways, he'd have heard everything that went on with Kristian and me just now. I imagined that after the conversation he and Kristian had had about cutting me loose, he was supremely pissed.

Kristian lifted his head from the newspaper he was reading and looked at me in that way new lovers do. "On whether we have family shit to do, or if we're on our own."

"You guys seem pretty tight-knit," I ventured, picking up an apple from the fruit bowl on the counter. I took a bite.

"You'd think. Especially since outsiders cause problems. Right, Kris?" Abbot looked at his brother who just kept reading the paper. Then he sighed and shut off the TV before standing up. "I'm going to Jazz's for a while. Have fun fucking." *Jesus. Bitter much?* He scooped up his keys and headed for the front door, pausing before he walked through. "For the record, brother, I think you're making a huge mistake."

The mistake being me. *Well, that really killed my after-sex buzz.* I hid my expression by taking another bite of my apple.

Kristian responded by saluting him half-heartedly. "And I think you're being a prick."

Abbot scoffed then left. When I heard his 4x4 fire up, I turned my attention to Kristian. "Still want me to stay?" I asked, leaning my butt against the bench.

Kristian looked at me and nodded slowly, smiling as his eyes did a little undressing. "He can stay somewhere else if he has a problem with it. Come here." He sat back in his chair, legs wide. I approached him slowly, seductively, curiously. I enjoyed the way his eyes felt on me, but it didn't escape me that I was now the cause of a disagreement with his twin. That was a pretty big deal and put me in an incredibly precarious position. Blood was thicker than water, after all.

"Closer," he urged when I stopped in front of him.

I smiled and shifted forward. "This close enough?" I stood in the space between his legs.

"That's perfect," he said as he placed his hands on my hips and wasted no time pulling my top from my shorts.

"I just put that on, you know."

"You want me to stop?" He paused, his fingers brushing lightly against my skin as he waited for me to respond, teasing.

I shook my head and held his eyes. "Not for a second."

"Then I want you naked on this table with your legs spread." He unbuttoned my shorts while I pulled my top over my head and dropped it on the floor. With a tug, my shorts fell to my feet. He released this little rumble of appreciation as he took in the lacy underwear and bra, the only decent set I owned, but I was glad I'd kept them. The look in his eyes was enough to have warranted making the space for them in my pack.

Grabbing my hips, he spun me around, his hands moving over my thighs and the curve of my arse before pressing on my skin and sliding up my back. He unhooked my bra, and I let it fall to the floor. Then he hooked his thumbs in the sides of my panties and…tore.

"*No!*" I gasped as they fell to the floor. "They were my nicest pair."

He stood up behind me, his erection pressing through his shorts and into my back as he slid his arms around my waist and palmed my breasts with one hand, pulling my head back with the other. "I'll buy you five new pairs," he growled. "Or, better yet, quit wearing them altogether." Then his lips crashed into mine. The taste of him flooded my senses, causing my clit to cry out for attention. I whimpered, twisting myself in his arms and practically climbed up his body. I needed to be closer.

With his hands going to my arse, he lifted me then placed me on the table, the cool of the wood shocking against the heat of my skin. But I didn't care. I was lost in that mouth of his as it demanded more from me. "Fuck me, Kristian. Please," I begged, my insides aching for him still. *How is it that my enemy is the best lover I've ever had?*

"Not yet," he gasped, dragging his lips past my jaw and down my neck, sucking on my breasts as his hands roamed all over my skin. I could barely stand it.

"Please."

Still fully clothed, he pressed his erection between my parted thighs. "So impatient," he whispered. "Don't be in such a rush this time."

"But I really want to come."

He chuckled. "I love that you're so greedy. Incidentally, that's exactly how I plan to spend my weekend—making you come."

Oh my Lord! Did I just hear that right? What kind of a man is this?

He positioned me so my feet were on the edge of the table then withdrew from my body. I whimpered from the loss of his mouth, his touch, his heat. But then he pulled the chair closer and took a seat, his face right between my legs.

"This is what I wanted to do to you when you were standing there in those bikini bottoms cooking dinner for me last night." He ran his hand down my mound, teasing either side of my lips.

"Why didn't you?" I asked, my voice husky as I quivered with desire.

He chuckled. "Because we had an audience."

"They probably would have liked the show."

"Hmm." He slipped one long finger into my depths and we both moaned at the same time. "But I don't share these things. Some things have to be mine and mine alone."

I didn't even get the chance to process what that meant before his mouth clamped down on my pussy, tongue swirling around my clit as his fingers moved inside. I made some very unladylike noises as my fingers went into his hair and my thighs clamped around his head, my hips moving, fucking his face.

"Holy shit, holy shit, holy shiiiiit!" My orgasm built and hit so fast that it shocked me as my back arched off the table. Kristian had some sort of magic touch—or tongue—that pressed my buttons in *exactly* the right way. I had never come like that before. I wanted to worship that huge cock of his to express my gratitude.

Slowing the movement of his tongue and fingers, he brought me back to earth, and I released the hold I had on his hair. He stood and wiped his mouth, grinning down at me. "*Now* I'm going to fuck you."

My breasts tingled and my insides ached as I watched him pull that shirt off his perfect chest and drop his shorts, a condom seeming to appear between his fingers. "Do it. Do it now."

"I love how you're not even bothered by my size," he said, stroking his cock with his hand as he tore the condom wrapper with his teeth.

I sat up a little, licking my lips at the sight of his enormous dick. "I'm not complaining. Giant cocks are hard to come by, you know," I said, causing him to laugh as he sheathed his length and positioned himself at my entrance.

"I normally need to be careful."

Reaching forward, I ran my fingers down his ridiculously muscular chest. He shivered and let out a moan. "Not with me. I can take it. I can take it all."

With his eyes locked on mine, he pushed in, causing me to gasp as I stretched to accommodate his girth. It burned a little, but in the best kind of way.

"God, you feel good," he said once he was fully seated.

"So do you. I feel so…full."

"Hmmm." He placed a hand at the base of my neck then trailed his fingertips down the centre of my torso, all the way to my stomach then lower until he was tracing circles around my clit. "Think you can come again?"

I nodded, my body feeling alive and on fire in the most delicious of ways.

He pushed a little deeper before dragging himself back, excruciatingly slow, millimetre by millimetre, his eyes never leaving mine while his fingers continued to tease. Then he pushed back in with one fluid motion, grinding his pelvis against mine and making everything inside me say, "Ohhh." I had never felt so entirely full like I did with him. Every sexual interaction I'd had before this day had always been laced with this longing for more, an aching emptiness that was never filled. *Until now.* I didn't think it was possible to quench that need, yet here I was, full. I didn't know if I could ever get enough.

Every fibre in my body shuddered as he moved. Back and forth, long languid strokes as he circled my clit, around and around, applying the perfect amount of pressure until he had me screaming.

"Holy shit!"

He groaned as I came around him, my insides tightened against his shaft. Then he placed a hand on the table, the other hooking my leg over his shoulder as he picked up the pace, fingers gripping my hip as we collided, again and again and again. I couldn't come down, I just continued riding the high and howling with ecstasy.

"Kris-tian," I moaned, unable to say more than one syllable in a breath.

"You feel too good. Just a little longer. A little longer." Each word was a breath as he thrust and thrust. I thought I might die if I didn't come again soon, the pressure in my core so great that I thought I might literally explode.

"Oh God!"

He clenched his teeth as he buried himself deep. "*Fuck*!" He shuddered and I screamed, my entire body tightening and shaking. It was world-altering stuff.

I'm liquid. I've come so hard that I'm a puddle of liquid that can't even speak.

Kristian's hand pushed my curls away from my face. "You OK?" he asked, out of breath but smiling.

Smiling was pretty much all I could do. It felt ridiculous, but I literally had no ability to react in any other way.

He laughed then gathered me up in his arms, pulling out of me before carrying me into the bedroom and placing me on the bed. "I think I broke you," he said as I relaxed against the pillows. This was the kind of sex I'd only ever heard about, spoken of like it was some kind of mythical moment we mortals may never be lucky enough to experience, but here it was. The type of sex you always wished you were having. No wonder I'd never felt sated. Kristian was a god.

I reached up and touched the side of his face, which was strange, because twenty-four hours ago I was sure I hated this face. *Him*. But not now. Now I just wanted it between my legs. "Give me twenty minutes' rest, and I'll be good to go again," I mumbled.

He grinned and leaned down, kissing me as he inhaled deeply. "I'm going to enjoy not hating you, doll."

I smiled. "Yeah. Me too."

CHAPTER TEN
DOG ON A LEASH

WE DIDN'T SEE Abbot again until Monday morning when he showed up dressed for work with coffees in a tray and pastries in a bag.

"Thought you two might be hungry after your fuck-fest," he said, dropping the bag on the kitchen table. I grinned and glanced at Kristian who dove right in. There was no point in pretending to be modest, I supposed.

"I got you a pack of smokes too." Abbot reached into his pocket and pulled out a pack of the same brand he smoked, along with a pink lighter with cute little flowers on the side.

"This is really great, thank you," I said, holding up the lighter.

"Whatever," he said. "Just let me know when you're low and I'll get you more."

Emotion surged inside me as I looked at the gift in my hands. It was probably the nicest thing anyone had done for me in a really long time, and I was pretty sure Abbot didn't even like me. *Shit.*

"Oh fuck. Don't start cryin' on me. It's just smokes. I'm only being nice as a favour to him."

"I know," I said, feeling annoyed at myself for losing control. "I just can't handle people being nice to me at all. It's weird, and I'm too tired to pretend to be cool."

His gaze shifted to Kristian. "Bro, what the hell did you do? You fucked her so hard you broke her. She's got emotions and shit now."

I punched him in the arm. "Shut up, fucker. I still hate you."

Abbot grinned. "Yeah, I still hate you too. But he's into you, so I have to try and be OK."

"Hence the peace offerings," I stated, oddly feeling better that this was all a display for Kristian's sake.

He nodded. "Hence the peace offerings. And as long as you two keep your shit contained to this house, you won't get any trouble from me." He looked at Kristian. "Sound fair, brother?"

Kristian nodded once then turned his attention to me. "Eat," he ordered, holding an apple danish out to me. I took it then the coffee he gave me, right before he slapped me on the arse. I let out a yelp. "Now go sit outside while we talk a bit."

With a smile, I saluted him and sauntered out into the yard, eating, drinking, and smoking as I bathed in the morning sunlight. *This is the life*. Although, I wasn't too sure about the 'keeping our shit in the house' comment because it reminded me how temporary all this was, but for now, I was OK. And who knew, if this thing between Kristian and me didn't die down by the time I'd worked off my debt, maybe he'd want to keep me around. And if not, maybe Toby actually would help me out. I felt like I finally had some options in this world.

Snippets of conversation flowed out of the house and into the yard. I needed to remember what a trumpet that house seemed to be, because private conversations weren't really that private at all. There was something said about a job to help Nate that was high-risk. I strained my ears, hoping for more details, but they'd obviously lowered their voices and I got nothing.

What kind of job would they consider high-risk? My mind automatically went to something nefarious, but that could have just been my own experience talking. There was a high possibility that these guys really were legitimate businessmen. I'd known a lot of crooks over the years and none of them ran a legitimate business and lived in a house by the sea. But then, they'd had the power to block Johno's illegal activities after our first run-in. Did that mean they were into their own illegal shit, or that they were just rich enough to pay people to do the things they wanted?

I didn't know. And honestly, I didn't want to find out. I liked the idea of being involved with a stand-up guy. This past week had been a window into what seemed like a normal life. But I knew in my gut that wasn't the case. The business, the house, the way they spoke… I knew a criminal when I saw one. Hell, the fact I was even attracted to Kristian told me he wasn't a *good* guy. I had never fallen for a guy with a clean rap sheet. There was no way they were legit; that was just my sex hormones romanticising shit.

"You ready?" Kristian said as he and Abbot strode outside.

I stood and brushed the crumbs from my leggings. "Sure am, bosses." I smiled, heading toward the Ute.

"She is way too happy today. She's freaking me out," Abbot said once we were all inside.

"What can I say, mate? I possess the wand of happiness between my legs. I can give you some tips if your women aren't smiling when they walk out the door."

Abbot cocked an eyebrow. "She's your *woman*, now?"

Kristian met my eyes in the rear-view mirror and smiled. "Well, I don't hate her."

———

For the rest of the week, I didn't spot a single thing about the way the brothers did business that confirmed my suspicions that they were up to something illegal. It was really messing with my head, because I *knew* something was going on, but they were good, and I couldn't spot any cracks in their façade.

Kristian and I fell into an easy kind of peace treaty. We spent our days mowing and gardening then we dropped Abbot off at that big house before returning to the beach shack to spend our nights fucking out all that excess energy. Maybe it was hate fucking, maybe it was something else, but damn, it felt good.

When the surf was decent, we hit the waves either in the morning or after work. More often than not, the call of the sea took a back step while we opted to answer the call of our bodies. It was early days, but I couldn't stop wanting him.

"I'm gonna come," I gasped, my hands on his chest as

I rode his cock, my movements getting faster the closer I drew to my conclusion.

"Wait for me, doll. I wanna come with you." Kristian held me at my hips, guiding me along his shaft and slamming against me to deepen each thrust.

Was it possible to have sex that was too good? If there was, I was definitely having it. I was going to die from too much pleasure.

"Oh God. I can't. I can't. I'm so close, so close."

"*Now*," he grunted, grinding his cock deep inside me as he held me still. I threw my head back and called out to the gods who made orgasms a thing.

"Holy fuckballs," I gasped, running my hands through my hair as we finished. I was buzzing all over.

Kristian cupped my breasts and chuckled. "Fuckballs?"

I rocked a little over him, still feeling the last waves of my orgasm receding. "Mmm, holy fuckballs."

"What does that even mean?"

I laughed. "I have no idea."

Grabbing me around the waist, he lifted me off him and rolled us until he was holding himself over me. He sucked slowly on one of my nipples, forcing it to a peak. "You think it means being balls deep in a tight little pussy?" He shifted and moved to the other nipple, giving it the same attention.

I moaned lightly, becoming aroused all over again. "It could also mean putting your balls inside someone while you fuck."

"Hmm, that would take talent. I don't think it would work to tuck your balls in with your dick."

I reached between us and took a hold of his shaft. It

was semi hard, but he had fantastic recovery time, so I knew he'd be fully erect in no time. "We could try it out."

"Or we could *not.*" He laughed, nuzzling my neck. "I think I'd rather bend you over and pull your hair while I fuck you from behind."

"I think I'd prefer that too."

"Roll over."

"Holy fuckballs, no!" Abbot yelled, suddenly bursting through the bedroom door.

"What the fuck?" Kristian yelled, pulling the blankets over us both to block Abbot's view. "Get out."

"We don't have time for you two to be *so close* and come together all over again. It's romantic as fuck, but I'm not sitting out there and listening to it a second time." *He was out there the whole time?* We had no idea.

Abbot stopped then pointed with his thumb over his shoulder, looking directly at his brother. "Did you have *any* idea how thin the walls are through here? I could hear every slap of skin."

Kristian lifted a brow as he took in the information. "Did you jack off to it?"

Abbot tilted his head a little. "I thought about it, but no, that would be weird." Then he picked up the clothes on the floor and started throwing them at us. "Now get up, get dressed, Jazz is expecting us. And I don't think you should be bringing your pet with you. Family only."

I sat up, holding the sheet to my chest. "His *pet*?"

Abbot stopped. "What else are you? His girlfriend? Sorry, sweetheart. You're nothing but a distraction."

Kristian sat up and pulled some briefs on to cover his manhood. "Shut your fucking mouth, brother. You don't get to talk to her like that."

"Seriously? Last week you wouldn't piss on her if she was on fire. Now you're fucking her and suddenly she gets *my* respect? No. It doesn't work like that. You need to get her out of your system and move the fuck on, *because we have work to do.* And she can't be here." The level of his voice rose with each word. I hid behind the sheet, knowing not to interfere with family. I'd only lose.

Kristian stepped towards him and stood to his full height, a tiny bit taller than Abbot. "Get the fuck out of here, Abbot, before you say something you'll regret. We'll meet you there."

"*We?*"

"We."

"You know Jazz is gonna flip if you show up with her."

"She can hang out with Holland. It's not a fucking problem."

"It's a huge fucking problem. Put your pet on a leash and tell her to stay put like a good little dog. Let's fucking *go.*"

Kristian launched himself across the room before I even had a chance to react. "Apologise to her," he growled, grabbing his twin by the front of his shirt and almost lifting him off his feet.

Abbot laughed. "You know that's never gonna fuckin' happen."

"Then get out of my sight. I don't wanna explain why I was forced to break your face." He released his hold and Abbot tightened his jaw while he straightened up his shirt. *Explain to who? Their mother?*

"You're thinking with the wrong head here, brother. I'm trying to stop you from making a gigantic mistake."

"I don't need you making decisions for me. Get the fuck out. Fuck off. *Leave*."

Abbot shook his head and looked my way. "You're a smart girl, Ronnie. Don't let him bring you. It won't end well. I promise you that."

I had two problems with what was going on. Firstly, I didn't like being told what to do. Kristian did it all the time, but that was different because I got off on his bossiness. But Abbot had no right to tell me to do anything. On top of that, he'd called me a dog. As far as I was concerned, he could go fuck himself.

I lifted my chin in defiance. "Tell your mum to set an extra place for lunch."

Abbot pressed his mouth into a tight line and shook his head. Then Kristian shoved him out the door and locked it behind him. "Fuck," he said, running his hands through his hair. I sat and watched as he paced back and forth. This was it. This was the moment where I knew all my suspicions were correct. Abbot was trying to keep me from learning anything about the nature of the family's true business, and Kristian was railing against them. Why, I didn't really understand. I just knew he felt disquiet deep inside him, and something about what was going on between us was helping him deal with that.

"Why did you do that?" I asked, shaking a little from the whole altercation. "Why are you fighting with your brother?" It wasn't the first time I'd seen him and Abbot put their hands on each other, or argue for that matter. They wrestled and argued all the time at work, but it was different this time because it was about me. He'd just gotten physical with his twin over a girl he was just meant to be fucking. *That* meant something.

"Because I don't think I *can* get you out of my system. Now, get dressed," he commanded, tension in his shoulders as he stood in the centre of the room. "I need to try and figure this out."

Getting up, I dug through my bags, trying to find something suitable—and clean—to wear while I mulled over his words. This thing between us was intense, that was sure, but was it worth fighting his family for? Was *I* worth that? I pulled on a pair of cotton panties before I found my black Roxy dress with the flyaway design that hung loose to my mid thigh and had thin straps that criss-crossed down the open back. *Too sexy.* I dropped it on the bed and hunted through for something else.

Kristian stopped pacing for a moment and picked it up and held it in front of him. "You wear a bra with this thing?"

I glanced over my shoulder at him, noticing that he'd already pulled on a pair of jeans, but had yet to add a shirt.

"No," I said, grabbing it from his hands, about to stuff it back into my bag.

"Put it on."

I stopped and turned to face him. "To go and see your family?"

He nodded. "And lose the panties."

I clutched the dress against my chest, suddenly feeling very uncomfortable. "No."

Moving closer, he held my chin so I couldn't look away. "Who are you dressing for? Them or me?"

I snatched my chin away. "Me."

He pulled the dress from my hands. "Wrong answer." He held it up like he was going to force it over my head.

"Don't you dare." I held up my finger to stop him. "I'm not your whore."

"No. But you're the woman I like to fuck." He dropped it over my head, putting my arms through the straps like I was a child. "And I want you as naked as possible at all times." I stood there and let him do it, feeling confused and a little numb. He'd just fought with his brother, told me he couldn't get me out of his system, and now he was labelling me as 'the woman he liked to fuck'. What the hell? My head was spinning from all the back and forth. We'd had a great week, we'd laughed and enjoyed every moment together. Then suddenly, he was being an arsehole again. *Typical.* I never was a good judge of men.

Once my dress was on, he dropped to his knees and pulled my panties down my legs with excruciatingly slow movements. There must be something wrong with me, because I was kinda turned on, his touch forcing a light whimper to burst from my lips. When my underwear was gone, his hand slid up under my dress, cupping my breast and rolling my already erect nipple between his fingers.

"I hate you again," I whispered as my eyes fluttered closed and his tongue swept between my thighs. My entire body shuddered. My knees went weak.

"No. You don't," he said, lowering me so I was lying back on the bed. He pushed his fingers inside me, massaging my walls as he looked into my eyes. "In fact, I'm willing to bet that you like me a hell of a lot."

"I don't," I gasped, causing him to chuckle before he brought his mouth to mine while his fingers worked their magic inside me. I couldn't take it anymore, coming on his hand and groaning into his mouth. When he tore his lips away, he looked down at me, grinning and triumphant.

"You were saying?"

"I really don't like you at all," I whispered.

He laughed. "Liar."

I shook my head. Then he fucked me until I agreed. It took almost an hour for me to admit I liked him, and we arrived late to his mother's house, but I didn't really think he cared. Why? Because he won. I was wearing the dress and nothing else. Well, I won too. Three orgasms wasn't anything to shrug at. I just wasn't going to tell him that since he seemed so pleased with himself. *Men.*

"HARK! A VAGRANT."

"Excuse me?" I asked the woman sitting on a pool lounger. She wore sunglasses and had her bleached-blonde hair twisted in a bun on the top of her head. I was fairly sure she was the matron of honour from the wedding. Although I couldn't remember her name.

"It's nothing," she said, waving her comment off. "Just a silly joke for the drama geeks." She sat forward and held out her hand. "I'm Holland."

"Ronnie," I said, smiling. It was the most welcomed I'd felt since arriving.

Abbot hadn't been wrong when he said I wasn't wanted in Jasmine's house. I'd kind of expected a bit of a temper tantrum on arrival, but I'd been greeted with calm indifference. Six sets of eyes had swung in my direction as I stood at Kristian's side, telling me I shouldn't be here. No one spoke except Jasmine.

"You're vouching for her now?" she'd asked with her ice-blue eyes on Kristian.

"I guess," Kristian had replied.

"You *guess*?"

He sighed. "Yeah, OK. I am. I'm vouching for her. I want her here."

I was ridiculously confused listening to the exchange. "Listen, I'm not here to cause any trouble," I started.

Jasmine smiled in a way that wasn't at all welcoming. "Yet here you are." Her eyes shifted from me to Kristian. "We need to talk." Then she told me to go wait by the pool.

The whole exchange screamed insanity. I felt like I was being presented to the *fucking mob* for consideration, with Jasmine the obvious boss. I'd asked it before and I'd ask it again—who the fuck *were* these people?

Holland tilted her head to the side. "Are you part of the 'blissfully unaware' or the 'hated by Jasmine' group?" she asked, releasing my hand before I took the seat next to her.

"Ahhh, both?" I laughed. "Me showing up seemed to cause a bit of a stir in there. I have a feeling I was brought here to prove a point or something."

"Hmm. Those Cartwright men are good at pulling stunts to get their point across."

"I'm not sure what Kristian's point is."

"Probably that he wants change. If he's anything like his older brothers, I'd say he's become restless with the status quo."

"Was Nate restless too?" She gave me a quizzical look. "I was a waiter at the wedding a couple of weeks back. I saw you there."

"Ahh, of course. Well, yes, Nate was very restless when we met. He had everything a person could want in life, but he was missing one very big thing."

"The love of a good woman," I finished for her. She gave me a smile and a nod. "That's ridiculously cliché, don't you think?"

She shrugged. "Possibly. Doesn't make it any less true." She took a moment to regard me. "You're the girl who scratched up Kris's car, aren't you?"

"The one and only."

"Seems you've been forgiven."

"Oh, I don't know if he'll ever forgive me for that. I've kind of been messing with his car for a while."

"Oh dear." She laughed. "What did you do?"

"Messed with his tyres a few times. Once, I siphoned off his petrol. I'm a bit of a vindictive bitch when I want to be."

A chuckle burst from her lips. "Remind me never to get on your bad side."

I shrugged and watched the reflection of the sun on the surface of the pool. It was peaceful out here.

"He must've forgiven you somewhat; bringing you here is a bit of a big deal."

"I don't know what his thought process is. But we've definitely found some common ground."

She lifted her brow, her expression telling me she knew exactly what that common ground was. "I'll bet." She grinned.

To my surprise, I felt myself blush. I had *never* blushed over a man before. *What is wrong with me?* "It's not just that, we…I don't know, we seem to get each other. It's working for the moment."

She smiled as she regarded me with a nod. "I get it. It was like that with Nate too. The beginning of our relation-ship was absolute chaos. But there was that instant connection. Cartwright men are very good at taking what they want with no regard for anyone else. Still, I can't imagine myself without him. His family, I could do without most days. But they have this fierce devotion to each other that won't be eclipsed by anything external. Either we all get drawn in or we get our hearts broken."

I took a deep breath and looked towards the house where the family was convening. It had only been a week of fucking for convenience, so I didn't think Kristian Cartwright had the ability to break my heart. I'd make sure I didn't get too attached, though. A woman in my position couldn't afford to get caught up in feelings. It would just make it harder to go back to what I was before.

"Was it the same for Alesha and Sam?" I asked for the sake of making conversation and learning more about this family I'd fallen in with. "Did they have a chaotic beginning too?"

She thought for a moment. "I would say they had a chaotic middle. They got married before they knew each other, and there was a steep learning curve after that."

"That's crazy. What'd they do, get drunk in Vegas?"

A musical laugh burst from her lips. I kind of liked her, which was odd for me. I'd never been great at getting along with other women. Or anyone, really. I was fantastic at burning bridges. Never go back, I always said.

"Not quite. There's a very involved story about how they came to be. It'd be best if she told you herself. I'd bet she could write a pretty interesting book about it if she tried."

I smiled. "I'll have to keep my eye out for it."

Comfortable silence fell between us for a moment, and I took the opportunity to look around the yard. Although, yard didn't seem the right word as much as *property* did. Close to the house, there was an outdoor kitchen with a long wooden table. Just beyond that was the large kidney-shaped pool we sat by. Behind a detached garage was a tennis court as well as a manicured lawn that went on for days. It was secluded and screamed money.

"Do you know what's going on inside?" I asked after a while.

"That all depends on what you know." She smiled but I could tell she was wary.

I decided that if I was smart and pieced together what I *did* know, I might be able to get her to tell me something more about the Cartwright's business.

But what did I know? Not much.

They had pull. They had enough knowledge of the local criminal element to implement a roadblock when they wanted to. And they—meaning Toby—could find things out about people that those people didn't want known. They were obviously a powerful crime family of sorts. But what kind?

Wracking my brain, I formed my speculation based on the conversation I'd overheard between Kristian and Abbot and the things I assumed.

"Your husband messed up and needs money. Fast. They're trying to plan a job with a big pay day." I held my breath, hoping she couldn't see how pulled from my own arse that summation was. I could have been wrong, but the admission was all over her face. I was right.

"You can't blame Nate, though. It's my fault, really," she started, talking as if she really needed to confess but was never given the opportunity to say her piece. I was more than happy to listen. "If I hadn't been so obsessed with making him go straight, he wouldn't have felt the need to do what he did so we could leave. He pissed off the wrong people, and now we need to pay those people to leave us alone. To leave *all* of us alone."

"What did he do?" I was risking giving away the fact that I had no information at all, but I hoped being provided a sympathetic ear might spur her on.

"You don't know that part?"

I shrugged. "I just know the basics, and I didn't want to pry into the details since I'm not family. Really, it's none of my business and you don't have to tell me, either. I shouldn't have asked."

"It's fine." She waved her hand in the air. "You're bound to find out eventually. There's a lot of family tension because of it, so it may as well come from me. Nate had a side job going. Did you know that part?" I nodded, even though I didn't. "He was growing poppies for some big drug manufacturers. You know, *Breaking Bad* level shit. When I found out about it, I left. Because while I could handle the stealing, I couldn't handle his involvement in drugs—I'd witnessed the damage heroin addiction can do to family first-hand. So I ended things. It was horrible on both of us. But, to win me back, he burned the field to the ground and faked his own death. We ran away together and everything was peaceful for a while, but then the shit hit the fan. That's what they're dealing with inside."

"Wow. That's some crazy shit. Although, I guess if a guy is willing to fake his own death for you, you never have to question his devotion."

She laughed a little and nodded. "That's true. He just didn't fully think it through." She let out her breath slowly.

"You know, it's nice to be able to talk about this to somebody. It gets real lonely out here when they're all in there."

"Why *are* you out here?"

"Honestly, I just don't want to know the details of what they do. I know what happens, I know when it happens, but I don't want to know how. It's easier for me that way."

"The life of crime isn't for you?"

She shook her head. "Hopefully it isn't for this little guy either," she said, running a hand lovingly over her belly.

"You're pregnant?"

"About ten weeks in. I have to tell you, it's scary."

"Because it's early days, or because of the drug dealers?"

"Both. But mostly the dealers. Nate made a deal with them, but I'm worried what will happen if it doesn't work out."

"Do you think they'd really come after *everyone*?" *And did everyone include me?*

Holland nodded then sat back and crossed her feet at the ankles. "Sometimes being a Cartwright has its perks. Sometimes it really doesn't."

"Guess I should consider myself lucky I'm not a Cartwright." I wasn't sure I was up for dealing with the bloodlust of a drug lord. No dick was worth that shit.

She chuckled. "Not yet."

I scoffed at the insinuation. "I think I can pretty much guarantee you that Kristian *does not* want me to be a part of his family."

"Really? Then why do you think you're here?"

This line of questioning caused my stomach to flip. "Kristian and Abbot had a fight over whether I should be here or not. It just seemed like regular dick swinging to me. You know, men throwing their weight around to prove who's boss? I came because, I don't know, Kristian said I had to." I wasn't sure if she was fully appraised of Kristian's and my master-slave relationship, so I gave her the vague details.

With a smile playing on her lips, she looked at me for an uncomfortably long time. I wanted to yell, "What!" but then her gaze flicked to a point past my shoulder. "Looks like you're wanted," she said, nodding towards the house as Kristian came walking in our direction.

I laughed. "Hardly." Because no one really wanted me. They might have wanted *something* from me, but never me as an individual.

Holland just smiled and laced her fingers behind her head. "Welcome to the family, Ronnie. You might want to put some panties on for this next part."

It was pretty obvious at this point in my life that I had a really shitty moral compass. But at least I knew who I was and never pretended to be anything else (Except that hour at the beach shack where I tried to act like a 'nice girl', and we all knew how that turned out.) I also didn't have a problem associating with others who had a murky relationship with the legal system. I didn't judge people for the way they decided to make their money. At the end of the day, we all needed it, and we all preferred to make it the easiest way possible. It was a fact of life.

That being said, I did have a limit to how deep into the criminal world I wanted to go. Stealing cars, selling weed, even pirating movies from the cinema, those were all things I could get behind. Anything deeper and I started getting uneasy, because that's when guns got involved. And I *hated* guns.

Back when Johno and I were dating, we used the contacts his mate Dazza had to fence some jewellery we found in the glovebox of one of our cars. There was a watch worth nearly five grand and a pair of diamond earrings, worth…I couldn't remember. Anyway, we met with the guy while he was having a 'house party'. It was hooker city in there, tits out, open-air fucking, and drugs all over the tables. I wanted to leave the moment we got there, but I sucked it up because we needed the cash. I went with Johno and Dazza into this guy's office, he took a look at the merchandise and bought it from us, no trouble. But when he paid us, he opened one of the safes in his wall. Fucking guns. At least ten handguns and one of those little machine guns you only ever saw in movies, on top of piles of money. He made a big deal about showing them to us and made it clear he had the power to hunt us down and fill us with bullet holes if we ever crossed him. I immediately agreed and then got the fuck out of there, telling Johno I would never fence jewellery again. I'd rather throw that shit out than enter that man's home, or whatever the fuck it was, again.

That was close to how I felt when Kristian called me into the house. Scared shitless. It really was a terrible idea to forgo underwear.

"What have you gotten me into?" I hissed as he led me to a bar area on the house's first floor.

"Nothin' you can't handle, doll. Relax. I got you."

While the sentiment made my chest flip happily, the

giant moths in my stomach flapped clumsy wings, making me feel ill as I was presented to Jasmine, the big boss, the matriarch. *Fuck.*

She sat on a stool and held a crystal glass of clear liquid with a wedge of lime inside it. Everything about her positioning—the crossed legs, the way she rested her forearm along the marble-topped bar—was designed to make her look casual, welcoming. Even her smile appeared to draw me in. But her eyes? Her eyes told me to watch out. I was standing before a predator.

"I don't think I need to point out that your presence wasn't expected today," she said, placing her glass on a coaster without it making a sound.

"Honestly, ma'am, no one expects me. They just kind of deal with the fact I'm there," I said, offering a smile and a self-deprecating joke. She didn't seem to see the humour in it and just looked at me like she was trying to figure out how I got on the bottom of her shoe. *Yikes.*

"I need to know why you *think* you were brought here today."

"Uh, I think Kristian brought me here as a big *fuck you* to his twin brother. He and Abbot seem to be at logger-heads over what to do with me."

"So, you consider yourself a trinket, arm candy?"

I swallowed. Calling me *that* really made it seem like I was a hooker. But I couldn't really argue with the facts. "Yeah," I said quietly. "That about sums it up."

"You weren't hoping to get yourself involved with our business?"

What business is she talking about? The legitimate or the criminal? I decided it was best to be safe and act dumb. "Are you franchising the mowing business or something?"

I hoped the sheen on my upper lip didn't give away my nerves. I had a feeling that if I said the wrong thing to her, I may regret waking up that morning.

She laughed. "No franchise plans. Although, I heard you were a great worker this week. A job, and a handsome man's bed to rest in. You must be feeling very pleased with yourself."

"I'm just doing as I'm told, ma'am."

"It's Jasmine."

"Jasmine. But to be fair, the bed part isn't part of the deal, per se. He's not making me sleep with him." I didn't want her to think her son was forcing himself on anyone. Although from the disinterested look on her face, I assumed she didn't care.

"Do you smoke, Veronica?"

"I prefer Ronnie."

"Veronica. Do you smoke?"

Okay. So my preferences didn't seem to matter here. That wasn't anything new.

I cleared my throat. "Occasionally."

She picked up a pack of cigarettes and offered me one. I honestly didn't feel inclined, but took it anyway, not wanting to say no to the woman who had previously wanted to kill me.

I held it between my lips and she sparked a flame, holding the silver lighter out for me. My fingers itched to take it and put it in my pocket. But I refrained.

"Thank you." I blew out my first inhale as she lit her own cigarette.

"No one smokes anymore," she mused. "I'm running out of people to share them with. Do you have that problem? There's something about the act that needs to be shared, I think. Even if you aren't speaking. Company is good. It's during the moments of deep inhales that clarity comes. Problems are solved, plans made. Don't you agree?"

I nodded.

"Most of them don't even want me smoking near them. Especially Holland since she's pregnant now." She held one hand up to shield her mouth. "Don't tell her I told you. Early days."

I made the shape of an O with my mouth, even though I already knew. I wondered what this woman's game was. What did she want from someone like me? I couldn't imagine she just wanted to get to know me. I was on tenterhooks waiting for the other shoe to drop, listening while she prattled on.

"Abbot is the only one, really, but I'm sure you've already learned his conversational skills aren't the greatest. We can talk shop though." Her eyes moved to my toes then returned to my face. *What the hell am I supposed to say here?* I thought it best to say nothing unless she asked me a direct question. "Tell me, Veronica, what is it you want most out of life?"

Wow. Straight to the deep stuff.

I shrugged. "Nothing out of the ordinary."

"Care to elaborate?"

My mouth opened then closed before I pressed my lips together, trying to work out what to say. I knew exactly what I wanted: more than what I had. I wanted to stop worrying. I wanted to stop struggling and fighting. I wanted someone to care about me.

"I just want to belong," I said, finally. It was probably

the most honest sentence to ever come out of my mouth, but why I told *her*, I wasn't quite sure.

A sage nod bobbed her head. "I actually see a lot of myself in you, Veronica."

"Seriously?" Was that based on the fact I was smoking? We had barely had any contact before now—unless of course Toby had shared his findings with her, then she'd know a hell of a lot.

"Yes," she said, standing as she finished her cigarette and stubbed it out in a glass ashtray. "You see opportunity and you grab hold of it with both hands."

Should I be offended by that? "This isn't exactly a choice I was given."

"No. But you're certainly making the most of it. I admire that. It takes a lot of guts to be exactly the woman you need to be in any given situation—a lot of talent too. I have my eye on you."

"OK," I said, not sure if that meant I needed to watch out, or that she wanted me to impress her.

"Now, come. Lunch is ready, and I hear I was to save you a seat."

Abbot dobbed? Ugh. "That was just me ribbing Abbot. He really didn't need to pass the message on."

She smiled. "Still. There is a seat. Let's see how the rest of the family reacts to you."

"HOPE YOU'RE ALL HUNGRY," Jasmine said as she carried out a giant bowl of salad and set it in the middle of the table. "There's enough food here to feed an army."

"The way these guys eat, we'll be lucky if they don't bite my arms off trying to get at this. Look at their eyes," Alesha joked as Sam and Toby both rushed to help her carry a tray full of chicken schnitzel. She was taller than me, super slim, and had dark brown, almost black hair.

"Well, hurry up then, woman," Abbot said. "We're hungry men." He snapped his teeth in her direction.

It was obviously a joke, but Sam hit him up the back of his head. "Don't speak to my wife like that, douchebag."

With a scowl, Abbot rubbed the sore spot. "She knows I'm only mucking around."

"He was only joking, Sam," Alesha said, her brown eyes soft as she gazed toward her husband.

"I don't care, peaches. When he gets his own woman, he can command her around and call her 'woman' all he wants. But he doesn't get to do that to mine."

"What's up *your* arse?" Abbot groused, frowning at his older brother.

"You. You're a pig lately."

"How? Because I'm not so desperate for a girl that I kidnapped one?"

A flurry of motion involved two brothers launching themselves at Abbot, while the other two jumped to hold them back. I took a step backwards to avoid the commotion.

"Enough," Nate barked, his arm blocking Kristian.

"Yeah, enough," Abbot said with a smirk. "The queen has gathered us to eat."

I glanced at Jasmine who pursed her lips and leaned forward on the table. "I don't know what's *up your arse* at the moment, Abbot, but you're going to need to unclench those cheeks and start playing nice before your attitude starts to hit you in the hip pocket."

He lifted his brow in surprise. "Are you seriously threatening to cut my allowance like I'm some kid?"

"That's exactly what I'm doing, child."

"This is fucking bullshit," he yelled, standing up and flipping the tray of schnitzel over on the table. "Enjoy your lunch, dickheads. Enjoy your stolen women too. I'm out of here." Then he turned around and took off. *What the hell?* Was that outburst because of me? I didn't understand what his deal was. Why was having me at a family lunch such an issue for him? It wasn't like I was marrying into his precious family. I'd been clearly relegated to the spectator seats.

"What's with you lot and flipping shit over whenever you're cranky," Alesha commented, grabbing the tray from the table while Sam and Nate helped clear up the mess.

They kind of murmured and shrugged sheepishly. I heard something about testosterone.

"Well," Jasmine said, taking a deep breath. "That was exciting. Why don't you all sit down? No point in wasting a good meal just because it fell on the table."

After we all got settled and the food was passed around, Alesha was the first one to make conversation, her expression telling me she'd been mulling something over in her mind. "I happen to think it was really romantic," she said, cutting into her chicken. "Fate pushed us all together in the craziest of ways and we found love in the middle of an epic mess. So it doesn't matter how it started, just what grew out of it. And honestly, I wouldn't trade this family for the world—even Abbot."

Everyone smiled, and Sam kissed her shoulder. Meanwhile, I slid a cherry tomato in my mouth while I tried to work out what was going on. *They were kidnapped?* If what I was piecing together was true, this all sounded a little Stockholm Syndromey to me.

"It's cool, Leesh," Kristian said from beside me. "He's not pissed at you guys. He's pissed at me."

"What did you do?" Holland asked, holding a glass of sparkling water to her lips.

"I broke the twin code."

"The twin code?" Toby asked with a frown. This was obviously a new thing to them. "What the hell is the *twin code*?"

"Ah, it's a code of conduct between twins, obviously," Kristian deadpanned.

"Why don't we know anything about this?" Nate asked.

"Because you're not a twin. We don't share our code with other people. That would defeat the purpose."

"Kind of like fight club," I said, nodding my under- standing. *First rule: Don't talk about it.*

Kristian looked at me and grinned. "Yeah. Just like that, but between twins."

"All right. So how did you break it?" Jasmine asked.

He pressed his lips together as he addressed the table. "No girlfriends unless they're best friends, sisters, or preferably identical twins."

Sam laughed. "Why is that even a rule? You two have *never* had girlfriends."

"That's partly because of work, but primarily because it's hard to find girls we both like who fit the mould," Kristian said, wiping his hand over his face in slight frus- tration. "We came up with this code when we were like, sixteen, and he's pissed I'm not sticking to it. He's citing twin law that I can't bring a girl into our house for more than one night without her fitting the 'aforementioned criteria', and I'm telling him to grow the fuck up because we aren't kids anymore. But as you can see, he's pouting. I don't know why it's such a big deal for him. Ronnie's only staying with us for a month until she's worked enough to pay off the damage to my Ute, and who the fuck knows what happens from there? It's early, right?" He looked at me for clarification, but I was still reeling over the fact he called me his girlfriend in one sentence then gave a time limit to our arrangement in another. The gist of it though, was that I was causing the tension between the brothers. Something I already knew, but felt uncomfortable having aired during a family meal when I was the outsider.

"I, uh, can leave now if it's a problem," I forced out,

not really wanting to say it but feeling it was best in the situation. I could talk to Toby, maybe find some other solution. And if Kristian could still be bothered with me, well, we could work that out too. It didn't have to be all or nothing.

"No." Kristian's hand landed on my thigh and he squeezed my bare leg under the table. "You're not going anywhere. He can grow up and get the fuck over it." Then he leaned a little closer, his hand sliding up my thigh as he spoke so only I could hear. "*No one* is taking away my access to this." His fingers brushed lightly between my legs, and I nodded so it looked like he said something reassuring instead of doing something dirty. I had to look down to hide the flicker of heat in my eyes. Although, maybe there was a little hurt there too. Holland had suggested there could be more between Kristian and me, and I read a little too deep into his words. But it was clear why I was still around now. *Sex.* I was there to pay off a debt and to provide Kristian with an outlet for his insatiable sexual appetite. Best to keep that in mind, and ensure my heart stayed safe. Untouchable. The way it always had been....

"You know, it sounds to me he could do with finding a woman of his own," Holland put in. "I reckon Jasmine should match him up." She giggled as she looked Jasmine's way.

"Well, I'm obviously fantastic at it," Jasmine said with a shrug, and everyone laughed. I didn't really get the joke, so I just sat there trying to decide if I actually liked these people.

It didn't take long for the awkwardness of Abbot's outburst to disperse. Despite the overturned schnitzel, we ended up having a fairly nice meal. Conversation flowed freely, as did the alcohol, and by the end of it, I was feeling a little buzzed along with everyone else. I was loosening up a bit, participating in their discussions, laughing along with their jokes. Despite the odd circumstances surrounding the way we all met, no one treated me like I was a piece of shit, or like I didn't deserve to sit at the table with them—which really, was how I expected to be received. And while it was weird sitting at a table eating a meal with people I had a messed-up history with, I was actually having a really great time.

"I like your family," I said when the table was cleared away and Kristian had lured me upstairs with a wink and smile.

He flopped back on the queen-sized bed that dominated a grey-schemed room. "Like how you like me?" Leaning up on his elbows, he offered me a cheeky grin.

"I said that under duress, so it doesn't count in my opinion."

"Nah. Sorry, doll. No take backs. You said you like me and that's fact now."

I laughed. "You are so full of yourself."

"I think you have that one wrong. It's you who's about to be full of me." Reaching out, he caught my hand in his and tugged me closer, flipping me back so I bounced on the bed. He was very quick to lean over me.

"You're a jackass," I told him, although the smile on my face told a different story altogether.

He brushed his nose alongside mine, lips teasing as his hands slid down my side until he hit my bare skin.

"You seriously want to do this right now with your

family downstairs?" I gasped as he pressed his erection into my side.

"You have *nothing* on underneath your dress."

"Speaking of," I said as his fingers began to lift my hem. "I think your sister-in-law saw what I had for breakfast."

He chuckled. "Which one?"

"Holland."

"Lucky her." His mouth moved down my chest, pressing kisses against the swell of my breasts as his hands made it to my hips, exposing my skin. I closed my eyes, trying to focus on how wonderful I felt whenever he touched me, but the events during lunch kept tapping against my mind.

"Your mother is interesting. She made it feel like lunch was some sort of an audition."

He slid down my body and pressed his lips against my stomach. "Jasmine is wary of outsiders."

"Why? And why do you call her Jasmine instead of Mum?"

He stopped what he was doing and sighed before meeting my eyes. His hair was sticking up, and in the afternoon light, his blue eyes seemed even more piercing against the tan of his skin. *My God, he's so beautiful.* "Can we *please* stop talking about my family? It's kind of awkward when I'm about to eat out your pussy and have a raging hard-on."

I ran my fingers through his silken hair, smiling as I sighed happily. "Of course. I'll shut up."

Burying his head beneath my dress, he ran his tongue around the edge of my belly button then down the smooth skin, a damp trail toward what I knew would be mind-numbing pleasure. And I tried to relax and enjoy it. I really did. But the uncertainty of my situation wouldn't allow it. Too much was happening in my mind.

"Kristian?"

"Hmm?"

"What did Abbot mean when he said you all had to kidnap women to find a girlfriend?"

He stopped what he was doing, coming out from under my dress and sitting back on his knees.

"He was being a dick," he said, straightening my dress.

"You don't have to stop," I said.

Releasing a humourless laugh, he wiped a hand over his face. "Yes, I do. You have questions. Ask them."

"I can ask them later."

He lifted his brows. "Oh, I don't think you can. Ask now. I can fuck you later." He flopped down beside me on the bed and flashed his charming smile. "Just don't expect to be gettin' any sleep tonight."

I rolled onto my side and leaned up on my elbow, eager to understand anything about these mysterious Cartwrights.

"Explain the kidnapping comment."

"Like you, Holland and Alesha posed a...*problem* to our family."

"Like me? You mean they kept fucking with your cars?"

He smiled and shook his head. "No. They got involved in things that weren't theirs to get involved with."

"Like what?"

His tongue poked out, wetting his lips before he rubbed them together. "I can't really say."

"Because it was something illegal?"

This time he pulled his lip between his teeth. "I never said that."

"You don't need to. It's obvious. Even if I wasn't of dubious character myself, I'd be pretty sure something villainous was going on."

"Dubious. Villainous. All you've seen is a family and a gardening business."

I scoffed. He was playing me for a sucker. "You're obviously used to a certain type of girl, Kristian Cartwright. Newsflash: I'm not one if your bimbos who will giggle and push my tits in your face because I think you're hot. I have a brain, I have eyes, and I have ears. The very fact you felt comfortable making me your slave would be enough to tell me you had more going on than *just* a gardening business. Top that with the fact you had no trouble tracking and stealing your car back, that you completely blocked any trading partnerships Johno, Dazza and I had created, *and* that your mother flippantly suggested killing me to get me out of the way at the wedding, I have a pretty compelling case."

"Do you have any evidence to support your *case*?" His expression was so impassive that I wanted to slap his face.

"Are you seriously going to tell me I'm wrong?"

He shrugged. "All seems pretty circumstantial to me."

I sat up and frowned. "Fuck you, Kristian. I'm not stupid. Don't try and treat me like I am."

He laughed at me and held out his hands. "What? If you're gonna accuse me and my family of something, make sure you have some fucking proof first."

"What more proof do I need? The cloak-and-dagger shit, getting presented to your mother and questioned. It's a fucking test. For what, I don't fucking know—to see what I know, to see if I fit in, or if I'm useful? Which one? What the fuck is going on?"

"Why don't you tell me exactly what you think is going on?"

"What? I just… Oh my god. My brain is going to explode. You know what?" I scooted to the edge of the bed. "I don't have to put up with this shit."

"Really? Where you gonna go? We've got your house. I mean, car."

I stood up and pulled my dress down as far as it could go, glaring at him. Clearly there were no secrets within this family. I'd practically begged Toby not to tell anyone. Why had I thought I could trust him? *Arsehole.*

"Yeah. I can figure shit out about people too. And you were just a little too desperate to sleep with some guy you supposedly hated."

"And what does that say about you?"

"That I have really low standards."

My mouth fell open. I could have scratched his face off. "Screw you, Kristian. I'd rather live on the street than share a bed with you."

"Back to hating each other then?"

I stuffed my feet back into my sandals. "Maybe I never stopped. Maybe I was just faking it all because I'm *so fucking desperate.*"

"You're a shit liar, Ronnie."

"And you're a shit human being. Good luck with Nate's big score. I hope you all have a really great time pulling that one off. Unless of course someone else gets in there first."

"What the fuck do you know about that?"

I held up my middle finger. "That you can shove it up your arse. Have a nice life, Kristian."

With that, I opened the door and flew down the stairs, the sound of the slamming door and what I imagined was a fist against the wall following me.

I may not have had a lot in my life, but I had my pride. And sticking around to be insulted and used just wasn't working for me anymore. I wasn't stupid. I wouldn't be treated that way.

Like you, Holland and Alesha posed a...problem to our family.

Knowing my outburst probably turned me into an even bigger problem than I already was, I jolted to a stop before I hit the bottom of the stairwell, flattening myself against the wall.

Kill her. I'm not having our family threatened again because some girl doesn't know her place.

I couldn't just run out there. That would be stupid. From what I'd gathered, these people were willing to protect their family's secrets by any means necessary. I might not have meant much to many people, but I wasn't ready to die because I'd had enough of my boyfriend. *Boyfriend*? No. That was never who he was. I was just a girl he kept in the house too long who didn't fit some criterion.

Because I'm not so desperate for a girl that I kidnapped one?

Kidnapped. Was this a regular thing for the Cartwright men? Did they take women and keep them under constant guard, the same way Kristian was with me? Was that how it was? And what happened when these kidnapped girls fought back? It may have seemed like things worked out OK for Holland and Alesha, but how many girls came before them? Was there an ex-girlfriend cemetery out there somewhere? A place they disposed of all the girls who learned too much or didn't fit the family mould? *What the fuck is going on here!*

Holding my breath, I tried to calm the beating of my panicked heart so I could listen. I was freaking out. I'd gotten myself into something I didn't understand and it was scaring the shit out of me. I needed to get out before it was too late.

Voices floated up the stairwell, laughter, and cama-raderie. The stairs opened out in the entry foyer right between the kitchen and the formal living area. I'd need to be careful before stepping into the open or I'd be seen.

Taking a deep breath, I looked back the way I came. Kristian hadn't followed me. Why? Was he counting on the rest of his family to stop me from leaving? Did he just not care?

Of course he doesn't care. You're a thing to him. Just go.

Staying against the wall, I made my way to the ground floor as silently as possible. I peeked down the hallway where I'd heard the voices. I felt sure the rest of the family were either in the rumpus room near the bar or outside by the pool. The front of the house seemed thankfully quiet. If they'd heard Kristian and me arguing, they didn't seem too concerned. All I had to do was casually walk out the front door and I could be done with this. Done with being used, done with being dragged into a world no one would explain to me, done with Kristian. It didn't matter how he made me feel. I had to let him go. Like every other man in my life, he was no good for me.

He didn't want me.

Saying a silent prayer to a god I didn't understand, I stood up straight and strode towards the oversized wooden door. I was going to walk out and just keep walking. I didn't need to get mixed up in their shit—whatever it was.

Reaching out, I gripped the handle, took a breath, and turned it.

"Fuck."

It turned, but the deadlock was bolted. I couldn't get through.

No wonder no one's paying attention. I'm locked in.

Looking over my shoulder cautiously, I moved into the lounge room and began trying the windows. There had to be a way out of here.

"Don't bother," a female voice said.

Startled, I turned around and found Holland lying on the couch. She looked half asleep as she sat up.

"I…" I started, looking for some sort of excuse like needing fresh air, but she just waved her hand at me.

"Don't waste your breath either. I've been in your position, babe, and they're not stupid enough to leave the front door open."

Holding my hands in front of me, I twisted my fingers together as I approached her. "Are, um, are you feeling all right?" I indicated the fact she was lying down.

"Oh yeah. Just tired all the time with this pregnancy. I'll be fine." She propped a cushion at her back and got herself comfortable. "Why were you leaving? You and Kris have a fight?"

I pressed my lips together and glanced toward the staircase. Still no sign of him. *Arrogant bastard.* "You could say that," I said. "I just don't think being together is the right thing for either of us."

She laughed. "It's a bit late for that now."

"It's never too late to walk away from a shitty relationship."

"It is when you know everything you know."

"Well, as far as he's concerned, I have no idea what I'm talking about, and I'm too stupid to see what's going on right in front of me. He might have picked a blonde, but he neglected to make sure I was a bimbo."

Playing with the tassel on the corner of the pillow, she smirked. "I like you, Ronnie."

"Really? Wanna help get me out of here then?"

"That would cause some massive problems. And I'm not the most liked woman around here."

"I'm not going to tell anyone anything if that's what you're worried about. I don't have a good relationship with the cops myself. I'm not interested in getting mixed up in anyone's shit. I just want to get the fuck out of here and forget I ever met Kristian Cartwright."

She looked at me for a long moment before she glanced around the room, checking that we truly were alone. Then she lowered her voice to a whisper.

"The laundry has a doggy door. Maybe you're small enough to fit through."

"There's a dog? What kind?"

"A Boston terrier named Rogue. He's Toby's, and he doesn't bite unless he's commanded. I learned that the hard way." She scowled and rubbed a hand over her butt cheek.

"They sicked their dog on you?" I gasped. "Maybe you should come with me." I felt genuinely concerned for her being pregnant and in the care of a family who used attack dogs to keep their women in line.

She shook her head and chuckled. "I'm here by choice. I love Nate and have no interest in leaving. But I understand why you want to go. It's a lot to deal with. Just do me one favour: if you go, keep going. I can't and won't help you again."

"OK," I said.

She smiled. "Now, ask me where the ladies' room is."

I looked around then raised my voice to a normal tone. "Do you know where the bathroom is?"

"Down the hall towards the kitchen. It's on your right."

"Good luck with your baby," I whispered. "I won't forget this."

She nodded then looked away as I left.

Passing the bathroom, I stopped in and flicked on the light, turning the tap on lightly so you could hear a trickle. Then I locked the door on the inside and pulled it closed on the outside—it would work as my cover for a while, or at least until they realised I couldn't possibly pee for that long.

Then I went into the laundry, a small oblong room that was gleaming white without a single article of clothing in a pile looking messy. I had a quick look around, and I couldn't see any sign of the dog besides the water and food bowls on the floor.

Squatting down, I eyed the size of the dog door and tried to work out what the best way to try and get through it would be. I figured my shoulders and chest were the widest point in my body, so if I led with that, at least if I didn't fit at all, it would be easier to crawl back out.

"Let's do this," I whispered, giving myself a pep talk

as I pressed on the Perspex and placed a hand through it, onto the pavement on the other side. I had to wriggle and push to fit through, but it was doable. I knew I was almost free when I slid out to my waist. All I had to do was twist to my side, wriggle out, and I'd be there. That's when something cold nudged me on the arse.

Oh God. No.

I froze in a panic as the nudging turned to nuzzling.

"No. No. No. No," I gasped, gripping at the ground to try and pull myself free as fast as possible. I *would not* be violated by a dog today. No, sir.

That's when I felt the tongue.

"*Eek!*" I let out a squeak and jerked my body away as fast as I could, thankfully bursting through the doggy door enough to get to my knees and jump to my feet, holding my hands out in defence. The dog followed through wagging its tail and licking its chops as it looked up at me expectantly.

"You are *disgusting*," I told it, while trying to shoo it away as I looked around and tried to work out which way to go.

The dog started whining and sat at my feet.

"Go *away*," I insisted, still waving my hands about. "Shoo."

It scooched a little closer, tail still going. It looked like it was smiling. "You are disgusting," I whispered. "Go find someone else to lick." It totally ignored me.

Deciding I'd just have to ignore the dog or have it draw too much attention, I moved to the edge of the house and looked out. This side of the property was separate to the rest of the communal areas. There was a patch of grass with a quaint sitting area near a clothes line. Beyond that, there was a line of trees. I wasn't sure what kind of fencing, if any, was past that. But it looked like that was where I had to go.

Sprinting across the yard, I heard the tinkling of dog tags as my newest admirer followed along behind me.

"You can't come," I told him, walking through the thick scrub, hoping there wouldn't be any snakes or spiders to make this my very own living nightmare.

Rogue didn't seem to give a shit what I wanted and actually ran ahead of me, showing me somewhat of a path through the trees and down to the aluminium boundary fence that faced the street. He let out a little bark as a magpie strutted back and forth just outside of his reach.

"Are the birds tormenting you?" I asked him. He just panted and looked at me expectantly.

I shrugged then gave him a scratch behind the ear. "I'm afraid this is where we part ways. I'd say it's been fun, but I think both you and I know it's been weird." Then I wedged my foot against the fence and hoisted myself over the top. When my feet landed on the other side, I let out a sigh of relief. "You take care of yourself, Rogue," I said, giving the dog a little wave before I set off on foot, hoping I'd at least make it to the nearest bus stop before they realised I was gone.

CHAPTER THIRTEEN
HOLY FUCKING PISSFLAPS

AFTER HITCHING A RIDE INTO TOWN, I walked quickly to the beach shack, which wasn't fun when I was clutching at my dress the entire time. The wind was fierce, and I cursed Kristian's name with every gust.

The benefit of owning very little meant it didn't take me long to pack my things and change into a more travel-friendly outfit.

Sitting on the end of the bed, I laced up my shoes then pulled my hair into a ponytail, giving the room one last look over. I told myself it was because I was making sure I didn't leave anything behind, but when a surge of emotion slammed the backs of my eyes, I knew it was more than that.

Because I don't think I can get you out of my system.
Shit.

Shaking off my conflicting emotions, I pulled my bag over my shoulder and picked up my duffel, taking a steadying breath before walking purposefully out of the room.

Right into a human wall.

"Fucking hell, Ronnie! You scared the shit out of me," he said, catching me by the arms before I bounced backwards.

For a moment, my heart jumped for joy. *He came for me,* it sighed. Then my brain kicked in as my eyes lifted and noted something missing. A freckle.

"Abbot," I said with a gulp. "What are you doing here?"

"I was going to ask you the same thing, although I think the better question is where are you going? Where's Kris?" He looked behind me into the empty room.

"Listen, this doesn't have to be a big thing, OK?"

"Why? What's going on?" His eyes narrowed.

"Nothing. It's just time for me to go. Things aren't working out, which should make you super happy. So, if you'll just stand to the side, I'll be on my way."

"I don't think so." He reached for his pocket and pulled out his phone.

"Wait. Please," I said as he unlocked the screen. "Don't call him. Just let me go. It's what you wanted, right? Me gone? You don't even have to tell anyone you saw me. Just step to the side and pretend I wasn't here. Easy."

He considered my words long enough for his screen to time out and darken, causing hope to surge inside my chest. "Where are you planning on going?"

"I don't know. I'll buy a ticket as far away as I can afford. Start over. You'll never see me again."

His jaw ticked as his gaze flicked between my eyes.

"Please," I pleaded. "Just let me go."

With a heavy exhale, he stepped to the side. Freedom was in sight.

"Thank you," I gasped, brushing past him.

"Wait." I stopped at his voice. I really wanted to run, but for some crazy reason, I stopped and turned back around.

"Don't you want your car back?"

I shook my head. "Keep it. Consider us square."

He nodded then reached into his pocket, pulling out his wallet. "Go far and don't come back, OK?" he said, holding up a wad of cash.

I hesitated before taking it. Normally, I'd clear a place of all the valuables I could carry in a situation like this, but in this instance, it didn't feel right. But money given willingly, that was a different story. *He's paying me to leave. Yeah, that doesn't sting. Much.*

"It wasn't that bad having me around, was it?" I asked, slipping the cash into my jeans pocket. He was the second Cartwright to warn me not to come back. *He was the second Cartwright who didn't give a shit if I left.*

"It was complicated. It'll be better now you're gone."

Pressing my lips together, I nodded as I fought the growing lump in my throat. "Well, I'll be off then. See you round, Abbot." I lifted my hand in farewell.

"I hope not, Ronnie." *Ouch.*

"Right. See you never, then."

He nodded once. Then I left. God, why did I feel like crying?

MY WHOLE LIFE, I'd felt…tolerated. No one, not even my mother, had stuck their neck out for me. For years, I was overwhelmed by my loneliness. I tried to become important to people, to boyfriends, to friends, hoping they'd *see* me. They'd *care*... Ultimately, they all let me down one way or another. And I'd fallen on my face often enough to learn to get out before I got too deep. Every time I stuck around too long, I got my heart broken or my legs pulled out from under me. In life, there was only a single person I'd ever been able to count on, and that was me. I really hated asking for help or favours, and I saved doing so as a last resort. Like, when I was trying to leave town and my flight didn't take off until the following night.

"Ronnie." There was shock in Maree's voice when she opened her door and found me holding my bags.

"Can I crash here tonight? I didn't have anywhere else to go." If she said no, I was really going to cry. I just needed one night with a friendly face. Then I could leave this town and forget the Cartwrights ever existed.

Maree regarded me with kind eyes. "Of course. Come in. You can have the couch if Daz ever gets off it."

"You're a lifesaver," I said as I bustled through the door, dropping my bags on the floor inside.

"Who is it?" a male voice bellowed from the other room. I could hear the TV commentating the latest cricket match.

"It's Ronnie. She's staying tonight."

"Hey Dazza," I called out as Maree offered me one of her menthols. I took it gratefully and sat across from her at her kitchen table.

"She can't stay," he called back. "She'll never leave."

"I promise it's just for tonight," I said, rolling my eyes slightly.

"Ignore him." She got up and took a six-pack of beer

from the fridge. "He won't be a bother." She gave me a wink then took the beer to her husband.

I smiled and lit my cigarette, breathing slowly while I leaned back in my chair then blew smoke at the ceiling. Dazza was a chauvinistic pig. I'd never liked him. Only worked with him because of Johno. He was lazy, drank too much, leered too much, and took advantage of his wife's kind nature. Maree could do so much better. She was the best thing about the man. And even she wasn't especially *good*. She had pretty loose morals just like the rest of us.

When she returned, she took two mismatched tumblers out of the cupboard then filled them from a white wine cask in the fridge, setting one in front of me. "So what's going on, love? You on the run, or something?"

"Not so much on the run as down on my luck."

"Oh yeah?" She took a seat and gulped down some wine. "I'm all ears."

Letting out a heavy sigh, I wondered what I should tell her. She was basically the closest thing resembling a friend that I had, and even that was stretching it. But, she cared about the people in her life—even work colleagues like me.

I went with a watered-down version of what had happened since I last saw her. "Remember those brothers from last year?"

She shook out her own cigarette and nodded, speaking with it bouncing between her lips. "The ones who beat Johno up for takin' their car then fucked things up for the rest of us? Yeah, I remember."

"And remember those guys you were perving on during the last wedding reception we worked together?"

"Yes," she said slowly. "Wait. That was them!"

I nodded. "They busted me keying their car and have been making me work for them to pay off the damage— which is why I couldn't work the function centre anymore."

"Why didn't you tell me who they were at the time?"

"Because I didn't want you to lose your job if you did something."

"You still should have told me."

"To what end? I did something and look at me. Things have gotten so complicated that I need to get out of here, leave town for a new start."

She eyed me carefully. "Complicated as in you took something or complicated because you slept with one of them?"

I picked up my glass and took a mouthful of the wine, which was tart and acidic. It was a little hard for me to swallow, just like the truth. "The second one," I said through the burn.

She laughed and pushed the ashtray a little closer to me as I took my last drag. "Girl, you are a special kind of fucked up."

"I know. I need to learn to keep my legs together," I said as I stubbed out the butt and pushed the ashtray back her way. "Sworn enemies don't make good bedfellows."

Tilting her head to the side, she lifted her brows. "I don't know about that. A bit of hate sex can be bloody good. How was he?"

I groaned and slumped forward on the table. "*Ridiculously* good." Even that was an understatement.

Letting out a cackle, she pushed out the chair between us and put her feet on it. "Must have been if you want to run away from it."

"It's just time to move on."

"Falling for him, were you?"

I downed the rest of my wine. "No. Hard no. There's no way. It just needs to be over, and I need to leave."

Watching me through her veil of smoke, she lifted a hand. "No need to convince me. So what's your next move?"

"I fly out to Brisbane tomorrow night. I'll leave here in the morning."

"What about your car?"

"They still have it. And I don't care. They can sell it and consider my debt repaid."

She narrowed her eyes at me. "So these guys just get it all and we do nothing?"

"These aren't the kind of people you mess with, Maree. They're into way heavier shit than any of us are. Remember what they did last time? You guys nearly lost the house when Daz couldn't work."

"What kind of heavy stuff are you talkin'?" Outwardly, she seemed concerned for me, but there was too much interest sparkling in her eyes. I needed to shut this conversation down. I'd already said too much, and I wasn't a snitch.

"I honestly don't know. They wouldn't tell me anything."

"But you know *something*, right? That's why you're taking off."

"No," I said quickly. "I don't *know* anything."

Fuck. I was trying to warn her away, not get her more interested.

"Come on, Ronnie. These guys need to be taught a lesson. They can't just throw their weight around without consequence. They have *your car*. You can't do nothing. It's about respect. When you and Johno took theirs, they retaliated in a big way. We need to do the same, but bigger."

"Need I remind you of the state Johno was in after *they* retaliated? And then, that Johno basically tucked his tail between his legs and ran away in fear? It's the entire reason we broke up."

"Johno is weak. I hear he's doing time now. Armed robbery. Dickhead tried to hold up a 7-Eleven with a carving fork."

"I heard he'd gone in."

"And did you hear that Dazza is working with a new crew now? They have a way better set-up. Smarter. You should tell him all you know and they can hit 'em hard and give you a cut. A nice chunk of change to start fresh, love. You deserve that."

"What the fuck are you promising her, woman?" Dazza grunted as he shuffled into the kitchen, giving his balls a scratch.

"She has info on those brothers you hate for fuckin' with your business. Time for payback, I reckon."

His eyes lit up and he pulled out a chair. "What kind of information?"

Looking between them, I smiled uncomfortably, feeling even more trapped than I'd felt in that house. "You know, I think it might be better if I spring for a hotel. I don't want to be in your hair." I pushed back against the chair, but Dazza's hand clapped down over mine.

"No, missy. You sit right there and tell old Dazza everything ya know."

Holy fucking pissflaps. What have I done?

"LET ME GO, Dazza. You're barking up the wrong fucking tree." I looked to Maree for assistance, but she just sat back and looked on expectantly. *Bloody hell, why did I come here? Why did I vent to her? Stupid, stupid, stupid!*

"It's no big deal, love," she said, pulling out a new cigarette. "Those guys are obviously rolling in it. All we're asking is that they share the wealth a little as compensation. And maybe then they'll understand that they can't push us little guys around and get away with it. Justice needs to be served."

I jerked my arm back, trying to break free. "And I'm telling you that this is a terrible idea. I don't know anything that can help you."

"See, Ronnie," Dazza started, shaking his head. "You've always been a shit liar, so I don't believe you. The stench of bullshit is stinking up the joint. I know you know something. And we're gonna sit here until you tell us."

"There's nothing to tell," I yelled, wincing as he gripped my arm tighter.

He lifted my forearm then banged my arm against the table, pain radiating far more than I expected. "You can fuckin' talk, or I can force ya. But we aren't leavin' here until I have something to take to my crew."

"Mumma wants a Bali holiday," Maree said, rubbing her hands together and reminding me that a score was always bigger than friendship.

Fuck my life. Why did I tell Maree *anything* about what had happened? I should have kept my big mouth shut, slept on the couch, and left tomorrow morning. Now I was up shit creek without a paddle to my name, and I had no idea what I was going to fucking do.

Lie.

I could lie.

Or...

My eyes landed on the full ashtray. Thank God Maree was a chain-smoker. Grabbing it with my free hand, I flung the contents at Dazza's face, coating it in the black ash as he sucked in his surprise. He looked like Castle Grayskull with his mouth wide open and his blackened tongue poking out. A gasping wheeze took the place of his breathing as he released his grip and went into crisis mode. Although his crisis mode involved spinning in a circle and making a lot of noise.

"What the fuck, Ronnie?" Maree shrieked as she jumped up to help him. He was wailing and spinning so much that each time she tried to help him to the sink, he ended up turning in the wrong direction.

"He shouldn't have held me down. I told you both *no*," I yelled in return, backing towards the door. "I swear to you, Maree, this ends here. If either of you go anywhere near those brothers, I'll rain bloody hell down on you."

"What are you gonna do?" she spat. "You're a jobless, homeless nobody." *God. People loved throwing that in my face today.*

"Use your fucking brain, Maree. I won't have to *do anything*. All I have to do is give them your names. I'm sure they'll have a great time fucking with you, and everyone else you're in business with." I picked up my bags and opened the door. "Have a nice fucking life and thanks for nothing," I said, slamming the door behind me.

As I walked down the driveway towards the street, a slow clap punctuated the air and pushed through my anger. I swung my gaze to the sound, finding Toby standing against his BMW sedan with a smile on his face.

How the hell…

"Nice work." He opened the passenger door as I got closer. "Now get inside."

"I'm not going anywhere with you," I told him, continuing to walk.

"You don't really have a choice, Ronnie. You can fight me or cooperate with me, but you don't get to walk away."

Stopping, I closed my eyes and took a deep breath. I really was trapped between a rock and a hard place. "How the hell did you know where I was?"

"There's a tracking app on your phone. I can see where you are, listen to what you're saying, and who you're talking to. It's a brilliant tool."

"For a stalker." Fuck. When would I catch a break?

Looking the picture of a gentleman in his tailored pants and button-up shirt, he grinned my way then gestured for me to get in his car. "Come on, Ronnie. We're not so bad once you get used to us."

"Because Stockholm Syndrome will help me to sympathise with you?"

He chuckled and rubbed his fingers along his jaw. "I like you, Ronnie. You're a breath of fresh air."

"Wish I could say the same for you," I said as I headed towards his car, and possibly to my doom. "Are Abbot and Holland in shit for helping me?" I asked when he got in beside me.

"That information can stay between you and me."

"Like how my living situation was supposed to stay between you and me?"

"I didn't tell anyone about your living situation, Ronnie."

"Then how did Kristian know about it?"

"He probably found it out himself. Maybe Abbot looked into you. I'm not the only one capable of putting two and two together."

That made sense. Still, I didn't know how much trust I could put into Toby. I didn't know how much trust I could put in any of them.

"Toby?" I asked as we drove along the residential streets.

He glanced at me and lifted his brow in response.

"I'm never allowed to leave, am I?"

His eyes momentarily left the road and met mine. "No, Ronnie. I'm afraid you know too much."

CHAPTER FIFTEEN
DO YOU KILL A LOT OF PEOPLE?

"IF YOU'RE ALWAYS LISTENING, why did it take you so long to find me? I've been gone for at least three hours," I said as I stared straight ahead, being driven to the Cartwright's main residence.

"Listening constantly would be creepy as well as time consuming. Frankly, I've got better shit to do with my time.'

"That doesn't explain why took you so long to find me."

"Took us a while to realise you were missing. Nice touch with the trickling tap, by the way."

I bounced a shoulder. "I know shit."

"I don't doubt that. But I heard the way you handled yourself in there. You could've told them everything but you didn't. I'm impressed."

"I'm no snitch. I'm also not stupid enough to continue a war I know I can't possibly win."

"This isn't a war, Ronnie. If anything, it's a recruitment."

"A recruitment? Why the hell would anyone want to *recruit* me for anything? I'm nothing to nobody—a pain in the arse, remember?"

"I think you have a certain charm. Jazz does too. Actually, the whole family thinks you're a good fit, even Holland, and she doesn't really like any of us."

"What about the twins? Abbot seems to hate me, and I just told Kristian to shove your whole secret society up his arse. Am I really being welcomed back, or is this a lamb-to-the-slaughter type thing?"

He chuckled. "I guess you just have to trust me."

"Like you trust me?" I took my phone out of my bag and held it up as my evidence.

"We're the ones with everything to lose. From what I can tell, you have a hell of a lot to gain. Can't blame us for being careful."

"None of this makes any sense," I muttered.

"It will."

When we returned, the entire family was convened in the formal lounge, sitting around the L-shaped couch—couples flanking the twins—while Jasmine remained standing, resting her forearm on the mantel.

"Welcome home," she said with a smile when she saw us. *Home*?

Toby placed his hand on the small of my back and ushered me into the room. Then he left me standing and approached Jasmine, saying something quietly in her ear before he took a seat on the arm of the couch next to Sam.

Jasmine examined her nails while I just stood there, feeling like I was in one of those dreams where you're standing on a stage and look down only to realise you're naked and everyone is snickering at you. It was horrible.

"If you're planning on killing me, just get it over with. No one is going to miss me, anyway." It had become exceedingly more obvious of late exactly how alone in this world I really was.

"Go and sit with Kristian please," she said.

My stomach reacted for me, dropping a little because I was still really pissed at him for being such a douchebag. On top of that, nerves jittered beneath my skin. I didn't understand what their deal was and desperately wanted all the cards placed on the table.

Turning towards the gathered siblings, I moved to the couch, startling a little when I realised Kristian and Abbot were wearing *exactly the same thing*.

What kind of mind fuckery is this?

Frowning, I looked between them. They were almost a carbon copy of each other. But that was for people who hadn't spent any time with them. And I'd just spent the past week studying every inch of Kristian's body and two weeks in his constant company. I was *very familiar* with him.

"Is this some sort of fucked-up test?" I asked, looking between them. One shrugged, the other licked his lips. Besides the freckle on the chin, there were other subtle differences in their appearances—a softer jawline in one, a tiny bump on the nose of the other, hair that grew differently. But mostly, it was the way they carried themselves that set them apart. I could tell at a glance, even without the simmering heat in Kristian's gaze.

I stopped in front of Abbot, my bare legs brushing against his bare knees. If they were going to mess with me, I was going to mess with them too. "Am I supposed to sit on his lap?" I turned and asked Jasmine.

"Do whatever you like."

I turned back and let out my breath as I leaned forward and placed a hand on Abbot's shoulder. He knew I could tell them apart. I didn't once think he was Kristian back at the shack before he gave me money. *What gives?* "Can you move, Abbot? I need to sit beside Kristian?"

A grin curled the edges of Abbot's mouth while Kristian let out a relieved chuckle. "I fucking told you," Abbot said, pointing his finger in his twin's face.

Kristian handed over a hundred dollar note with a shake of his head.

"You bet against me?" I asked, deeply offended.

His gaze swept over my face, softening with each passing moment. "Not against you. Against your actions. I said you'd probably spit in my face, Abs said you'd try to fuck with us. He was right, I was wrong."

I folded my arms across my chest. "You were almost right, I considered it."

"Sit down, doll," Kristian said, taking my hand and pulling me to his side. Despite feeling churlish toward him, electricity simmered beneath the surface of my skin.

Why does his touch need to feel like that?

It was like heat against ice, a breeze against hot skin, instantly changing my temperature and providing relief at the same time. I closed my eyes. "I'm still pissed at you," I said, pulling my hand free.

He grinned and placed his arm on the back of the couch, meaning that in order to sit, I was forced to be within his embrace. I huffed out my breath. *So fucking sure of himself. He knows exactly what he does to me, and I hate that I don't stand a chance against him.*

"Sit please," Jasmine said with a clap of her hands.

"We've got a lot to get through. Needless to say, this information does not leave this room." She hit a button on the side of the mantel, causing the windows to change from clear to opaque and the lights to dim. A whirring sound caused me to search for its source, finding a screen lowering from the ceiling. *Are we watching a movie?*

"Relax," Kristian whispered near my ear, the warmth of his breath feathering my skin. "This is what you wanted."

I turned and met his eyes. "Are you sure about that?"

His eyes smiled for him. "Positive."

"We'll start from the top for new members and the lesser informed," Jasmine said, looking at me then Holland as she stepped in front of the screen. In her hand, she held a small device that when clicked, made a photo of four men appear. "Meet our local drug lords. Heroin is their game." She lifted the device in her hand and a small blue dot appeared on the forehead of a solid-looking man with receding brown hair and a Tom Selleck moustache. "Robert Conway. He's the main man behind the curtain. He controls almost eighty percent of the drug's production in the country. And will do anything to keep it that way. He's rarely seen in public, but when he is, he's flanked by his personal security." She moved the pointer along the photo as she continued. "Yani Verboten, the man to his left, is ex-SAS, and Thomas James on his right is a thug for hire, trained pretty heavily in both weapons and hand-to-hand combat. The man in front, Bruno, is no longer of consequence."

I raised my hand.

"Yes, Veronica?"

"Why?"

"We killed him," she stated simply.

They killed him. "Oh."

"Do you have a problem with that?"

"He was a drug dealer, right?"

"Essentially, yes."

"Then, no. Not really."

Jasmine smiled. "Good. Moving on." She turned her attention back to the screen. "Previously, Nathaniel was supplying these men with only a fraction of their raw product. Even so, since a fire decimated that crop, we're paying them for what they consider loss of revenue, and frankly, it's bleeding us dry. These men need to go. Their organisation needs to go with them. I think we're all in agreement there."

I raised my hand again.

"Yes?" Jasmine asked. Was that a twitch in her eye?

"Do you kill a lot of people?"

"Only if they keep interrupting when I'm talking," Jasmine said, that pleasant smile still fixed upon her face.

My mouth made an O shape then I pressed my lips together and did the locked-lips gesture.

Kristian chuckled and leaned in. "Relax, doll. We're thieves. Not killers. This is just a necessary evil to repair some old damage."

"So, you don't get rid of people who know too much?"

"We're careful who knows what, but if that person poses a threat, yeah, that's a real possibility. The family always comes first."

"I see. And how many girls came before me? What did you do to them?"

An amused burst of air left his nose. "You're the only

girl I've ever brought home. And you have nothing to worry about. You're mine. No one's gonna touch you."

You're mine.

Mine.

Most girls longed for *three* little words. All I needed was two.

You're. Mine.

Fuck. I swallowed hard and took a deep breath. Then I reached over and slipped my hand in his.

Mine.

Someone wants me. I could forgive this man anything as long as I was *his*.

God, I was a pushover with this guy.

Lifting our joined hands, Kristian pressed a kiss to my knuckles then rested both hands against his thigh. I leaned a little closer then turned my focus back to what Jasmine was saying.

"The problem we face is that it can't look like us. If we can find something on Conway, someone he's pissed off, or owes something to, then maybe we can use that to our advantage. I'm open to suggestions, but this is what we have so far." She clicked through a few slides, verbally detailing ideas. I was a little off balance due to the fact I was sitting *in the middle of an organised crime meeting talking about plans to kill people.* But other than that, I was doing OK because of all the handholding and whatnot. I got the gist of most of the ideas, which all had their pros and cons. First and least favourite was replanting the poppy field to re-establish supply. It would take some time, but it would release everyone from the monetary strain and feed more income into the family. The catch there? We'd be right back where they started, beholden to Conway and his crew.

The next idea was to ask them for an exit figure, then liquidate Cartwright assets to meet it. It turned out they had an absolute fuck load, which when liquid, was in the many millions. Obviously, that idea was met with grumbles about needing to work twice as hard to rebuild. No one wanted to go backwards. My personal favourite was hiring contract killers to go in there and decimate the lot of them. It'd bring a shitload of media attention and was certainly the most risky, but it would get the job done, and if all the breadcrumbs were swept up, we'd be free.

We?

A few hours ago I was hell-bent on leaving Kristian and the insanity he called family. Since when did I start thinking like I was one of them?

Since they gave you what you wanted and treated you like you belong. I knew the answer right away. All I'd ever wanted was to belong. I'd told Jasmine as much earlier. Now, here I was, being given exactly what I'd wanted. Could I trust it?

"If anyone has a better idea, I'm all ears," Jasmine said to the room. "I want this dealt with as soon as possible. We're pulling off too many high-risk jobs to meet payments, and I'm not willing to have another family member go to prison during my lifetime for these rat bastards."

"Our father is in for life," Kristian whispered, filling me in. "Job gone bad. Someone died."

I nodded, that probably sucked. I had had zero relationship with my dad, so I didn't really understand the loss.

But if they'd been as close to him as they were with Jasmine, I imagined his incarceration was quite the blow.

Jasmine looked my way and waited. "Is there something you can think of, Veronica?" Why was she singling me out? Was this another test? Something I needed to do to prove my worth? I furrowed my brow and dug deep, wanting desperately to impress.

"Uh…maybe."

"Then tell us. There are no stupid ideas when brainstorming." Her smile was encouraging, but I'd seen it slip into indifference to know it wouldn't take much to lose her favour. Still, I could think of one other option.

"Have you heard of the smuggler around here? His name is Brendan Grey, lives on this big property farther inland. It's basically this den of pleasure—drugs, whores, gambling. Anything you want, this guy can get it, *or* he already sells it."

"We know the name. What about him?" Sam asked, his long legs crossed at the ankles.

"Well, maybe we start a rumour that Grey is planning to take over the heroin supply now that Conway's running low. Maybe even put the idea in Grey's head and he'll do it for real—start a turf war where any deaths that come after that are blamed on either side. If we're lucky, Grey will take out all these guys for us. I met him a while back, and he's very keen on killing anyone who gets in his way. If it works, you'll get what you want, and it won't cost a thing besides some well-placed word of mouth."

Jasmine's eyes narrowed thoughtfully. "How long do you expect this plan would take to come to fruition?"

"I…" Suddenly, I felt very stupid for suggesting such a long shot. "You know what? I think the contract killer idea is the best one. A group of mercenaries—*bang, bang,* they're all gone. Ignore me."

Kristian gave my hand a gentle squeeze. "Don't backpedal. Your idea is crazy enough that it could actually work."

"Kristian's right," Jasmine said. "I think this is worth pursuing, at least as a backup, even as a cover story. We know enough people to start talking about whispers we're 'hearing'." She used air quotes. "Anything about conflict spreads like wildfire. Do you know anyone in Grey's camp?"

"I know someone who can get to him."

She nodded. "Then make contact and tell them all about Conway's lack of product to get the ball rolling. Meanwhile, we'll look into this mercenary business. Toby, Nate. I want you both on that." They both bobbed their head in understanding, with Toby giving Nate a sidelong, slightly wary glance.

"What if they realise the rumour came from us?" Alesha asked. "If Grey's side turns around and says it's bullshit, it could get traced back this way. *Or,* Conway hits back hard and takes out Grey, putting us in an even tougher position than we're in now."

Way to poke holes in my scheme, Alesha. I was pretty sure she would pull apart any plan I suggested. She'd been the only Cartwright to refuse direct eye contact or conversation with me so far. Seemed she still harboured ill feeling towards me since our first meeting, which was kind of shit, because I was the one who got fucked over while she got all of this.

"Grey has more than just a few goons," I said, glancing between her and Jasmine.

"So has Conway," Alesha put in.

"Well, I've never heard of Conway before today, so I have to defer to you on the size of his operation. But I have seen Grey's outfit, and at any given time, he has at least twenty guys around him, not three like Conway. And those guys are packing some serious heat. Plus, I'm pretty sure the guy I used to run with, Dazza, is working for him now. He was real eager to take something to his new boss. If I go to him tomorrow, apologising for putting ash in all his"—I held my hand up and gestured toward my entire face—"face holes, then offer him some information out of 'guilt'"—it was my turn to use finger quotes—"then he'll get the ball rolling for us. I really can't imagine a man like Grey passing up this kind of opportunity. In fact, I'd be surprised if he wasn't already looking into it. We can just help bring that information public."

"I like this plan a lot." Jasmine grinned as she looked at me. "She is so smart, Kristian. Wonderful choice. Make sure you help her do that, OK?"

Kristian nodded and smiled my way, his fingers brushing lightly against the back of my neck. "Great work, doll. Told you this was what you wanted." He leaned a little closer, his lips brushing my ear. "And for the record, I never called you a bimbo. I happen to think you're fuckin' perfect."

I turned and looked into his eyes, trying to find the truth in his words. *Perfect?* No one had ever called me that before.

"I thought I was a shit liar."

He grinned. "You are. But that's part of your perfection. I know what's real with you. And what's fake."

Closing my eyes, I pressed my lips together for a

moment, the hurtful words I spat at him earlier revisiting me. "I said a lot of really shitty things to you today."

"Nothing I didn't deserve."

"I went too far," I started before he silenced me with his lips against mine.

"It's OK. You were scared."

"You think I was scared?"

He nodded.

"Of what?"

Taking a deep breath, he tucked my hair behind my ear. "Of what this is."

I sucked in my breath as his words rang true. I was scared. I was scared of falling too far, of becoming too reliant, of *needing* someone more than I needed myself. That was why I ran. Out of fear.

But then this family of misfits dragged me back. It was all so ridiculously fucked up, and I probably deserved a spot in a mental institution for thinking this, but today ended up being the best day of my life.

Why? Because I felt useful, I felt wanted, and most of all, they didn't let me go. No one had ever brought me back before. They'd always been glad I'd left. Because of that, I wanted to stay.

I want to belong.

"Can I ask a question?" Holland yelled over the ruckus while everyone talked excitedly about plans. The room quieted as we waited for her to lower her hand and speak. "Do they have to get married now too?" She looked over to where Kristian and I were huddled together, and my eyes went wide. *Married*?

Jasmine laughed. "I don't know that we have time for a wedding right now. But, yes, I think you should make her a

Cartwright, Kristian. The family is a lifetime commitment."

"Whoa. Back up a bit," I said, holding up my hands in front of me. "Married? Don't I get a say in this?"

Pretty much everyone in the room gave me this look that said 'Sorry, luv' as they shook their heads like it was no big deal. Meanwhile, I wanted to vomit.

I think I finally hit my threshold of crazy.

"It's tradition," Alesha said with a smile. "When you catch the eye of a brother and learn about the business, you have to become legally bound to the family. It means you can't be subpoenaed to stand trial if the shit ever hits the fan—you know, that whole 'spouses don't need to testify' thing."

I looked at Kristian, blood pumping in my ears as I processed what was going on. *I just have to accept this?*

"Am I at least going to be asked?"

Then he got down to one knee in front of me, and grinned the most dazzling grin I'd ever seen on his face. I was already a puddle of anticipation, and I wasn't even sure I wanted this. "Veronica Sutton, will you do me the honour of becoming my criminally minded wife?"

I couldn't explain my reaction even if I tried. Blame it on the fact that I never thought any man would propose to me, and the fact I'd had the craziest of crazy days, but when he met my eyes and I saw legitimate hope inside his, tears formed in my eyes and I nodded my head.

He really does want me.

"Yes," I whispered, sniffling. "I'll marry you. Let's do *terrible* things together."

A joy-filled laugh bounced out of his chest. "I don't have a ring, but I do have this." He pulled one of the twine bracelets from his wrist. It was blue and had small shells woven into it. Then his family cheered as he tied it around my wrist before he cupped my face in his hands and kissed me like the fool I was.

But, I was a happy fool. I'd always dreamt of belonging. I thought I hated the Cartwright family because of their strong-arm tactics toward me over the last year. But since the wedding, my view of them had shifted. They loved each other. Gave a fuck. And I wanted that for myself. Like Kristian, I was ready for my life to change. I was tired of *surviving*. I wanted to live. Maybe with Kristian's offer of marriage, and *their* offer to join the family, everything I ever wanted would finally come to fruition. Maybe it was *my turn* to get some good in life.

CHAPTER SIXTEEN
KNIGHT IN STOLEN ARMOUR

"YOU FREAKING OUT YET?" Kristian asked when the meeting was over and we were alone in the upstairs room. We'd seamlessly moved from the proposal to planning the next big job and breaking down tasks. It would be the first job I was actively involved with—an initiation of sorts. And it involved driving to Sydney and infiltrating a cult-like religious group that operated out of Katoomba. They didn't believe in banks and demanded new members liqui-date their assets and offer that money to the communal pool. We were being divided into teams—Sam and Alesha were our inside couple, Nate and Toby were surveillance, the twins and I were in charge of acquiring vehicles and sourcing tools. Jasmine and Holland would remain behind to keep the businesses they used as their front, running smoothly. Seemed there was quite an art to stealing then laundering your profits so you could safely use that money. It sounded like a lot of hard work to me, but it was exciting at the same time. I had the buzz of anticipation vibrating within my bones.

"I'm not freaking out," I whispered, leaning against the closed door. "Just...decompressing. This. You. Us. It's all pretty intense for me."

His mouth curved up on one side, his playfulness cutting through the tension of our situation. "Because you like me?"

This so was not the time to joke, but I smiled despite myself. "Well, I don't hate you as much as I thought I did."

"I knew it." Letting out his breath in a weighty sigh, he held his hand out to me. "Come here." I moved so I was standing in front of him, placing my hands on his shoulders as his hands landed on my thighs then slid upward, over my arse before he dropped his head against my chest.

His hands on me feel so damn good. If he hadn't made me his slave before, I certainly was one now.

"I was an arsehole earlier. I shouldn't have thrown your housing situation and our relationship in your face like that." His voice was muffled in the fabric of my shirt.

"If you're apologising, can you at least look me in the eye while you do it?" I asked, my fingers urging him to tilt his head back.

Meeting my eyes with a mirthful gaze, he pulled me a little closer. "I'm not apologising, just admitting to wrong-doing. Cartwrights don't ever say sorry, doll. That's something you'll have to get used to."

I smiled and ran my fingers over the golden stubble on his cheeks. "That's funny. I don't do apologies either. But for the record, I was an arsehole too. When I was asking you questions and you wouldn't answer, it made me feel like you didn't really want me here, that you didn't really want me."

He gripped me a little tighter and growled. "I want you, doll. Can't stop wanting you."

I placed my hands on his shoulders and pushed a little. "Not just sex, Kristian. Me. I want you to want *me*."

His eyes grew serious as they stayed locked with mine. "I do."

"Then why did Toby come and get me? Why didn't you?"

His tongue wet his lips before he released his breath. "Because I was here convincing Jasmine you could work with us."

"Because I knew too much?"

"Partly. And because after spending a couple of weeks with you, I'm nowhere near ready to let you go."

"So you needed permission from her to what? Keep me?"

He nodded. "Like I said earlier, we're careful who we bring in. Toby thoroughly vets every person we do business with—he thought you were a good fit. But Jasmine needed to work through the pros and cons with me."

"Because she wanted you to marry me?"

He nodded. "That's kind of how it works with us. We don't really do relationships because love can turn into hate, and hate wants revenge."

"We started out hating each other."

"Yeah. And you've been a fucking pain in the arse this entire time. But you know what? I wouldn't change it. Because it proved to us you had guts, tenacity, and some serious skills."

"I liked being mean to you. I blamed you for everything that happened to make me homeless."

"I get that. But even so, you never sold us out. You had

the connections to fuck us over but you didn't. Why is that?"

I shrugged. "That's not who I am. And I fight my own battles." He nodded at me, yet he had no idea how true that was. His family wasn't like anything I'd seen before. I'd *never* had anyone fight my battles for me...*with* me. But before he could press too hard, I added, "And also because Grey scares the shit out of me."

"And we don't?"

Grinning, I leaned into him. "You're too pretty to be scary."

His response was to laugh. "God, I like you, Ronnie. I like you a lot."

"Enough to marry me, it seems."

He nodded.

"This is insane, you know? It's even crazier than those people who get married in Vegas—at least they're wasted when it happens. We're making a conscious decision to get married after sleeping together for only a week."

"It's been a great week, though. And people have gotten married for a hell of a lot less and had it work out. I say we jump on board the crazy express and ride it all the way to the station. I have no fucking clue if it'll work out, but maybe Jazz knows what she's doing. She made the others marry, and they're happy as fuck. Maybe we'll be the same."

"And if it doesn't work out?" I was pretty sure that wasn't an option, but I really needed to be sure.

He shrugged. "I honestly don't know. It would depend on Jazz and the circumstances at the time."

I get it. Family is for life. This marriage really will be till death do us part. Guess I just need to work hard at this thing.

I ran my fingers through his hair, silky brown strands brushing against my skin. Up until this day, I never thought marriage would be an option. I thought I was destined to struggle all my life, to be a loser with no home, no hope, and no one to care for her.

I want someone to care for me. To care about me, and whether I fail or thrive.

I wanted to have a place in this world. I wanted to have a chance at being more than the 'problem' I'd been repeatedly called. I wanted to take a chance. How often did a knight in stolen armour come along and invite you into his criminal organisation? For a girl like me, that might just be the fairy tale.

"Crazy together forever, huh?" I whispered, too afraid to give volume to my voice in case it made me think too hard.

"When you know, you know, right?"

"Yeah." And I did know. This past week had been the first week in my life where I actually wanted to remember every detail. "But am I supposed to be afraid?"

He let out his breath. "You're supposed to be terrified."

I closed my eyes, because he was right. I was. "Just shut up and kiss me, Kristian, and we'll worry about the rest of this shit later."

Doing just that, our emotions quickly intensified, our clothing shed until he hooked his fingers into my panties and paused. "I thought I told you no underwear today."

"Well, you shouldn't have pissed me off."

"I can't promise I won't do it again," he said, dragging said panties down my legs.

I reached between us and wrapped my hand around his cock. "That's why I only kind of like you," I gasped as I sank myself over it, taking him inside me with a shudder.

"Really? I'm fucking crazy about you," he whispered, holding on to my face as he kissed me and I rode his length, my movement growing faster as I pushed his words to the side and chased my orgasm.

I could handle his family. I could handle *being his*. I could handle marrying him, even. But having him tell me I'm perfect and he's crazy about me? It freaked me the fuck out.

"Slow down, doll," he whispered, flipping me over so I was on my back and he was in control. "I don't want this over just yet. I've been waiting all day to be inside you."

His hips swivelled, slow and deliberate. His eyes focused on mine, hands searing heat all across my skin. This wasn't fucking. It was something else. I'd never been treated so carefully by a man where the experience of fucking transported us to another plane of existence all together. In that moment, there was only us. We were *everything*. And I didn't know how to process that. *What is this? What is he doing to me?*

Then he leaned in and kissed me, thrusting one last time, both of us coming undone. And I couldn't help it. I fucking cried when we came.

As soon as it happened, I shook my head, and pushed him away. "I can't. I can't," I gasped.

Immediately, he pulled back then gathered me in his arms, placing me so I was sitting across his lap, curled against his chest. "It's all right, doll. Shhh. I've got you. I've got you. You don't need to fight anymore. Let it go."

"This is too much. *You're* too much."

"I know," he whispered. "I know."

I pushed against him a little, but honestly, there wasn't much fight left in me. I was exhausted, going through life scrambling and scrounging, hoping to make it just *one more day*. I'd wanted it over more times than I could count, and now that it was, my emotions were all over the fucking place.

"I'm not perfect," Kristian said as he rocked me gently within his giant body. "And I can't promise you that this thing we've got going on will be any sort of easy. I'm gonna piss you off, and you're gonna piss me off too. But that's OK, because I have no intention of ever sending you away, so you don't need to run. You have somewhere to live. You have a family who's always gonna give a shit. And you have me." He hooked his finger underneath my chin and lifted. "It took one day with you, and I was already gone. A week having you, and I'm never letting go. You got me?"

"Yeah." A smile crept across my face, just before more tears filled my eyes. "Fuck," I said as they splashed down my cheeks. "My eyes are leaking. You broke my eyes."

"Oh doll," he said with a chuckle as he gathered me closer, and I cried into his chest. It was the first time I had cried properly in so long that I couldn't seem to stop. "Marrying me can't be that bad, can it?"

I shook my head. I wasn't a stranger to jumping into situations with both feet, but I was a stranger to feeling wanted. I was a stranger to having hope. But fuck, if it didn't feel good to have those things. "Does this mean I get a ring?" I sniffed, wiping my eyes as I looked up at him.

Placing his hands on either side of my head, he

brushed my hair away from my face and smiled. "I'll take you shopping for one tomorrow. You can pick whatever you like."

"You might regret saying that," I said with a smile."

"You know, I don't regret a single thing in my life so far. Something tells me I'm not gonna regret you either." I could only hope to live up to that claim, but I wasn't sure I had it in me to not end up being a regret. But fuck it. I was going to try because this felt worth it. I'd run away out of fear and been brought back and welcomed with open arms. This felt real to me, and I was going to do everything I could to be the best me I was capable of.

I just hoped it was enough. *Hoped I was enough.*

CHAPTER SEVENTEEN
BATTLE CAT

"WAKE UP," Kristian whispered while nuzzling my neck. I groaned and kept my eyes closed, causing him to laugh. "Come on, sleepyhead, wake up."

"I can't." As much as I loved fucking him, my body literally couldn't take any more. He'd fucked me into exhaustion.

"You have to. I want to show you something really cool."

"Is it your cock?"

An amused chuckle bounced his chest. "No, doll. It's not my cock."

"Then what?" I groaned as he pulled me to sitting.

"It's a surprise. But you have to get ready quick or we might miss it." He started handing me clothes and helping me get them on my sleep-heavy body.

"You could show me a few hours of sleep. I'd like that."

Grinning, he kissed me on the temple. "You'll like this too. Come on."

He pulled me out of the bedroom and held his finger up for me to be quiet so I didn't wake up the others. We'd all spent the night at Jasmine's place, which seemed to be tradition whilst the family was planning a job.

Hand in hand, Kristian and I crept down the stairs and through to the kitchen where he handed me a thermos of coffee.

"You've already been up to make this?" I whispered, clicking the mouthpiece open and taking a sip.

"Yeah. I was gonna go surfing while you slept in."

"Why didn't you go?"

He grinned again, the boyishness I loved about him showing through. "You'll see."

I harassed him a little more as we climbed into the Ute and drove the short distance to Bells Beach. "You brought me to the beach you banned me from surfing?" I asked.

"Consider this your official invitation back," he said, unbuckling his seatbelt and jumping out of the car. He jogged around to my side and pulled open my door faster than I could myself. He was definitely eager about something. "Hurry."

"OK, OK," I said, taking his offered hand as I got out and he pulled me towards the wooden stairs. "What's going on down there?" I asked, noting the small crowd of people gathered on the beach below. They were all looking out to the water and pointing.

"Out there," he said, pointing to the water like the rest of them. There was a big splash and suddenly a cheer went up.

I beamed. "Dolphins."

With his eyes dancing with excitement, Kristian nodded and hurried me down the rest of the stairs. "I was checking the surf report when this popped up. At first they thought sharks, but then they realised it's a whole pod of dolphins playing."

There had to be at least twenty of them putting on a show and leaping out of the water, flapping their fins and tails, lifting their heads like they were laughing. A couple of surfers were still out there, and so was a dog! It was an amazing sight.

Joining the gathered group at the water's edge, Kristian stood behind me and wrapped his arms around my shoulders as we smiled and watched, hooting and hollering with each leap.

"They're so beautiful," I exclaimed, my cheeks hurting from smiling so much.

"Worth getting out of bed for?"

"Definitely." I turned to look up at him and meet his eyes. "Thank you for including me."

He brushed his fingers through my windswept hair and secured it behind my ear. "Always, doll. You were my first thought." Then he brought his mouth to mine, and I twisted my body in his arms so I could press against him chest to chest. God, I loved kissing him. I loved being in his arms and just generally being around him. *His first thought was me.* I'd never been someone's first thought before. It was something I'd have to get used to, but definitely something I liked.

"What is this?" a familiar voice said from a few feet away. Kristian released me and turned to find Nate, Toby, Alesha, and Sam. They were all in wetsuits, their hair wet obviously from getting out of the water not long before.

"Dolphins," I said, gesturing towards the water.

"Oh wow," Alesha said, taking Sam by the hand and walking closer to the shoreline.

"How long has this been going on," Toby asked, staying beside us while Nate joined the other two.

"About thirty minutes. I didn't realise you were all up and out of the house already," Kristian said.

"We went to Winkipop. Didn't want to disturb the newly engaged couple, so we left you both sleeping," Toby replied, quirking his brow.

"Where's Abs then?" Kristian asked. "It's not like him to skip a morning surf."

"He's gone back to the shack to grab some shit since we're staying with Jazz until this job is done."

Kristian's brow furrowed as he nodded. "Reckon you can take Ronnie back to the house for me? I wanna have a talk with him alone."

Toby nodded once. "No problem."

Kristian leaned down and kissed my forehead. "Stay with Tobes. I'll come back to take you ring shopping a bit later, OK?"

"Sure," I said, feeling a little disappointed that he was handing me off so fast. We'd just had a moment where he said I was the first thing he thought about, and now he was racing off to have secret conversations with his brother, who'd been an absolute arse for most of the time I'd known him. I knew they had some shit to sort out, but I'd hoped after the craziness of yesterday that Kristian and I could spend today just being *us*.

"You seen anything like this before?" Toby asked as Kristian jogged up the beach. I watched him until he hit the stairs.

"Like what?" I asked distractedly.

"This many dolphins. I've lived here all my life and I've never seen this many in one place."

"Must be a lot of fish there," I said, my eyes still straying back to Kristian's receding figure.

"He'll be back, you know."

"I know," I said, even though I had this terrible feeling twisting at my stomach. Call me crazy, call me high-strung. But, I hadn't had a great track record with men sticking around. All of them said the right things in the beginning, but their actions ended up telling a different story.

"They're twins, Ronnie," Toby said as if reading my thoughts and knowing I needed reassurance. "For thirty-three years, they've been two sides of the same coin. I know you need him, but they need each other too. Do you get what I'm saying?"

Swallowing my misplaced jealousy down as far as I could, I focused on Toby's face. "I get it," I said. "I'm just...I'm not used to all this."

"I know." He put his arm around my shoulders and pulled me in. I stiffened for a moment, then he gave me a friendly squeeze, and I relaxed against his side. "Family isn't always easy, especially when you aren't used to having it. It takes work to keep this many people functioning well together. But, we do it because this is bigger than any one of us. No matter our differences, we're all committed to the job, and we're all committed to each other. Which means we're here for you too. You're one of us now, Ronnie. OK?"

I had to swallow again, but this time from emotion. Then I took a deep breath. "OK," I said, hoping to hell I could believe him. God, they gave good speeches. I so badly wanted to whole-heartedly believe everything they said to me. Only time would tell if their actions aligned with their words.

Toby smiled then released his hold. "Good. Then let's go join the others. See if we can get you and Leesh talking. I think you'd really get along."

"I NEED you to stay out here," I said to Kristian as we pulled up outside Maree and Dazza's. As promised, he'd returned with Abbot only a couple of hours later, breezing into Jasmine's place like they were the best of friends, which was interesting to me because I hadn't seen them that at ease together since watching them at the wedding. It seemed they had come to an understanding. And in a move that chased some of my demons away, the first thing Kristian did was plonk himself on the couch beside me and haul me onto his lap, kissing me like he'd just returned from war. *What a way to make a girl feel special.*

Before we could go and choose my engagement ring, we decided it was best to do our part for the backup plan first. That involved a little grovelling to Maree and Dazza on my part. As a peace offering, I had a case of beer, a cask of wine, and a carton of cigarettes sitting on my lap.

"What if they decide to get you back for turning Dazza into Castle Grayskull yesterday?" Kristian asked as he looked toward the small house.

"I don't know. I'm hoping the years I've known them and the gifts will count for something."

"Well, if they don't go for it and you're in trouble, call out Battle cat."

"Battle cat?" I laughed. He was really enjoying the He-Man references.

With a serious look, he nodded slowly. "Yes. Battle cat."

"OK," I said, dragging out the sound as I pushed the door open on his Ute and swung my legs out, trying to figure out how I was going to get down with everything I carried.

"At least let me carry all that shit to the door for you."

"Nope. I'm fine," I grunted, snaking my way out of the cab by leaning back and sliding on my butt until my feet hit the ground. When I managed the move successfully, I turned around to Kristian and gave him a triumphant smile. "Ha! I'm awesome."

Shaking his head, he laughed. "Be careful in there, doll."

"Yeah, yeah. I'll be fine," I said, taking a step toward the house. My foot hit the edge of a concrete manhole, causing me to trip and shriek, the slab in my hands slipping free. The beer hit the concrete with a *thwack*, causing the aluminium cans to crackle then hiss. Then beer sprouted up through the cardboard, saturating my shirt and hitting me in the face. "Battle cat!" I yelped, using my hands to try and stop the assaulting spray. "Battle cat!"

"Don't just stand there taking it." Kristian grabbed my arm and pulled me to the side of the fountain of beer, chuckling the entire time. "See, that was pretty easy, wasn't it?" he asked, looking down at my dripping face. I stood in front of him, stinking like a brewery, my clothes wet, my hair ruined, trying not to breathe too deep so I wouldn't suck beer up my nose.

"Battle cat," I whimpered, feeling awfully sorry for myself.

"Come here," Kristian said, then he leaned in and ran his tongue up my cheek, smacking his lips together. "Needs more hops," he said. "Maybe some barley."

I shook my head, unable to keep my smile in check. "You're an idiot."

"I'm not the one who stood there while beer sprayed me in the face."

Rolling my eyes, I looked down at my now see-through pink shirt. "Maybe we should come back later—after I've had time to change." I pulled the fabric away from my chest so he couldn't see the bra underneath.

"No need to hide from me," he teased, pulling my shirt free from my hands so he could see through it again. I slapped his hands away, causing him to playfully slap back and the next thing I knew, we were cartwheeling our hands at each other and laughing.

"Stop it. It's not you looking I'm worried about."

He playfully slapped my hands away again and smoothed his hands down my shirt so it stuck to me like glue. "You should always be worried about me," he teased. Then he leaned down to kiss me.

"Ronnie?" Maree's voice floated down the path, stopping us before our lips could touch.

"Oh, hey Maree," I said, looking around Kristian's big frame.

Kristian cleared his throat then shoved a balled-up shirt in my direction. It was the top I'd been wearing that first night I slept at his place. The one we'd properly fought over. I didn't know why, but I was really touched that he still had it. I thought he'd burnt it after our fight. I turned my back and pulled the beer-soaked shirt off with Kristian jumping to shield my body from view. "I thought that maybe we could talk," I called out to Maree. "I hated leaving things the way we did yesterday."

"Yeah? Well, we been friends a long time," Maree said, her voice curious as she eyed Kristian's massive form. "Who's he?"

"He's Kristian." I pulled the shirt over my head and tied the hem into a knot at my side so it didn't look quite so massive on me.

Her eyes moved over him, head to toe then back up again. "Looks like one of them brothers from the other night? You didn't bring a Cartwright here, did you?"

"I did," I said. "I hoped we could talk. Maybe even give Dazz what he wanted yesterday."

She folded her arms and pointed her chin at Kristian. "I don't want him in me house. He can wait outside."

"OK." I turned and looked at him, even though he already knew he wasn't coming in with me.

"It's cool. I'll see if there's any cans worth saving and clean the rest up. Call out if you need me."

"Battle cat." I smiled and he gently tugged on my hair.

"That's the one."

Picking up the wine and the carton of smokes, I headed up the path and handed them to Maree. "A peace offering. I accidentally dropped the beer."

Maree wrinkled up her nose. "I can smell that." Then she turned her head to the side. "Dazz. Ronnie came back."

"You fuckin' serious?" he hollered, appearing in the doorway in about two seconds flat.

"Hey Dazz. I thought we could finish our talk. Maybe I *do* have something for you to take to your boss."

"This better not be some trick."

"It's not. It's good intel."

He stood up a little straighter and tilted his head to the side. "I'm listenin'."

About thirty minutes later, I was outside again, walking quickly towards Kristian who waited against his Ute the same way Toby had the day before.

"Well?" he asked as I powered toward him and he opened the car door.

"Let's go. It's not gonna work," I said quickly, jumping in my seat.

"Why? What happened?"

"I was wrong. They don't work for Grey at all."

"Bullshit," he said, closing his eyes for a moment. I could tell he already knew the answer, but he asked the question anyway. "Who do they work for, doll?"

I bit my lip. "Conway. They work for Conway."

CHAPTER EIGHTEEN
STAND HERE AND LOOK PRETTY

I HAVE NEVER SEEN a person move as fast as Kristian did when he ran back up the pathway and into Maree and Dazza's house. He didn't even knock. He just jump-kicked the door and flew right in.

"*No*," I yelled, chasing him into the house.

I caught up just as he snatched a phone out of Dazza's hand then punched him in the face. "Sit the fuck down," he yelled.

"Oh shit," I gasped, covering my face as blood poured out of Dazza's nose and ran down his chin. This was *not* supposed to happen.

Maree started screaming, and I ran over to her and begged her to be quiet. When she wouldn't, I clamped my hand over her mouth, holding her in a headlock so she couldn't escape and scream again.

I was the worst kind of friend for this. And it was going to take way more than a case of beer to fix it. "Kristian, stop!" I yelled, still holding a struggling Maree. "*Stop hitting him*. You've got this all wrong."

He froze, one hand holding the front of Dazza's shirt, the other pulled back ready to punch. "*What*?"

"Whatever you're thinking right now. It's wrong," I repeated, looking right into his eyes. "Please. Let him go and listen to me."

With his eyes darting and his brow creasing, he released Dazza's shirt then wiped the blood from his hand down the front of it. "Don't fucking move," he commanded as he looked to me and inclined his head to the side.

"Can I trust you not to scream?" I asked Maree, who nodded and relaxed in my arms. I released her to a grateful silence. "OK. It's OK. Everyone is OK. This is just a big misunderstanding."

I moved to the corner of the room where Kristian joined me, keeping his voice low as he said, "What the hell is going on?"

"I said it wouldn't work, not run in here and beat them up," I whispered harshly.

"They work for Conway. You said so yourself."

"Yeah. And the moment I found that out, I backed out and told them some shit about hitting an evidence transport that I heard about in the news the other day. I didn't even mention Grey."

"You what?" He wiped a hand over his face as he registered what I was saying. "Fuck."

I nodded my head. "Fuck."

"What do you want me to do?"

I placed my hand on his chest and pressed against it. "Just stand here and look pretty. Please."

With a clench of his jaw, he nodded then leaned against the wall.

"This wasn't my intention, guys," I said as I walked to the sink and grabbed a clean cloth. "I just wanted to make things right between us, and I thought that if I brought you in on that job it could help *all* of us earn a little favour with Conway." I ran the cloth under cold water then took it to Dazza and started cleaning him up. He looked at me with wary eyes. I'd never seen him afraid before. I'd be lying if I said I didn't get a small kick out of it.

"I thought you *were* givin' us the job," Dazza grunted. "What do youse need Conway for?"

I glanced toward Kristian, who had his arms folded across his chest as he waited to see what I was going to pull out of my arse. This could go horribly wrong for me, but after the way Kristian burst in here... There needed to be some major damage control or else *everything* would get so much more fucked up.

"Well," I started. "I probably shouldn't have brought you in on *that* particular job. I made you think I was *giving* you the job, then Kristian thought you two were trying to cut his family out of something they've been working on." There was a lot of nervous laughter and hand movements while I tried to unjumble the mess. "This is all crossed wires and miscommunication. And that's on me. I'm just trying to think of a way we all benefit."

"Go on," Dazz said, taking the cloth from my hand and holding it to his nose. I didn't know if he was acting interested because he was worried Kristian would break his face, or if he really wanted to hear this. Either way, I had a captive audience and needed to come up with something and fast.

Come on, brain.

"OK. So, we heard that Conway is looking for a way to re-establish his coke supply."

Daz lifted his brow. "You didn't hear that. You know because it's his stupid brother who fucked supply up."

Kristian growled and shifted forward like he was going to attack, so I quickly moved between them and held up my hand to stop Kristian while I continued talking. I felt like the red flag between the bull and the matador. "OK. So you know they're on the hook. And we know you're looking to improve your position. We can scratch each other's backs by doing this job together. The Cartwrights are expert thieves, and this transport won't be an easy mark. Inside it will be over a billion in coke. If we take this job to Conway together, maybe, just maybe, it'll be enough that he'll release the Cartwrights from their debt, and give you two enough of a cut that you'll never have to work again. That could work, right?" I looked between Kristian and Dazza, who weren't really giving anything away.

Maree looked from me to Kristian, her arms folded tight around her waist. "Your family is indebted to Conway?"

Kristian glared at me a moment then turned to Maree and nodded without elaborating further. *He hates this idea! Ugh. I'm in the shit now.* Bye-bye, engagement ring. Goodbye hopes for a family. Goodbye fairy-tale life. Fuck. I should have kept my mouth shut.

"Why aren't you just taking this to him yourself?" Dazza asked, his eyes bouncing back and forth. "Why do you need me?"

Fuck. That's a really good question. And one I hadn't thought of an answer to.

"Because we owe you too," Kristian piped up, surprising me by joining in. "We went way overboard when we fucked up your business last year. This is our way of making things right." OK. Maybe this was going to work after all. *Thank you, baby Jesus!*

"So *I'm* the one taking this to Conway?" Dazza asked, the cloth muffling his voice.

"I think we all should," Kristian said, stepping forward.

Dazza nodded. "That would be better. I'll set up the meet?"

"Not right away," Kristian said. "We need to gather some more details first, make sure the job is viable before we present it to the big boss. It may be too risky. Even for us."

Dazza nodded, understanding. Maree frowned. "Hang on," she said. "This is less than what she offered us before. And why the fuck did you kick our door down and beat into Dazza?"

"I gave you a job to take to his boss, Maree," I explained. "There was no guarantee you'd get anything from it. But this way, you will."

"But the job needs to be planned to perfection," Kristian added. "It needs to stay between us until we're almost ready to go. We can't risk anyone else swooping in to claim the score. No one wins if anyone talks too soon. Got it?"

Daz nodded, his greedy eyes twinkling. "Billions, hey?"

Kristian nodded. "We'll give you the credit, and we'll do the grunt work."

Daz held out his hand. "You've got yourself a deal."

With a few more details hashed out and numbers exchanged, Kristian and I left with a resolution that didn't involve spilling any more blood. If I hadn't just thrown the family into a massive job that could see us all before a grand jury, I'd be feeling proud of myself.

"What were you thinking?" Kristian asked after we drove away. My chest tightened as I prepared to be abused for making such a stupid call.

"I'm sorry, I—"

"Don't apologise, doll. It was a good plan."

"Oh." I exhaled, relief flooding my system. "You're not angry?"

"No. I just want to know where it came from. Is it real?"

"The transport? Yeah. I read about the seizure in the paper. It was getting smuggled into the country on a shipping container. Border Force and the AFP need to transport it to a secure location to be destroyed."

"When?"

"I'm not sure. After the trial I guess."

"That's something we need to find out."

"OK."

He reached over and took a hold of my hand. "It's a good plan. And if we can pull it off, it's a great plan." He lifted my hand to his lips and kissed my knuckles. "Time to go get that ring, hey?"

A laugh burst from my chest, partly out of relief, partly out of surprise. I'd been so sure he was going to yell at me and tell me I couldn't be in the family any more that I was stunned silent.

"You don't want a ring?"

I gasped then nodded, still struggling to find my words.

Kristian laughed. "I'm gonna need some more information here, doll."

Taking a deep breath, I forced my words out. "I stink like beer."

"I love beer."

"You have swollen knuckles and some blood spatter on your shirt."

He glanced down. "So I do."

"They'll think we're there to rob them and probably call the cops."

"The irony." He smiled my way. "The one time I plan to buy jewellery and I look like a hobo. Won't they be surprised when I pull out the platinum Amex."

"They'll probably think you stole that too."

"Then I'll be gracious when they verify it and start apologising."

"You don't want to go back and tell Jasmine what just went down?"

"I promised to take my girl ring shopping. That's exactly what I'm gonna do."

His girl.

Holding a hand against my face, I smiled. "OK. Let's go get a ring."

Then I ran my fingers along the still damp edge of my shorts. If I'd thought yesterday was crazy, today was setting itself up to completely insane. I looked forward to what was going to happen tomorrow. How one man had brought so much purpose to my life was mind boggling.

How can he already mean so much to me?

CHAPTER NINETEEN
ALL HANDS ON DECK

"THAT IS STUNNING," Alesha cooed as she inspected the diamond ring on my finger, cushion cut with a double halo of both pink and white diamonds. All up, the diamond weight was just under a carat. Kristian had pushed for the bigger centre diamond—I think he was really enjoying making the salesgirl freak out—but against the size of my hand, I felt this ring was perfect. I had barely been able to take my eyes off it the entire way home.

Home.

The thought entered my mind and surprised me.

"Wow. It really is beautiful," Holland agreed. "I'm so happy you've decided to stay. We need to balance the ratio of boys to girls, you know."

I met her eyes and smiled knowingly. We hadn't been able to speak since my return, and I needed to express how grateful I was to her for helping me. I was in her debt—despite the fact they'd tracked me down and brought me back anyway. I also owed Abbot a big thank you, even if he was just trying to get rid of me.

With everyone gathered, Jasmine insisted on taking photos, making Kristian and me assume various poses until she felt she had the perfect series of shots.

"Those'll go straight to the poolroom," Nate said, and everybody laughed.

"Why is that so funny?" I asked Kristian in a whisper, not understanding why it was hilarious to put a picture on the wall of the room with the pool table in it. Although, I'd personally call it a rumpus or a games room instead of a poolroom.

Kristian grinned. "You've never seen *The Castle*?"

I shook my head. "Is it on TV or Netflix? I don't get to the movies much."

Holland laughed. "It came out in like, 1997. You would have been six or seven at the time. It was raved about as a quintessential Australian film."

"I didn't get to the movies much then either. I watched TV. Otherwise, I was too busy fucking up my life."

Both Holland and Alesha exchanged glances and frowned. "Have you at least seen *Pretty Woman*?" Holland asked.

I shook my head then she clutched her hand to her chest. "*Clueless*?"

"I've seen *Mean Girls*."

She gasped. "We need to fix this, and fast. If she hasn't seen all the movies, how is she going to understand all my pop culture references?"

Kristian laughed and slung his arm around my shoulder, drawing me in close. "Tell you what, next time we get a break between jobs, you and me are having a pop culture marathon." Then he leaned closer and spoke into my ear.

"You can eat popcorn while I eat you." I squirmed at that very appealing idea.

"Oh my God. That would be so awesome. I can't wait," Holland squealed, clapping her hands and bouncing on her toes.

Nate slipped his arm around his wife's neck and pulled her against him. "I think they want to have the marathon a little…privately?"

Her face fell. "What? Nooo, don't take this away from me. Leesh, back me up."

"Maybe we can show her a few of the girly movies and Kristian can focus on whatever floats his boat?" Alesha suggested.

"Sounds good to me," I said with a smile. Alesha and I had barely exchanged more than a few words and this was a step in the right direction. Toby had made it clear that everyone needed to get along, so I wanted to live by that notion too. Plus, people were actually jonesing to spend *time with me*. That had never happened before and was kind of cool.

"OK," Jasmine called over the commotion. "I need your daily reports before dinner. Alesha and Holland, if you can show Veronica where everything is, she can help out too. Nate and Sam, you're manning the barbecue, Abbot and Kristian on table and drinks. Toby, I need you in the office first."

"Actually, Jazz. I really need to talk to you first," Kristian said, giving me a reassuring squeeze as a silent exchange occurred between mother and son.

Jasmine pursed her lips and nodded. "Toby, if you'll trade with Kristian?"

Toby nodded then everyone dispersed like the dutiful soldiers they were.

"We're prep and salads?" I asked once we got to the kitchen and Alesha started pulling food from the fridge.

She nodded. "Sort of. The guys do the meat, but we make everything that goes with it."

"OK. Where do you want me?"

"You can start washing the salad ingredients," she said.

"The strainer is in that bottom drawer," Holland pointed out helpfully.

Moving to do as I was told, I got myself set up before Alesha spoke again.

"Do you know what's going on with Kris?" she asked, glancing at me for the barest of moments.

I tore the core out of a lettuce and started breaking up the leaves before responding. "I, um, depending on how you look at it, I might have messed up."

"Messed up how?" Holland asked.

Am I allowed to tell them before Jasmine does? I wasn't sure of the protocol for information sharing within the family.

"It's probably best if you all find out at once," I said. "It will involve everyone."

"Does this have anything to do with the rumour?" Alesha asked, obviously not willing to wait.

"We couldn't get that going. But we did come up with another solution."

"Is it dangerous?" Holland asked. No one was doing anything. We were all just standing at three points in the kitchen with our backs against the benches, facing each other.

I nodded slowly, pulling at my lip with my teeth. "Very."

A LONG NIGHT stretched ahead of us. *Us* being the three partners—Holland, Alesha, and me. Dinner didn't end up happening. Jasmine called all of her sons into the office and instructed us to order Chinese. They needed to work.

"Why aren't we included in this?" I asked, holding a cushion against my chest as I watched the credits roll on the second movie of the night. I'd just sat through Holland's all-time favourite, *Pretty Woman,* followed by *The Princess Bride.* I think I would have enjoyed both if I wasn't freaking out over what was going on inside the office. I didn't understand why, when this job was both my fault *and* my idea, that I wasn't allowed to sit in. Seemed my inclusion within the family business would only go so far. "This is some sexist bullshit."

"They've been working as a unit since forever," Alesha reminded me. "This is what they do. How they brainstorm and whatnot. Once they have a solution, they'll come out and tell us. Don't worry about."

I'd since caved and told Holland and Alesha all about the visit to Maree and Dazza while we ate dinner. Now they knew as much as I knew.

"What if they all hate me for putting them in this situation?" I asked, biting the inside of my cheek.

"If they don't hate me over poppygate," Holland started, "they won't hate you coming up with a risky plan to fix it. Plus, if Kris hadn't run in there half-cocked, you wouldn't have needed to go into damage control." *Well, that's true.*

"Jasmine will nix the plan if they can't pull it off," Alesha added, looking at her nails.

"Then what happens to Maree and Dazza? Jasmine said family only. One day and I've got someone else involved with our business…"

"Family has access to the kind of information that could take down the entire operation. There are stacks of people—contacts and inside men—who do specific tasks when needed. What happens will depend on whether Maree and Dazza are the sort of people the Cartwrights can work with," Alesha explained.

"And if they aren't?"

Alesha took a deep breath. "It'll depend on what type of a problem they are."

Holland mimed a hanging and an involuntary shudder rolled through me.

"I don't want them to hurt Maree," I said. "She's been good to me. In her own way."

"Then pray it all works out and everyone gets what they want," Alesha said.

"And you know, Ronnie," Holland started. "If this does work out, you've singlehandedly come up with the way to free us. That's a big deal."

I closed my eyes. *Then why am I so afraid?*

"Let's watch *Encino Man* next," Alesha put in, obviously feeling it was time for a subject change.

"And I think Ronnie could do with a drink a little harder than Pepsi," Holland added.

"That's a great idea," Alesha said, jumping up. "I learned how to make Mai Tais recently. If you haven't had one before, Ronnie, they're lethal, but delicious. It'll take the edge off in no time."

That definitely piqued my interest. But, before Alesha could leave the lounge room, Sam appeared and caught her by the arms so she didn't slam into him.

"What's the outcome?" she asked when she found her feet again.

"It's a mess," he said, looking at all of us. "But it's doable. I hope you're all up for this, because it's going to be our big Hail Mary."

"I'm not up for *anything*," Holland said, which was ignored.

"Absolutely," I said, standing up like a soldier being called into battle. "I'll help in any way I can."

"What about you, peaches?" he asked Alesha. "Think you can help hijack a police transport?"

She took a deep breath then blew it out with a whoosh, nodding as well. "I will do anything to get us back to general thievery," she said. "This drug shit needs to be over."

Sam hooked his arm around her neck and pulled her close, kissing her on the forehead as I sat back down on the couch and released my breath to ease the tightness in my chest.

"It'll be the biggest job we've ever pulled," Jasmine said, appearing in the entryway along with Kristian and the others. Kristian came and sat beside me, sliding a hand along mine and entwining our fingers.

"Are we cool?" I asked, referring essentially to my relationship with him and everybody in the house.

"I told you, doll. It's a good plan." They all seemed so

tired, but Kristian was smiling at me, so I felt like it would be OK.

Jasmine spoke again, "It'll take meticulous planning and all hands on deck. Even you, Holland."

Holland sat forward in shock. "No way. I'm pregnant."

Nate sat beside her and took her hand in his. "We need you, duchess. Nothing too dangerous for you, but we'll need you involved."

Twisting her lips like there was a sour taste in her mouth, she nodded. "If it gets us free of Conway, then fine. I'll do whatever you need."

"How long do we have to plan?" Alesha asked. "And what about the Sydney job? We're all set to go on that."

"The Sydney job is still going ahead," Toby said, rubbing his palms together as he addressed the room. "Based on what we've been able to learn, this transport isn't going to happen until the court case is through. That gives us at least six months. Maybe even a year if it gets dragged out."

"That long?" I gasped.

Holland let out a squeak, fear in her eyes as she touched her stomach. Nate slid his arm around her and murmured softly, reassuring her that she and their baby would be kept safe.

Abbot ran his fingers through his messy hair. "It's a massive case. It'll be months just for that discovery shit they do. Then there's jury selections... But it's good. It gives us time to prepare 'cause it's gonna be fuckin' hard."

"So, what? This is the backup plan to something we might be able to pull off faster, like the mercenaries?" I asked, confused because another six months to a year seemed like a long time to keep paying someone who was milking you dry. We also had to explain the need to wait to Maree and Dazza, but the money at the end of it would be worth their patience.

"No, doll. This is *the* plan. There isn't a single permanent option that's going to take less time to set up," Kristian explained. "It might shock you, but finding a group of mercenaries willing to risk their lives by going in and shooting up a drug cartel isn't easy to find. This is the most feasible of them all."

"As long as Conway goes for it, of course," Sam said.

"He will," Jasmine said, knowingly. "In the meantime, it's business as usual. Once this Sydney job is done, there'll be no time to rest. We'll need to spend every working hour preparing for the transport gig. And of course, we have a wedding to organise, and that's all before Christmas."

"What? We're still doing the wedding?" I asked, shocked it was still a priority.

"You want to be a Cartwright, don't you?" Kristian asked.

"Of course. But, it can wait," I said. "Isn't planning this job more important?"

Jasmine smiled and shook her head. "There is absolutely nothing more important than family, Veronica. Nothing."

CHAPTER TWENTY
A COMPLETELY FUCKED-UP
KIND OF RIGHT

"YOUR FAMILY IS INSANE," I said to Kristian as I leaned on his chest and played with the smattering of hair across his pecs. "In a good way. I've never been involved in something like this before."

"A bit bigger than nicking cars and shoplifting, hey?"

I nodded. "Way bigger. It makes me nervous. And excited. But I guess this is all normal for you."

He shrugged. "In a way. I remember the first jobs we pulled. They were exhilarating because it was a new feeling. But, I still get nervous. I even still get a buzz of excitement out of it. But that crazy high I had in the beginning has calmed right down. There's nothing like your first score."

"What was your first score?"

"I'll tell you mine if you tell me yours." He grinned.

"OK. Mine is pretty lame. When I was thirteen, I went into the department store and changed the tags on this really expensive dress. I got it for five dollars then sold it for five hundred. I thought I was so badarse because of it."

He chuckled, his eyes shining. "Why didn't you just take it in the first place?"

"Because it had one of those anti theft tags on it and I needed them to take it off."

"Makes sense."

"Not long after that, though, I did manage to grab one of the magnets to remove them myself. That made the whole scam a lot easier."

"I'll bet."

"Now tell me yours. Put my first time to shame."

"Mine is way lamer than yours. Abbot and I went around with those card readers that allow you to duplicate credit cards. It was real easy. We'd go to a busy shopping centre, stand too close to people on the escalators. Boom. We could capture an easy fifty cards on a good day." He shrugged like it was no big deal.

"That's actually way cooler than mine. You had tech. I just had a greedy mind."

Running his fingers lightly along the edge of my jaw, he pressed his teeth into his bottom lip. "Nah. I've read your file, I don't reckon you were greedy back then at all. Just stuck." That was an interesting way to look at it, although, it felt strange having someone know things about me I hadn't told them. This was all stuff I kept hidden from people. Only a select few knew a little about my past, none knew it all, and the Cartwrights had pieced together more than most.

"What excuse do I have now?"

"I don't know. Do you still feel stuck?"

Stuck. Many would feel that in the position I was in, taken by a man, told I couldn't leave, tied by the promise of marriage. But no, I didn't feel stuck at all. I felt...afraid.

Not of them, not of what they wanted me to do. Afraid that this would all go away. It felt like a timer ticking in my mind, waiting for the moment I wouldn't be seen as useful anymore.

"I don't feel stuck," I whispered, just as he ran his thumb over my bottom lip.

"Even though you are?"

I looked away. What was the point of this? "What do you want me to say?" I asked, meeting his eyes again. "I want to be here. I don't feel stuck."

"I want to be sure you understand the situation."

"I do. I can't leave. I'm being watched all the time. Even though you asked me, I didn't really have a say about marrying you. If I fuck up, my life could be over. I'm quite literally in bed with my lover, my captor, and my enforcer. Does that about sum it up?"

He nodded and took a deep breath through his nose. "Do you hate me?"

I shook my head. "You want me to keep playing that game with you, or do you want the truth?"

"The truth."

I traced a circle in the centre of his chest with my index finger, watching it instead of looking into his eyes. Because I couldn't. *I'm not brave enough to watch his reaction to my words.* "I haven't hated you since the first day I worked with you and you kept sneaking looks and telling me about yourself. Before then, you were this enigma I blamed for fucking up my life. Then I saw you as a person looking for something more in life. Same as me. I felt connected to you." I laughed to myself as I remembered some of our earlier interactions. He'd tried so hard to stay angry at me for keying his car, but always ended up slipping into the easy-going, kind-hearted guy I knew now. It was the person we were when we thought no one was looking who defined us. "Plus, you couldn't be mean to me. You kept trying, but you failed so hard."

"That's your fault for being so fucking gorgeous. I kept looking at your arse and wanting to bite it."

"You really think I'm gorgeous?"

"You don't think you are?"

"I don't think I'm ugly." But compared to him, I was plain.

"Yeah, doll, I think you're gorgeous."

"So, this is all about my body?"

He reached down and pinched my arse. "Too right," he said with a chuckle, lightening the mood. I was grateful, because while I wanted to know exactly what he saw in me, it was getting a little too deep into feeling territory for me.

"Explain to me how this whole marriage bargain came to be," I said, changing the subject to a broader topic. "I'm trying to make sense of it."

It was early in the morning, but with my head still spinning from recent events, I wasn't tired. I wanted to keep talking. I needed to know everything about this family I was becoming a part of. I wanted to embrace their world the way they seemed to be embracing me. *Me*. The girl no one ever wanted. I didn't care that they were the bad guys by typical standards. To me, they were a major step up. I wasn't sure I deserved them to be honest.

"Let's see," Kristian said, running his fingers up and down my arms causing the fine sun-bleached hairs to stand up against my tan skin. "Nate and Holland had this fucked-up game going on. He spent the night with her then cleaned out her apartment while she slept."

"What?" I laughed. It sounded so ludicrous. "He took everything? No way."

"He did it to her twice, actually. Furniture, car, books, and clothes. But Holland hid some tracker in her stuff the second time, and then she and Alesha used it to find our operation and followed us here. Since they knew enough to get us all sent to prison, Jasmine ordered them killed."

"She sounds like the queen of hearts. 'Off with their heads!'"

Kristian chuckled. "Yeah. A bit drastic if you ask me. Of course, Nate didn't want that because he was crazy into Holland. He offered to marry her instead, make her one of us, so that even if she did go to the cops, she couldn't testify against her husband—not that I think that really would have worked out, but Nate sold it pretty hard, and Jasmine relented. Sam and Alesha got the same deal, although they had no say in the matter, but it worked out great for them. And Leesh is the perfect Cartwright, really. I think any of us would have stepped up to save her from the red queen."

There was an uncomfortable feeling associated with that comment. *Jealousy*. Another first for me. "If I wasn't the one lying here naked with you, I might think I had some competition with Alesha."

"I already told you she's like a sister."

"You also just said you would have married her."

"It's hypothetical, because it would really suck if she wasn't around. She's Sam's, always was, always will be."

"You talk about her like she's the standard by which all women should be measured."

He laughed and ran his fingers up my spine. "Are you jealous, Veronica Sutton?"

My eyelids fluttered closed involuntarily. It was hard to be even slightly annoyed when something so simple felt so good. "Do I need to be?" I whispered, inhaling deep before my eyes landed on his. They were sparkling with mirth.

"No," he whispered. "I only have eyes for you, doll. Just you." Placing his hand on the back of my head, he pulled my mouth to his and kissed me deeply. *God, this man can kiss.*

"Why do you call me doll?" I asked, licking my bruised lips as we parted.

He wrinkled his nose. "You probably don't wanna know."

"Why? Do you think I look like a sex doll?" I made the face.

He laughed. "No. Not at all. But you know that movie *Annabelle*?"

"The one where the porcelain doll kills everyone?"

Pulling his bottom lip between his teeth, he nodded. "You're beautiful to look at, but you've got this ferocious side—like the doll. It's kind of stuck in my head."

"I don't know whether to love it because it makes me badarse, or whether I should be offended that you're likening my personality to a horror movie plot."

His hands slid down my body and he gripped my arse while he smiled. "You're badarse, doll. This thing between you and me wouldn't be workin' so well if you weren't. I like the fire inside you."

"I think this is working well because you finally picked a woman with some brains."

"Well, you can certainly think on your feet. You proved that when you sorted out both Nate's and my fuck-up without breaking a sweat."

I lifted one shoulder. "That was nothing. I just blurted the first thing that popped into my head. I could have seriously messed things up."

"But you didn't."

"I got lucky."

"Wasn't luck. It was smarts." He tapped the side of my head.

"That must be odd for you when most of your girls can't chew gum and walk at the same time," I said, poking fun and deflecting at the same time. I wanted him to give me compliments, but I also struggled listening to them. It was like I needed to balance each one out with a self-deprecating joke so I didn't forget my place or become too complacent. There was that old saying: 'if something seemed too good to be true, it probably was.' That was how I felt here. I wanted all of this to be true so badly, but there was this little voice in my head that kept telling me to watch out. There are wolves behind those smiles.

"You think you know all about the kind of woman I used to date, huh?" Kristian said with a chuckle, cutting through the maze of my mind.

"Well, I'd hardly call it dating if the busty blonde and the brunette with the arse were an example of the calibre of girls you and Abbot normally *party* with. I can completely understand why you're both still single at thirty-three."

"It's not easy finding a girl who ticks all the boxes."

"Best friends, sisters, or twins?"

"Nah, my personal boxes. Abbot and I might be twins,

but we don't like the same women. It's why that stupid code was never gonna work out."

"OK. So what's your personal checklist?" I suspected this was about to get interesting.

"I'm pretty shallow. Are you ready for this?"

"Yeah." I grinned, placing my hand under my chin as I looked down at him.

"Great tits is at the top."

Smiling, I rubbed my chest against his. "Check."

"Great arse."

"Check." He pinched me and I giggled. "Or, so I've been told."

"Gorgeous smile. A body I want to sink myself into."

"Wow. You're *super* shallow."

"Told you I was," he said, grinning as his fingers dug into my skin, tickling me until I tried to squirm away.

"Stop," I cried, laughing as tears poured from my eyes. "I'm too ticklish." I twisted my body, trying to escape his torture, finally jerking back so hard I fell out of the bed with a thud.

"Ow," I said, still laughing as he leaned down to help me up.

"Oh dear. Great arse might have to get unchecked now," he said while trying not to laugh too hard at my mishap.

I slapped him against the chest as he picked me up and settled me back against the pillows. "Is that really *all* you want in a woman?" I asked.

"A sexy thigh tattoo is a definite bonus," he said, tracing his index finger over the elvish script that wound around my thigh.

"So, so shallow," I whispered, my voice getting a little

thicker as his hand danced closer to my pleasure zone. My clit was probably going to need a break from all the friction soon, but with the way he made me feel, I would risk having to walk around like a cowgirl for one more orgasm by his touch.

His fingers made contact and I moaned lightly, my hips squirming. He leaned down, his tongue running down the centre of my chest, starting at my collarbone and going down, down to my belly button where he paused. "I also want someone I can laugh with," he said, pushing his fingers inside me. I gasped. "Someone I can play with." He looked up at me, his hand working my insides while his lips brushed against my stomach, featherlight. Our eyes locked, but I had trouble focusing. "I want someone I don't have to pretend around." He filled me a little farther, pumping his fingers in and out until I was gripping the sheets and arching my back. Then it hit. I called his name and came around his hand while he pressed a slow kiss between my breasts, his breathing heavy as he brought me back down. "Someone who understands my life and doesn't expect me to leave it or to go straight because they're scared of the consequences."

Looking at him, my chest heaving, I asked the obvious questions. "Is that why you want me, Kristian? Because you like to fuck me, and because I'm a crook like you?"

He lifted his head and looked at me quizzically. "That's a massive oversimplification, doll. I like *you*. I like everything about you."

"Why? You might have looked into my past, but you don't really know anything about me."

"What's to know, doll? We're the same, you and me. And this *feels right*. Are you tryin' to tell me it doesn't?"

Running my hands over his impressive shoulders, I shook my head. "No. You're not wrong. This *does* feel right. Inexplicably, nonsensically, a completely fucked-up kind of right." His strong body was above mine and he was leaning up on his elbows.

"Yeah," he whispered, looking at me with a perplexed understanding in his eyes. "That's *exactly* how it is." And then he entered me in one hard thrust, and I was filled…in more ways than one."

CHAPTER TWENTY-ONE
TAKE IT

"READY?" Kristian asked as I double-checked the contents of my bag.

"Looks like it," I said, tapping my jeans to make sure I had my phone. "I'm all good."

"No phones. Jazz will give us burners when we get in the car."

I dropped my phone back on the bed. Then I tightened my ponytail, and blew out my breath while hooking my bag over my shoulder. "I'm ready." It had been ages since I'd boosted a car, so I was a little nervous, but mostly, I was excited.

"Relax. You're gonna do great," he assured me, holding out his hand for me to take.

"I just don't want to mess this job up. You look amazing by the way," I said, taking in the suit-sans-tie look he had going on. He was very businessman chic, and all I really wanted to do was find a tie and get him to tie me up and have his wicked way with me. But, we had a job to do: stealing cars from long-term parking at the airport. A contact there had given us the details and exit passes for two SUVs and one station wagon. These were the cars we'd be driving to Sydney so none of our personal vehicles were picked up by traffic cameras. And since no one would know these cars were gone, there was no one to report them stolen. We'd have them back in their designated spots before anyone even looked for them.

"Here are your phones," Jasmine said, handing us all ancient-looking Blackberrys as we got in her black Chrysler sedan where Abbot was already waiting. "The SIMs are activated, and the only numbers on there are each other's. Anything goes wrong, you hit the home button three times and an alert goes out to everyone else, letting them know to dump and run."

"What happens if we need to dump and run?" I asked.

Jasmine turned in her seat. "You get out. You go dark. Then you make your way home when it's safe. No traceable calls, and no unnecessary risks. If you get caught, you say nothing."

"So basically, you're on your own," I said.

"Only if you get caught," Kristian said. "Otherwise, one could go down and we'd all go down too. On a job, emotion needs to be set aside."

"I get it," I said, turning the phone over in my hands. "You know, I don't even know how to use this."

"They're new to us too," Abbot said, showing me his screen as he pulled up contacts and made out like he was going to make a call then send a text, explaining as he went along. "We started using them when we began pulling riskier jobs. They've been modified and everything we send or say gets encrypted along the way so no one else can intercept it or track us." He hit send on a message that scrambled on the screen then popped up on mine, still scrambled.

"How do I read it?"

Kristian pointed to the navigation buttons on the keypad. "No touch screen, just buttons."

Once I selected the message and hit the enter key, the message unscrambled, the words, 'Don't fuck this up' popping up on my screen.

"Thanks, arsehole," I said to Abbot, rolling my eyes as I worked out how to send his message to the trashcan. "I'm probably better at stealing cars than you are, you know." I patted the pack on my lap that had my handy tools inside it. I had some shanked keys, a slide hammer and a slim jim. As long as I wasn't breaking into any luxury car, I could be in and on the road in thirty seconds.

"Seems to me you'd be better off with one of these," he said, pulling out a boxlike device from his inside jacket pocket. He was dressed in jeans, a button-up shirt and a blazer, a slight departure from the board shorts and T-shirts he normally wore.

"Holy fuck. Where'd you get that?" I asked, reaching out to grab it so I could take a closer look. I'd heard about these magical little boxes, but I'd never seen one in real life before. They basically scanned for a car's frequency and de-activated the locking system. He could take any modern car he wanted with that thing.

Holding it out of my reach, he twitched and slid it back in his pocket. "It's not a plaything. It's serious tech."

Kristian laughed. "That's the most pretentious thing you've ever said, brother. Here, doll, take a look at mine. When we get a chance, we'll get you one of your own."

"Just don't hit any of the buttons," Jasmine said from

the front seat. "I don't want you messing with my car's electronics."

Kristian rolled his eyes and mouthed, "It won't do that."

I smiled and handed the device back to him. "It's cool. But what happens if the car needs a key?"

"That's what this is for," he said, pulling out a tool that looked kind of like an ice pick but had all these moving parts to the handle, reminding me of a bicycle lock. "Basically, you put this in the key slot and turn the dials until it forms the shape of the key and unlocks the door. It can be fiddly, but once you've got it, you can get in and put it straight in the ignition."

"Wow," I said, taking it from him and twisting the dials. "You guys are impressively kitted out."

"It's just smaller and faster than old-school methods. Both work just fine though."

Returning the tool, I hugged my pack against my chest, suddenly feeling like a school girl in a room full of university students. But after all the cars I'd stolen with Johno, I knew I could hold my own.

Once at the airport, we went through the terminal and caught the shuttle out to the car park, pretending we didn't know each other the entire time—which was really hard when Kristian kept pressing his dick up against my butt whenever the bus jostled. I shot him a warning look, but he just smirked and kept doing it.

Our cars weren't all in the same section, so Kristian got off the bus first, and Abbot and I got off second, splitting up as we headed for our individual cars. We already had everything we needed, so it was a matter of getting in and getting out while looking as natural as possible doing it.

Walking along the massive rows of cars, I looked for spot number 435. In it, there was supposed to be a Ford station wagon. Instead, there was a Land Rover Defender, circa 1980s. I could take it, but I was worried about its ability to get us to Sydney, and the fact it was the wrong fucking car.

Since Abbot was the closest to me, I called his number, marked with a simple 'A', and put the Blackberry to my ear. "Can't get in?" he asked by way of greeting.

"Of course I can," I said in a low voice, "but this isn't the car I was supposed to boost."

"What do you mean? Are you at the right spot?"

"435. Right spot, wrong car. I can't see a white station wagon anywhere here. Do I take this one, or do we leave it?"

His loaded breath filled my ear, telling me he was trying to work out if we could pull this off with only two vehicles. "Take it," he said finally. "He probably just wrote down the wrong car."

"OK," I said before I hung up and took a quick look around the lot. The bus was approaching in the distance, so I made quick work of popping the lock and turning the ignition. The engine rumbled to life and I breathed a sigh of relief. It was in good nick. Actually, the whole car was pretty immaculate for something so old.

Putting it into reverse, I grabbed my hat and sunglasses from my bag—cameras were mounted high and the brim obscured my face, putting most of it in shade. They wouldn't be able to get a clear picture if they went looking.

There were no issues getting out, and we all got through the exit gate and hit the Tullamarine Highway without a hitch. Now, we just needed to get to the rendezvous point to pick up the others. I gripped the wheel with both hands. It felt good after months of being straight. This was all going to be just fine.

About fifteen minutes into the drive, the Blackberry started ringing, startling me a little. I hit the green answer key and held it to my ear. "It's illegal to talk and drive, and I don't know how to put this on speaker," I said quickly, keeping my eyes peeled for cops.

"You're worried about talking on your phone while driving a stolen car?" Kristian's warm voice rumbled in my ear.

"Yeah. It's the little things that get you busted, dude. What's up?"

"You aren't in a station wagon?"

"I know. I went to the spot and this was there instead. Abbot said to take it anyway. Do you think I should just dump it?"

"Jesus. I don't know… It should be fine. I'll call our guy and get him to find out how long we have on that one. We'll make a decision then."

We said a fast goodbye and hung up, the conversation doing very little for my nerves. After the damage control needed with Maree and Dazza, I really wanted this job to work out perfectly so they didn't think I was a jinx. Come hell or high water, we were coming back from Sydney with a buttload of cash.

CHAPTER TWENTY-TWO
BORN TO DO THIS

THE RENDEZVOUS WAS the car park of a massive home improvement store in Craigieburn. Mixed in with all the DIYers, were a handful of criminals, getting the things needed to lift and secure a safe full of money.

Minutes after we got there, Toby and Nate came out with trolleys loaded with chain, sledgehammers, a winch, and a concrete drill. Alesha walked along behind them eating a sausage sizzle.

"Oh fuck," she said when they reached the cars. "I got sauce on my shirt." She lifted it and sucked the red dot, making the stain worse.

"Where's Sam?" Abbot asked as he opened the back of his SUV and started loading in the tools.

"He's right there," Nate said, nodding towards Sam, who was walking over with everyone's duffle bags in his arms.

"We ready to get this trip on the road?" he asked, throwing the bags in the back of each car, knowing from our earlier planning which bags belonged where. "Why is this a Land Rover?"

"I called Randy and he said the spot is booked for a month. He reckons they probably booked one car then used another. Said it happens a lot," Kristian said, holding up his phone.

"Me and Leesh were supposed to be in that station wagon. It was more believable turning up in that."

"I know, man," Kristian said. "But I reckon take the Tucson. We'll take this one. Plenty of couples drive them."

Sam pressed his lips together and looked at the other cars before releasing his breath. "All right. Just make sure Randy double-checks the cars next time. We don't like surprises."

"Will do."

After loading up our bags and separating the tools between the three of us, we got on the road, Nate and Toby in one car, Sam and Alesha in the other, and the twins and me in the Land Rover. It was a ten-hour trip with stops and Kristian took first driving shift.

"We should get fake IDs so we can fly places," I said after the first hour of nothing but a radio to listen to.

"Flying is too regulated. Plus, they'd still see our faces. Not worth it. Road is always safer," Kristian said. "How about we play a game to pass the time? Remember those games we used to play as kids, Abs?" He glanced in the rear-view mirror to address his brother.

"Dirty license plates?" Abbot said, a smile in his voice.

Kristian laughed. "That wasn't what I was thinking, but sure."

Abbot chuckled. "Jasmine hated us playing that game.

She was trying to raise decent men, she'd say, not twisted perverts."

Kristian laughed. "Ten points for tryin'."

"How does the game work? I've never played before," I said, twisting in my seat so I could see both of them.

"What?" Abbot said. "How are you even alive? You seem to have missed *everything*."

I looked down. I knew he was just joking, but the answer still cut me a little—I'd never done anything because I never had the opportunity. No family, no life, no money. I was born, I went to school, I learned how to surf, how to party, and how to steal shit to party harder, then I quit partying and still had nothing. That was me in a nutshell.

"We didn't all have caring families to go on road trips with, you know," I said finally, and he at least had a moment where he seemed to feel bad for throwing that fact in my face.

"OK. It's really easy," he said. "You take the letters from the number plates of the cars in front of us and make something dirty out of them. Like that one for instance, ALM can be Arse Licking Monkeys."

I smiled. "Or Anal Loving Mormons."

Kristian almost spat. "I think she's got it," he said, chuckling.

"Kris, your fiancée has a filthy mind and is being culturally insensitive."

Kristian placed his hand on my knee and gave it a squeeze. "That's what I like about her."

"All right, Ronnie, you win that round," Abbot said. "What about that one there?"

A car changed lanes in front of us with the number plate ESG-173.

"Everybody Sucks Gonads," I said.

"Etching Sexy Geese," Kristian said, laughing at the absurdity of his words.

Then Abbot took his turn. "Eat Shit Gary," he yelled, cracking us all up.

The rest of the day went pretty much like that. When we got bored of one game, we started playing another —*never have I ever*, *radio roulette*, and *would you rather*. Between that, we told stories of our upbringing. The twins had lots of good ones about parties they attended, jobs that didn't go quite right, and family adventures. Jasmine had tried really hard to give five boys with an absent father the best life she could manage.

I contributed where I could, telling them a few stories about narrow escapes from the law and some of my surfing mishaps. I even trusted them with a few anecdotes about living life out of the back of your car and how McDonalds could always be counted on when I needed to pee—except that time I got locked inside one.

There was something special about being trapped in a car for ten hours with people you didn't really know a lot about. At the end of it, you felt a hell of a lot closer and a lot more like family.

"This is where we rest," Kristian said lifting his eyes to the crappy-looking motel on the Great Western Highway. It was basically a parking lot and a long white building with two levels that were populated with simple rooms.

"I always thought Katoomba would be prettier," I said, looking around at the concrete landscape, dotted with a few gnarly looking eucalypts. The sun seared hot against my bare shoulder even though it was late in the day. "And colder."

Abbot handed me my bag from the back of the Land Rover. "It is in winter," he said. "Gets freezing up here, even snows sometimes."

"It's pretty a little farther up, though," Kristian assured me, taking the bag Abbot just handed me out of my hands. "But, we're on the side of the highway, doll. Nothin' can make the stench of exhaust fumes pretty. Maybe I'll take you sightseeing if we get some spare time."

"No time, buttface," Sam said as he walked over, slapping an envelope against Kristian's chest. Then turning and doing the same to Abbot. "We're here to work. Not to have fun. In there are your room keys and a little play money."

Kristian grinned and stuck his tongue out. "Mate, you just said there was no time for fun. What are you giving me play money for?"

"Food, fuckface," Sam said, punching him in the shoulder. Kristian just laughed and pocketed the envelope.

With a shake of his head, Sam turned to me and held up another envelope. "You're sharing with Kris—unless of course you want to kill him after being in the car together ten hours?"

I laughed. "I still like him enough," I said, giving Kristian a sidelong glance. He made a show of putting his hand on his heart.

"Good," Sam said with a chuckle as he handed me the envelope. "This is some cash for you. Don't use any cards while you're here. Got it?"

I nodded. "I left my cards at home," I said.

Sam smiled and gave my arm a squeeze. "Good work,"

he said. "All right, people. Let's get settled. Meeting in my room at eight."

We all bustled about, grabbing our things and finding our rooms while making small talk about being glad that long drive was over. The general consensus was that we were all desperate for a shower and something greasy to eat. I'd noticed a fish and chip shop in the nearby strip, so Kristian and Abbot decided to go gather food while I took a hot shower. Thank God the water pressure was good.

Once refreshed, I headed into the motel room. All it contained was a double bed that would barely accommodate Kristian's bulk, a fabric couch, two small chairs, and a table. The walls were a soft yellow colour, and the lone art print was an Aboriginal dreamtime scape. A small flat-screen TV was on the wall facing the end of the bed, and that was as extensive as the tour of our accommodation got.

Wearing a pair of cotton shorts and a clean singlet top, I towel dried my hair as I walked over to the window and looked outside. Kristian and Abbot were on their way back with paper bags of food, plastic bags of drinks, and possibly a few other things. They were talking and laughing, their body language telling me they were having fun larking about. Kristian lifted his bag of food so Abbot could look inside, then Abbot shook his head and showed him what was inside his. They reminded me of kids arguing over whose lunchbox had the best treats inside.

Watching them made me smile. Now that they'd stopped being pissed at each other over me, it was easy to see how close they were. Two sides of the same coin, Toby had said. I thought that was no small feat for two people who'd almost spent every day of their entire lives in each other's company. Especially when the only other identical twins I'd known had absolutely hated each other. In the beginning, I'd actually thought they were the same person because I never saw them together. There was one girl in my class at school, I got along quite well with. But, every time I saw her outside of school, she pretended she didn't know me. Eventually I got tired of it and confronted her for the strange double standards. She laughed and told me I was seeing her twin. She then walked me to the other side of the school and showed me this identical-looking girl. I felt so stupid, but we laughed it off and she explained that they never hung out because they didn't like each other. Unlike Kristian and Abbot, who seemed almost symbiotic. I wondered when Kristian and I got married, if we'd continue living with Abbot too. I wasn't sure how I felt about that. It could get really awkward. Well, more awkward than it had already been. But at the same time, I didn't want to be the wedge between them. The fact they were so close was a testament to the Cartwrights ability to always stick together as a unit. And it was the same reason I'd felt so welcomed in their presence throughout a really crazy experience.

"OK. We have burgers. We have fish, and we have chips," Kristian said as they burst in the door. He set our food on the tiny table and Abbot plonked down on the couch, pulling out his before passing out drinks. The smell of hot potato and batter filled my nose, and my stomach growled. I couldn't wait to dig in.

"So, how does this work now? We did our part and got the cars—what's next? We're the getaway drivers?" I asked, pulling apart a piece of fish with my fingers, watching the steam billow out of the white flakes.

Kristian nodded. "Once we know exactly where the safe is and how to secure it, Nate, Abs, and I will go in there and get it. You'll keep a lookout with Toby and be our getaway drivers."

"What about Sam and Alesha?"

"They're our inside people, so they'll meet us and take us to the safe and help get the thing disconnected."

"They're also responsible for drugging the whole compound," Abbot added. "Sleeping marks are easy marks."

"Smart," I said. "How much do you reckon they have in that safe?"

"Ten mill?" Kristian shrugged and looked at his brother for confirmation. Abbot nodded. "People are sellin' their houses and shit to join up. They ask for a minimum of two-hundred K per person to join."

"Sounds like the path to enlightenment is a costly one," I said.

"Two-hundred grand to give up technology and live off the land? You could go bush and do that for free," Abbot said. "Don't need no fancy bloody commune to do that shit. I can't believe people get sucked in that bad. Serves them right getting hit."

"All the more profit for us," Kristian said, popping a tomato sauce-coated chip into his mouth. "If there weren't any suckers in the world, we wouldn't get to live like kings."

Abbot looked around the cramped motel room. "Sure, fucking kings we are."

I smiled. This room mightn't have been much, but I'd been in worse. "So we're here a week minimum, right?" I asked, making sure I had all the details straight in my head. They both nodded so I went on. "Sam and Alesha are going up there tomorrow. They have to go through the whole interview protocol before officially joining, but they're going to be scoping out the place to find the safe and get a look at security. Once they know what's what, they get in contact with us and we'll all go in?"

"That the gist of it," Abbot said.

"Nervous?" Kristian grinned.

"Fuck yeah," I said with a gasp. This was the most in-depth operation I'd ever been a part of.

"Relax, doll. You're gonna do great."

"I'm glad you've got faith in me."

Abbot spoke around a mouthful of burger. "You did a great job getting the Land Rover when you weren't expecting it, so don't sweat it. We plan well and improvise where needed. It always gets us by. Go with your gut. You were born to do this."

AFTER THE EIGHT O'CLOCK MEETING, Abbot and I stood outside and had a cigarette together. I'd barely spent any one-on-one time with him since I joined their lives almost three weeks ago. Of course, that was primarily because he'd made it clear he wanted me to fuck off. Although, it had crossed my mind that perhaps he felt his twin was pulling away from *their* relationship when I entered the picture. It made sense. They'd been a pair forever, and I was sure it didn't feel good being the lost sock.

But ever since they'd come back to the house together on the day the dolphins had played, things had been a lot better. Well, he wasn't openly hating on me, so that was progress in my mind.

"I want to tell you I'm gonna quit being an arse toward you," Abbot said, leaning on the railing as he blew smoke out of his nose.

"Is that something you're capable of?" I asked, teasing. "I mean, weren't you born like that?"

Watching him try not to laugh made me smile when I was trying to play serious. "Maybe you should be the one telling me that you're not gonna be an arse," he said.

"I would never promise something like that," I said, inhaling a drag as I pressed my back against the railing, looking up to watch the clouds disappear behind the building.

"I get why Kris likes you," he said, flicking ash into the car park below. "You're cool."

"That's probably the nicest thing anyone's ever said to me—who wasn't also trying to fuck me," I said as I finished up the smoke and flicked the butt into distance.

He shook his head and chuckled. As Kristian said, Cartwrights don't apologise. And Abbot hadn't. But he had offered me an olive branch, and internally I'd grabbed that with both hands. I didn't think it would be easy for a twin so close to his brother to watch a woman enter their shared realm. I understood that I was the intruder, so, I smiled. And then downplayed my inner happy dance.

"Thanks for the hit of nicotine," I said, sliding my hands into my back pockets. "I should get back to Kristian."

He nodded. "Why do you keep calling him that?"

"Calling him what?"

"Kristian instead of Kris like everybody else?" *Because only those he loved called him Kris.*

The thought came so quickly that the intensity surprised me. It was just a nickname at the end of the day, but this family was extremely loyal and fierce of its own. Somehow, offering a nickname seemed to mean more, and despite the marriage proposal, I wasn't entirely sure Kristian would ever offer me more.

I shrugged. "Because he hasn't asked me to."

THE THING they leave out in heist movies is the incessant waiting around. When you're a highly organised group like the Cartwrights, every move is meticulously planned before it's carried out. Before we arrived in Katoomba, Sam and Alesha had been in contact with the commune's recruiters, emailing back and forth and doing Skype interviews before they were finally invited to spend a few days to see if they were a good fit for the lifestyle. I thought leaving a digital thumbprint like that was a risky move, but I was assured that Toby was some tech-savvy genius who made it look like they were calling from a different location. I had no clue about any of that stuff, so I had to trust he could do as they said. Especially after the way he tracked me to Dazza and Maree's. Which reminded me— he could listen through my phone. I probably needed to make sure it was turned off in the bedroom.

"So, say the safe has like, ten million in it. How long is it going to be before we need to pull off another multi-million-dollar job to keep up with the payments for

Conway?" I asked, my feet on the dashboard as Kristian and I took a surveillance shift not far from the commune's boundary. I had a set of binoculars, but there wasn't a lot to see. Mostly, there were a fuck load of trees around, a multitude of squawking birds, and shrieking insects.

"About five months," he said, leaning forward and playing with the leather bracelet he'd given me. I'd transferred it from my wrist to my ankle, and he slid it around in a circle.

"*Five months?* Is that all? Fuck. We could relocate to Mexico or the Bahamas or something for less than that. We'd never have to worry again."

"Cartwrights don't run, doll. We stay and we fight for what's ours."

"Even though what's yours was stolen to begin with?"

He smiled then nodded. "Finders keepers."

I looked over and met his eyes. "Hey, I get it. Losers weepers."

"That's why we really need this plan of yours to work. Once Conway gets his hands on all that product, we should be off the hook for good. No more hunting down cash when cash is so fucking hard to come by these days."

"He won't let you wire the money offshore?"

"Nope. All cash."

"Huh. We should rob him next."

"Reckon he'd figure it was us."

I shrugged. "You know, I'm actually starting to think that growing poppies isn't such a bad plan after all. Seems there's a lot of money in it."

"Far too much risk involved in that kind of thing. We'd all said no to it, but Nate had gone ahead and done it without us. Made him rich, but look at the mess we're in now. They don't let you retire from that."

A walkie-talkie was on the dashboard, emitting a constant static hum. When it crackled, we both sucked in a breath and stared at it. We were essentially sitting there like a teenage girl, hoping the boy she was crushing on would call.

"When was the last time they checked in?" I asked.

Kristian checked the logbook. "Four fifteen yesterday afternoon," he said. "Seems to be around that time each day. They know where the money's being held. Just not how to get to it."

Looking at the time on the dash's clock, it was only two. I tilted my head toward the back seat. "You know, we've got a couple of hours of waiting around. I can think of something…a lot more fun to do." I grinned, moving my knees so they opened and closed.

His eyes immediately darkened as his mind joined mine in the gutter. "Doll, we really shouldn't on a job."

I placed my hands on my chest and squeezed my breasts, using a breathy voice to speak. "I'm just so hot, Kristian. I need to take off this shirt. It's sticking to my skin." I sat forward and pulled my T-shirt free from my cut-offs, lifting it up while he watched with great interest.

"Keep it goin', doll. You know I like what I'm seeing."

"But we're working," I said, lowering the shirt back down and pouting his way. "If only I wasn't so hot."

"You're a tease," he said with a laugh.

"Oh yeah? What are you gonna do about it?"

"Tell you to get the fuck out of the car and put your hands on the bonnet."

"For real?"

"For real."

Excitement trilled through my veins. "Please tell me you're planning on frisking me?"

Leaning a little closer, he lowered his voice to a sexy rumble and ran a finger down my cleavage. "Thoroughly."

I couldn't get out of the car fast enough, my body humming with desire as I placed my hands on front of the Land Rover. "Do you want me to climb up a little? I'm not exactly bent over here," I said as he came up behind me and pressed his lips to my neck, sucking lightly. My fingers went into his hair as I arched back into him.

"Like this is just fine," he said, gripping my hips and pressing his erection into my butt.

I moaned.

"Guys?"

We froze as the walkie-talkie came to life. "Terrible timing," I groaned, standing back up.

Kristian adjusted himself in his jeans. "You're telling me."

"Are you there?"

Kristian jogged around to the driver's door and leaned in through the window. "Yeah, we're here," he said, snatching up the walkie and holding it to his mouth. "Anything to report?"

"Yeah," Sam said, his voice crackling a little. "We're good to go."

"You can get us to the safe?"

"Yeah. Leesh got herself on cooking duty tonight, so she'll add the magic potion to the lentil stew."

"Lentil stew? That sounds disgusting."

"You're telling me. Reckon I could knock them all out with a well-timed fart at the moment. All peace, love and mung beans, baby. I can't wait to eat a nice juicy steak once we're out of here. This vegan stuff is killin' me."

Kristian chuckled and picked up the pen. "OK, brother, give me the details, and we'll get you that steak for breakfast in the morning."

Sam rattled off GPS coordinates and explained how the others needed to proceed once inside. Kristian wrote furiously and told him we'd mark a path through the bush to make our exit faster. It was actually a pretty cool idea. We were going to mark trees with iridescent paint so they could use black light torches to find the way. It didn't give off anywhere near as much light as a regular torch.

"I should get back. They don't like us being alone for long. See you tonight?"

"Sure, give Leesh our love."

"Will do."

"Time to go?" I asked, about to get back in the car.

Kristian looked at me with a devilish grin and shook his head. "Lose the pants," he commanded. "I'm not done frisking you yet."

———

"Drinks, snacks, and extra condoms. Gotcha," Kristian said as he kissed my cheek then strode into the petrol station. The Land Rover guzzled diesel like an eighteen-year-old drinking during schoolies week, and we needed to fill up. I stood against it as the meter ticked over.

Once it was full, I got back inside, checking my appearance in the rear-view mirror while I waited for Kristian to come back from paying. Just as I fluffed my hair, I noticed a blue and white sedan pull up and an officer in uniform get out.

"Oh shit," I said under my breath as I watched him stop and say something into his radio, looking my way.

Shit. Shit. Shit. Shit.

Grabbing my phone out of my pocket, I pulled up Kristian's number and dialled while I slid from the passenger side to the driver's.

"You read my mind. I'm already getting pies," he said as soon as we connected. If I wasn't so panicked, I would have smiled.

"Don't react," I replied, keeping my eye on the approaching officer.

"What's going on?"

"I need you to leave quietly and meet me back at the hotel."

"*What?*" There was a pause then he lowered his voice. "Oh. Shit. Is that a—"

"Cop. Yeah. But, it's OK. I've got this."

"Ronnie!" The sound of my name faded as I pulled the phone away from my ear and disconnected the call. "I've got this," I whispered to myself, hoping to hell I did.

Angling my knee so you couldn't see the slide hammer in the ignition, I kept my eyes ahead even though I really wanted to look for Kristian and make sure he wasn't trying to intervene. I didn't need us both getting collared over this.

Straightening the rear-view mirror, I took a steadying breath, sliding my sunglasses on my face. "You got this."

"Afternoon, miss," the officer said as he approached.

I pushed out my chest and flashed him my brightest

smile. "Oh hi, Officer. Do you need the pump?" I tried to sound light and airy.

"I actually need you to step out of the vehicle, please."

"Did I do something wrong?"

"Just step out of the car please, miss." The radio pinned to his chest announced that the Land Rover with our specific number plate was the car they were looking for.

I smiled and tried to stay calm. It wasn't the first time I'd been caught in a stolen car. And it probably wouldn't be my last. "Sure. I can do that for you."

He stepped back as I made like I was about to comply, then I quickly turned the ignition and slammed my foot on the accelerator while I threw it into gear. My biggest worry was the car stalling, but when the wheels spun and the Land Rover lurched sideways, I said a silent prayer of thanks. At the same time, I hurtled forward, fishtailing onto the main road, leaving a cloud of stinky burnt rubber behind me.

"Oh, I've still got it," I said, adrenaline coursing through my veins as I accelerated down the highway at top speed.

Sirens blared behind me, but I was yet to see the flashing lights. I had a slight head start, but not enough that I could remain on the highway without them catching up or blocking my way. *Fuck.* I needed to get off the main road and get rid of this car. *Fast.*

Seeing a residential turn off coming up, I veered to my left, my exit speed causing the old beast to tilt and slide. Thankful for my misspent teenage years joyriding and hooning around, I turned the wheel, shifted my weight then righted myself, downshifting as I took the next right, the next left. Then I pulled into an empty driveway, wiped every surface as fast as I could while shoving everything into my bag. Then I bolted.

We plan well and improvise where needed. It always gets us by. Go with your gut. You were born to do this.

Knowing it was stupid to stay in the same street as the Land Rover, I jumped a fence and ran through a few back-yards before the bark of a big dog sent me heading for the next street. Ideally, I needed a new vehicle. But with the sirens drawing closer, weaving through the streets, I didn't have the time.

I need somewhere to hide.

Running down the path, I spotted a house with no cars in front of it and sprinted towards it, my chest burning as the sirens suddenly stopped. *They've probably found the Land Rover already. Fuck.* I forced myself to slow to a fast walk. Running looked guilty, and people would be looking out their windows after all that commotion.

"That noise for you?" a male voice asked as I crossed a driveway.

Startled, I turned and saw a guy who appeared to be in his late twenties working on a motorbike, ratchet in hand. I didn't answer and kept going.

"You can hide in here if you like."

That made me stop.

"Better hurry and make a choice. They're moving again."

I turned and saw flashing lights between houses in the next street over. *Shit.*

Rushing towards him, I hoped to God he wasn't some kind of serial killer who liked to collect women in trouble then make lamps out of their skins.

"In you go," he said, holding up a fabric tarp that was covering another bike. I got under it and curled up against the body of the Harley Davidson, holding my breath as my heart bashed against my ears. *Calm down*, I coached myself. *You're OK. Everything is going to be OK.*

God, I hoped Kristian got away. I'd hate it if I took off and they got him instead of me. They needed to be able to finish the job. It was too important to give up all that effort. I needed to talk to him.

I can text!

Pulling the Blackberry from my pocket, I hit the home button to activate the screen.

Nothing.

"What the hell?" I muttered under my breath, hitting it again. Nothing. "Just work." I hit it again, spamming the damn thing with my thumb in frustration until finally, the screen turned on.

I let out a silent cheer then readied my thumbs to start texting. Then the screen blacked out again.

Fuck. I considered smashing the shitty thing on the concrete at my feet when the screen lit again, and a GIF started playing. *What is going on?* A cartoon character in a trench coat was opening a safe. When it popped open, a man with a moustache was tucked up inside, holding up a note. The guy in the trench coat read it and slammed the safe closed. Then the message exploded and there was a comical flash where you could see the moustache man's bones like an X-ray. After that, a little yellow dog popped out of a smaller safe that was on top of the bigger one. *Is that...Inspector Gadget?* It was. What the hell did that mean?

Anything goes wrong, you hit the home button three

times and an alert goes out to everyone else, letting them know to dump and run.

Dump and run. Would they do that? Would they burn the job and leave over a stupid GIF? Oh my god. *Fuck motherfucking fuck fuckery!*

I needed to get back to the motel. *Now.* I shoved the dead Blackberry back in my pocket and went to lift the tarp. If I was fast, I could steal a new car and be back up there before they'd zipped up a bag.

"Stay quiet. They're in the street," the guy said, causing me to immediately back out of that plan and stay very still instead. All I could hear was the clicking of his ratchet as he tightened a bolt. Then I heard the engine of a slow-moving car.

"You see a blonde girl come running by here?" It was idling in front of the house.

With my adrenaline causing my breath to come out louder than normal, I placed my hand on my mouth to force myself to breathe through my nose and calm the fuck down. They'd drive by. They'd leave. And I could get out of here the moment the coast was clear.

"Not today. What'd she do?" the guy hiding me asked.

"We just need to ask her a few questions."

"Sorry. Can't say I've seen any girls today."

"Call it in if you see anything."

"Will do, Officer."

There was a silence like they were staring at each other, then the engine whirred and slowly receded as the cops drove away. I was finally able to breathe again.

"All right, girl. You can come out now," he said after a few more minutes.

I slid my way out and stood up, pushing my hair back

from my eyes. He watched me carefully while he leaned on the seat of his bike and pulled a pack of cigarettes out of his pocket. He offered me one and I shook my head. Nicotine and adrenaline didn't go so great together in my book.

"I should go," I said, pulling my backpack onto my shoulder. "Thanks for the tarp."

He lit the cigarette and blew out the smoke. "Don't be crazy. You can't leave right now. They're only a street over. At least wait a bit. There're drinks inside. Take a load off."

"I really should get back. I'm expected."

"You're expected." He smirked and rubbed a hand over the full, neatly trimmed, dark brown beard. He wasn't of the lumberjack variety who grew it for fashion. He was of the biker variety who grew it to keep their face warm, or maybe because that's just what bikers fucking did. The tattoos on his arms identified him as a member of the Grim Order Motorcycle Club, a biker gang that had had more than its fair share of press over the past few years. *What have I gotten myself into this time?*

"Yes. My fiancé and his brothers. They'll be waiting for me to make my way back to them." I lifted my hand above my head to indicate how huge they all were. "There are five of them."

He chuckled. "Listen, babe, you don't need to make up a family of giant men to scare me off. I'm not gonna hurt you."

"Why would I make them up? They're real."

"Sure they are." He chuckled again. Why did he not believe I knew a family filled with mammoth men? "Listen, I'm just saying that you gotta lie low until you know if you're in the clear or not. What'd you do anyway?"

I didn't know if I should tell him, but figured, what the hell. "Stole a car."

"OK. I have a scanner in the house. We can listen to see what's goin' on. Once we know the coast is clear, I'll take you back to your giant brothers myself. Cool?"

Tightening my grip on the strap of my backpack I took a deep breath and nodded. He was right—those cops were still looking for me. I didn't have much choice but to sit, wait, and hope Kristian waited too.

Leading me into the house, he opened the fridge and pulled out two beers, handing one to me. "I'm Travis. But my friends call me Breaker."

"Do I dare ask why?" I asked as I took the bottle.

"Not if you're squeamish." He smiled, the corners of his eyes turning up a little and creasing in the corners. I decided to change my earlier assessment of his age and put him at mid-thirties. He was pretty good-looking actually—if you went for biker types.

"I'm Ronnie."

"Nice to meet you, Ronnie," he said, nodding his head as he took a mouthful of beer.

"Is it?" I asked, and he chuckled. He liked a good chuckle this guy.

I watched him open a cupboard door and pull out a battery-operated police scanner that he set on the table in front of me and switched on. There was a lot of nonsense being said that I didn't understand, but I did understand the part that said: "Be on the lookout for a Caucasian female, late-twenties, blonde hair, around one hundred and seventy centimetres." They were still searching the area, and noted I was assumed to be on foot and in Leura.

"They saw you," he stated.

"I was wearing sunglasses," I said, suddenly feeling as though the life of a hermit might be a really great alternative to my current life of crime. I just kept fucking things up.

He laughed, ran his hand over his beard, then picked up a remote and turned on the TV, flicking through channels. "You aren't on TV yet, but it's still early. Depends on how bad they want you, I guess. And if they got a picture..." He turned the volume right down and placed the remote on the table next to the scanner. "Since we've got some time, why don't you tell me about these giant brothers?"

ABOUT AN HOUR LATER, it seemed the search for the mystery blonde woman (me) had been called off. There was chatter about monitoring train stations and bus lines. They even thought I might have jacked another car.

"Ready to return to your giants?" Breaker asked as he stood and tapped his pockets for keys.

"Eager to get rid of me?" I responded, standing with him and slinging my backpack over my shoulder. As wary as I'd been, it turned out he was pretty cool to talk to. He told me how being in an MC was a lot like creating your own family. Loyalty was a big thing for them, as was the freedom to live the kind of life you chose. I guessed that was why they had a bit of a messed-up relationship with the law—too many rules.

Breaker shrugged. "You can stay if you like, but with the way you've been bouncin' your knee, I reckon you're gonna wear a hole in my floor if we wait much longer."

I laughed. But, it was an uncomfortable sound, because I was anxious as fuck. There hadn't been any mention of the cars they were driving over the police radio, and there hadn't been any mention of any one-hundred-and-ninety-three-centimetre men. The walkie-talkie was too far out of range for me to make contact, but, as far as I knew they were safe. Besides my accidental sending of the burn message, they had no reason to leave. *Please be waiting for me.*

"Put this on," Breaker said, holding out a smaller leather jacket. "Make sure your hair is tucked in the back of it."

Taking it from him, I slipped my arms inside the well-worn leather. A slight musky smell coupled with a rich, earthy scent filled my nose. This particular jacket was well used. "I like that you just happen to have a ladies'-sized jacket within easy reach," I joked, twisting my hair at the nape of my neck and sticking it in the collar.

He grinned. "Gotta be prepared for all situations, babe. I got a pretty pink helmet too if you wanna wear it."

"I thought we were going for inconspicuous."

"Good point." He grabbed a plain black helmet with a dark visor and handed that to me. "I actually don't have a pink one at all." He winked at me.

When we went outside, he pulled the tarp off the bike I'd been hiding next to and secured his own helmet to his head, sliding his arms into a leather vest that had his club emblem on the back of it. Then he got on the Harley and started it up, the engine roaring to life like some kind of animal warning. I felt the vibration in my chest just from standing beside it. It made me smile.

"You like that?" he asked, revving the engine.

"I've never been on a bike before."

"Then this'll be a treat. Hop on. Hold on tight. You're never gonna want to drive in a car again."

My day had been one from hell, but the ride on that bike was fucking fun. I smiled the entire time we were on the highway, weaving in and out of cars, the wind blowing my hair loose and letting it flap in the air behind us. I squealed and laughed, and when we pulled up outside the motel, my cheeks hurt from grinning so much.

"That's almost as awesome as surfing," I said as I took the helmet off my head.

"Surfin', huh? Can't say I've ever given it a go. Boards and bikes don't really go together."

I laughed at the mental image in my head. "Yeah, I can imagine they'd slow you down a bit."

He nodded towards the building. "So, where are your giants?"

That was a good question. The cars were no longer parked in the lot. My stomach dropped. I had a terrible feeling about this.

"They're probably inside," I said, sliding off the bike and unzipping the jacket.

Please be inside.

"You know, you might not wanna hear this, but when things go wrong—especially when the law is involved—most people don't sit around waitin' to get caught," Breaker said as I placed the jacket on the bike where I'd been sitting.

"I asked him to wait for me here. They wouldn't just leave me behind."

"I'm not sayin' they'd want to, but if your fiancé saw the cops go after you like you said he did, maybe he thinks it's too hot to stick around. Now, I'm not pretendin' to know what the hell a girl in a stolen car and five giant brothers were doin' here, but maybe there's somewhere you're supposed to meet or somethin'. You know, if the shit hits the fan, disperse and regroup when things cool down?"

"Maybe we were just here on a holiday and decided to go joyriding?"

He gave me a look that told me he thought I was full of shit. "Wanna know how I know that's a lie?" He reached into his back pocket and pulled out his phone, showing it to me. It was a Blackberry. Just like mine. "And since yours is bricked, I reckon someone hit the home button three times."

I pressed my lips together and looked away, breathing in deep to keep my emotions in check. *They should have waited. They should have trusted me not to get caught.*

"Let's go in and see if they're still around," Breaker said, his voice a little softer. "What room number were you in?"

"Twenty-nine," I said, my voice small.

I'd messed up really bad this time. All that work and my stupidity made the job a bust. *Fuck me sideways.*

Following Breaker into reception, I waited a step behind him as he asked if room twenty-nine was available for hire. The girl behind the counter smiled and said, "You're in luck. They just finished cleaning it. It was vacated about an hour ago." She opened a drawer and pulled out the keys. "How many nights you looking at?"

Breaker turned to me and lifted his brows. "How many nights are we lookin' at, babe?"

My chest tightened as I blinked rapidly, trying to keep my shit cool. "I, uh...I think I want to stay somewhere else, actually," I said, turning around and walking outside to suck the fresh air into my burning chest.

They left me.

He left me.

I was in a strange city.

I was alone.

Again.

Shit.

"OK. So what now?" Breaker asked as he joined me on the footpath.

I shook my head.

"Oh shit. You're gonna cry, aren't you?"

"No," I forced out, my voice obviously strained with unshed tears. "I don't cry."

"You are. Your eyes are fuckin' puddles."

I blinked and a tear splashed down my cheek.

"Ah shit," he said. "I can't handle tears."

"I'm not crying," I insisted even though rivers were streaming down my face.

"Bloody hell." He pulled me into a bear hug, and all I could smell was leather and dust. "Don't take this personal, babe. It's not about you. It's the way this kind of stuff works. You get that, right? Criminals are like cock-roaches. We scatter when the lights get turned on."

"They're supposed to be my family," I sniffed. "They could have waited an hour at least."

Placing his hands on either side of my head, he pulled me back so I could look up into his eyes. "How old are you, babe?"

"Twenty-seven," I sniffed.

"So you've got a lot to learn still. See, *my brothers* are my family, too. But when a ship is sinkin', everyone bails. You save who you can, and the ones you can't help, you hope to God they're strong enough to save themselves."

"SO, CARS, HUH?" Breaker asked as I took a mouthful of the instant coffee he'd made me. *International Roast, yuk.* It was bitter going down, so it certainly matched the tone of the day.

"Mostly," I said, leaning on my forearm as I moped against his table. "I was always about opportunity more than planning, though. I tend to think well on the fly."

"These brothers, they're about plannin'?"

"Down to the last detail."

After finding the hotel empty, Breaker told me I could come back to his place, and he'd help me get to Torquay since that was the only option left. I really hoped he was legit with that, because I didn't want to be forced into becoming some biker whore like what happened on TV. But, so far, he'd been nothing but helpful, and my gut said to trust him. *Go with your gut.*

"Are cars good business?" He slid a cigarette between his lips then lit up.

"They're OK. Do you mind?" I asked, pointing to the

pack in front of him, he pushed it across the table and held the lighter for me. "Thanks." I tucked my feet up on the chair and blew out some smoke.

"Seems you're a long way from home pullin' a job that just does OK."

"What's with all the questions?" I narrowed my eyes. "You the feds or something?"

"Just checkin' what kind of criminal I'm aidin' and abettin'."

"What kind of criminal are you?"

He inhaled deeply, and I took a moment to inspect the tattoos on his hands, the words 'respect' and 'honour' in script just above his knuckles. Each finger seemed to have a rune on it, partially hidden by chunky silver rings. There wasn't a lot of bare skin.

"You read the papers, watch the news? You already know."

I nodded. Drugs, guns, violence. It was all the media could talk about whenever the Grim Order MC was mentioned.

"How long have you been doing it?" I asked.

"Became a prospect at fifteen. A full member at eighteen. I don't know much else."

"Do you ever regret it, getting involved so young?"

He shook his head slowly. "You?"

I pulled at the inside of my lip with my teeth. "I don't know. This is really all I've ever known."

"Then I guess you're well ahead of most others your age."

"How's that?"

"You're already followin' your callin'."

"ALL SET," Breaker said, handing me a prepaid phone and a bag with some chocolate cupcakes inside it. "Buzzard'll take you all the way to Melbourne. You can make your way home from there. That work for you?"

I nodded. "Thanks for everything."

"Call me when you get back. I wanna know you're safe."

"Sure thing."

In the last few days, I'd learned a lot of things about bikers. Namely that, they did regular things like the rest of us. They didn't go around purposely trying to frighten the life out of people for fun, and when they did, there was a reason behind it. Essentially, they were doing their thing and providing for the people they loved—*just* like the rest of us. Sure, they smuggled drugs to do it, and some of the women at the clubhouse were pretty strung out on the stuff —I'd been there with him to 'pick something up'—but really, they were no different than the Cartwrights. Just way hairier and a bit more scary-looking.

And Breaker really liked to bake. I'd eaten more cake in his house than I've ever had at my birthdays.

"You ever decide to kick that guy of yours to the curb, my door's always open to you."

He'd also made it no secret that he was interested in me. But he didn't like to mess with another man's woman so never made any advances. Thank God. He was lovely. But my heart and body belonged to someone else.

"I didn't know bikers were such gentlemen."

He winked. "Don't tell anyone." Then he opened the

passenger door on the Mack truck that would take me home. I couldn't wait.

One of the other club members drove a truck to Melbourne once a week, transporting goods for a national grocery chain. I was pretty sure they were using him to smuggle drugs too, but with a BOLO out with a somewhat grainy image of me from the service station cameras, I had to take what I could get and cross my fingers.

Buzzard was already in the truck's cabin.

I figured he was called that because he had little beady eyes. He also looked about sixty and had questionable personal hygiene.

Another thing I learned about bikers—they weren't all hot like the ones on TV either.

"Let's go," he yelled.

A cool wind whipped at my hair. "Thanks again," I said, smiling at Breaker before remembering I was still wearing his jacket. "Oh, I should give this back."

Breaker pulled the collar of the leather jacket up around my neck and zipped me in. "You keep it. To remind you there's more to life than surfing and stealing cars."

"Like Harleys and cupcake-baking bikers?"

He chuckled and pulled me a little closer. "If you weren't already spoken for, I would have fucked you so hard you'd never want to leave," he said close to my ear. His lips brushed my cheek, and I placed my hand on his chest as a barrier.

"And if I wasn't already spoken for, I might have fallen for that line, but I think we both know you only want what you can't have."

He grinned, brown eyes twinkling. "You're good at reading people, Ronnie. Make sure you use that."

"I will."

He stepped back as I climbed into the truck. "I hate to see you go, but I love to watch you leave," he said, making me laugh.

"Goodbye, Breaker. I hope I never see you again."

He smiled. "Me too, babe. It's been real."

TEN HOURS in a car took more like fifteen in a truck, and Buzzard wasn't much of talker. He wouldn't even go for a game of dirty license plates. I wanted to stick a needle in my eye just to alleviate some of the boredom.

But once in Melbourne, I quickly made my way to Southern Cross Station and hopped a train to Torquay. Another hour and a half and I had the salt air of my home against my skin.

I closed my eyes and breathed in. It was only a week since we'd left, but God, I'd missed it. It felt like a lifetime had passed, the entire time I'd been away from Kristian, from my *family*, was a slowly ticking clock. I wasn't secure enough in my position with them to feel confident that my return would be parades and roses. I expected a little hostility over another job gone sideways, but I only hoped they'd hear me out and forgive me for sending them running unnecessarily.

Needing the comfort and reassurance that only Kristian could give me, I headed towards the beach shack, hoping that maybe he was there instead of all the way out at Jasmine's. The sooner I saw him, the better it was for my nerves.

My step was light, and I hummed a nonsense tune out

of hopeful comfort. I hadn't even walked that far when I saw Kristian's Ute parked at the curb. I wanted to clap my hands and jump up and down. I'd never been so happy to see that stupid vehicle in my life.

Elated, my heart light in my chest, I ran to it, hoping to find him—or even Abbot—inside it. But it was vacant, locked up tight.

That's OK. I can wait. I've already waited days, so a few more minutes won't hurt.

When the minutes stretched from five to twenty, I climbed up on the bonnet and sat with my bag beside me, the leather jacket bundled up to the side. It was late afternoon. I'd been travelling since late the night before, and at some point, I think I dozed off because a sudden noise scared the shit out of me.

BWOOP, bwoop

My eyes flew open, my heart lurching in my chest as the Ute beeped unlocked beneath me.

Darkness had replaced the sunlight, and it took a moment to register where I was.

Kristian.

Sitting bolt upright, I turned and saw him on the path, staring at me with his keys in his hands, telling me he beeped the car specifically to wake me up.

It was for that reason I didn't run into his arms.

"Why are you looking at me like that?" I asked when he didn't speak.

"I'm trying to see how many biker tattoos you accumulated. Although I see he gave you a different souvenir," he said, indicating the jacket.

I blinked twice. "Excuse me?"

He stepped forward. "I saw you. At the motel. It was touching, really it was."

"What are you talking about?" I gasped, my chest so tight I could barely breathe.

"You. The biker. The fact you went straight to him and stayed with him in his house. I saw you together, several times. I watched the way you were with him for days. I had to be sure." *Sure of what? What is he going on about?*

"You're talking out your arse," I whispered, my eyes burning. I already knew what he was accusing me of, and it felt like a knife in my gut.

"Tell me, was it planned the whole time? Was the cop even a real cop?"

"I got into a car chase with the cops to protect *you*, you motherfucking arse." I spoke through clenched teeth. "That *biker* took pity on me and hid me from them. Then, when the police quit searching, he took me to find you. *But you were gone.* I'd barely been gone an hour, and you were *gone*. Packed up and left. *He* convinced me that *you* didn't abandon me and then he gave me a place to stay. He helped me get home because the cops were *looking for me* and I was so *desperate to get back to stupid you.*" By this point, I was yelling, tears streaming down my face. I wasn't sure at which point it started, but the hysteria gripped my throat and coated my words. "I have been through hell and back because of some misguided notion that I was finding my way *home*. To my *family*. But now I see I was *wrong*. You're just like all the rest, Kristian Cartwright. You use people and throw them away when you're done with them." I hopped off the hood of the Ute, grabbing my bag and jacket. "You don't deserve me." I angrily swiped at the tears pouring from my eyes. "And you don't deserve my tears. Here." I pulled the ring from

my finger and pegged it at his feet. It bounced with a *ting*.
"*Rot in hell!*"

Then I turned and ran as fast as I could, barely able to
see through the tears. When I finally got to the point where
I couldn't breathe and move anymore, I dropped to my
knees and pressed the heels of my hands to my eyes.

I hated my life.

I hated my life.

I hated my life.

No one stuck around. No one trusted me. No one gave
me a *fucking chance.* They didn't care if I lived or if I died.
Whether I was safe or in danger, whether I could *fucking
breathe.* I wanted to squeeze my eyes so tight that I disappeared, popped like a bubble of nothingness and simply
ceased to be.

It would be so much easier.

Balling up my fists, I hit them into the concrete ground
and screamed. Again and again and again, slapping and
crying until a set of hands wrapped around my upper arms,
and I jumped to my feet defensively.

"Oh my God, Ronnie. What happened to you?"

I met Holland's concerned eyes for only a moment
before I crumbled again, this time crying into her shoulder.

"Come with me," she said kindly, her hand rubbing
circles on my back. Let's get you cleaned up, then you can
have a stiff drink and tell me all about it."

TAKING me to a property farther down the coast right near
Bells Beach, Holland stayed quiet until she stopped her car
in front of a quaint farmhouse.

"Here we go," she said, unclipping her seatbelt. "Nate should be back later. He has some meeting at Jasmine's and quite frankly, I'm sick and tired of being there. So, here we are."

I sniffed. "Are you supposed to be at this meeting too?"

She waved her hand dismissively and shrugged. "I'll text so he knows I'm safe and having dinner with a friend."

That just made me cry more.

"Shit, Ronnie. Come inside. I'm a lot bigger than you but I'm sure I have something you can wear once we clean up those bleeding knuckles.

I didn't even realise... I turned my hands over in my lap, seeing the damage I did punching the concrete.

"OK," I said, sniffling.

Once inside, she directed me to the bathroom and showed me how the rainfall shower worked before leaving me to it.

"You have a beautiful home," I said as she was leaving. I wiped the side of my hand across my nose, taking in the rustic décor that looked carved from nature. It was a home that belonged in magazines.

Holland thanked me. "You should see the library."

Stepping into the shower, I let the water wash over me, the heat seeping into my aching muscles and stinging my scraped hands. I'd never felt as out of control as I did right now. To be offered your dreams, to hold it in your hands and wear it on your finger, believe it was real before losing it all again was the cruellest of cruel. They should have let me go when I ran. They should have never interfered in my life at all. They should have *left me be*. They were cruel, heartless people who called you family one moment then treated you like a pariah the next.

Why? Why am I surprised? I was my mother's unwanted pregnancy, and from there, life never improved. *Why didn't she just abort me to save me all this pain? Why do I keep expecting—hoping—someone will actually give a fuck?*

When my pity party started to hurt my brain, I closed my eyes and shook my head, repeating the only good advice my mother ever gave me. "You can't rely on anyone but yourself, Ronnie. No one will give you what you need. You have to take it for yourself. Do you understand? *Do you understand?"*

I covered my face with my hands, tears bursting the dams of my eyes. I had never cried this hard and had no idea why this was hurting me so much. "I'm better off alone," I chanted. "I'm better off alone. I don't need him." My voice cracked and I slammed my hand against the tiles, trying the line again. "I don't need him." That wasn't strong enough either. *Come on, Ronnie. Say it like you mean it.* I cleared my throat and went again. "I don't need him," I said with force, feeling it in my chest. "I'm better when I'm alone."

I don't need *them.*

I don't need anyone.

CHAPTER TWENTY-SIX
AS GREEN AS GREEN
CAN BE

"FEELING BETTER?" Holland asked when I emerged from the bathroom with Band-Aids on my knuckles. I was wearing a sundress and an oversized cardigan several sizes too big for me, but there was a sash about the waist of the cardigan, so I wrapped it around myself like a robe, and it did just fine.

"Much. Thank you for that. A shower and some clean clothes really does the world of good."

With a nod, she smiled and picked up a teacup that had a little saucer and everything. "I made you this. I wasn't sure if you would prefer tea or alcohol, so I made you a Hot Toddy. My aunt—she raised me—loved them in the evenings. Said they could cure anything. It's tea, honey, lemon, and a splash of whiskey."

Taking it from her, I lifted the cup to my nose, smelling the concoction. It reminded me of Lemsip. I took a sip, tasting all the flavours she'd mentioned, and felt the warmth of the alcohol spread as it hit my belly. "That's actually pretty good," I said, placing the cup on the saucer

I was still holding in my other hand. I wasn't sure where she wanted me to drink it.

"Why don't we sit?" she suggested, gesturing toward the overstuffed couch in the lounge room. It faced a fireplace and there was one of those distressed wooden coffee tables in front of it. Around it, bookcases, a sideboard, a large window with an ocean view, but no TV.

I sipped at the tea and tucked my feet beneath me, my body getting lost in the dress. "I suppose you want to know why you found me screaming in the street," I said, clearing my throat as I straightened my spine.

"You can talk if you want. Or, we can just sit. I can put the television on."

"You don't have one," I said, frowning slightly because she should have known that—it was her house, after all. Wasn't it?

She grinned and reached to the side, picking up a remote that she aimed at a large landscape painting on the wall. It slid up and there was a flat-screen television behind it.

"Classy," I said.

"It's very *Get Smart*."

"Get Smart?"

"It's an old TV show. It was always on after school growing up. Haven't you seen it? They made a movie of it a few years back—bumbling spy who takes all the credit while his female assistant does all the work? You know, like every workplace everywhere?"

I shook my head. "I think I missed that one."

"We'll have to add it to our list of things to watch."

I looked into my cup, watching the gentle ripples move over the tea's surface. "I don't think we'll be doing that anymore. I'm thinking I might get out of town. I probably should have left years ago, anyway..."

"No, Ronnie," she said, touching my arm. "Don't run away again. We're only just becoming friends."

I looked out the window, her words hitting me in the cracks of the wall I kept trying to put back up. "It's not really up to me. Kristian doesn't trust me—and I guess I don't blame him. We didn't exactly start in a way that builds trust. But still...I can't be in a relationship like that. So, it's best I go. Especially since, well, who knows what the Queen of Hearts will do."

"Is the Queen of Hearts Jasmine?"

I nodded and mimed chopping my head off.

"I hear that, sister," she said with a chuckle. "Although, I don't think she'd do that. She likes you."

"If she believes Kristian's version of events, I can't see how that could possibly be true."

"What do you mean?"

"You don't know?"

She shook her head. "All I know is that they returned early and you and Kristian didn't. I actually expected to see you tonight. They were meeting because Kris got back this afternoon. You didn't come back with him?"

"No. I came back *for* him. But he made it very clear that he doesn't want me around anymore."

"Those Cartwrights can be absolute stubborn arses when it comes to matters of the heart. Lord knows I went through it with Nate, and Alesha went through it with Sam. They like to cut their own noses off to spite their face."

"Well, he can go around looking like Voldermort for all I care."

"There you go," she said, patting me on the knee. "There's a movie reference we can all get on board with."

I sniffed and laughed a little. I liked her humour and was glad in a way this was ending early. With her kind eyes and understanding nature, I would have grown too attached to her. Perhaps it was because she was a teacher and used to guiding all kinds of people, but she really seemed to get me. I was going to miss the friend I never got to have.

"He thinks I cheated on him," I said after a while, finding that I really needed to get that detail off my chest. The injustice of it, the weight of his accusations... They had me feeling sick and twisted up inside. I felt that if I could just get one Cartwright to listen and understand, then at least I'd get my say. Then I could leave and close the door on this chapter of my life.

"Why would he think that?"

"Because he saw me with another man. We weren't doing anything. In fact, he was actually hugging me out of comfort. But Kristian saw it as something else, and now he's convinced I ruined the job on purpose. That I had planned on the cops all along." Frowning, I shook my head.

"You got *caught*?" she shrieked, her eyes going wide as the colour drained from her face.

"No. *They* didn't get caught at all. I did. The intel on the car we took must have been wrong, because it was reported stolen." I then proceeded to tell her about my ordeal—the car chase, running on foot, doing everything I could to make sure I kept the police away from them so they could finish the job, the fuck-up with the home button on the Blackberry. I told her how Breaker helped me, how horrible I'd felt when I realised they'd left without me, how I travelled back with a truck driver who didn't talk, and stank—all so I could get back to Kristian. "The thing that kept me going was the thought of running into his arms and having him hug me and say, 'Thank God, doll. Thank God you're home.' But he didn't say that at all. He accused me of fucking another guy. But I didn't. I fucking didn't." I shook my head, swallowing the lump in my throat, because I refused to fucking cry over that man again. He'd gotten all the tears he would from me.

Holland was quiet for a moment, her brow furrowed as she studied my expression. "I'm sorry, Ronnie. It sounds like you've been through an ordeal and Kris is being a complete and utter cunt monkey."

I chuckled a little at that. "He really is."

"You know, when Nate and I were first married, we had a few problems with jealousy. Another man declared his love for me and kissed me. I pushed him away and slapped his face, but Nate saw the whole thing and lost his mind. He beat the crap out of poor Toby and barely spoke to me for weeks afterward, even though it wasn't my fault. He was just so deeply hurt that another man dared to touch his toy that he couldn't see the forest for the trees. I was livid."

"Back up a minute. The other man was *Toby*?"

"Did I say that?" She frowned like she was trying to rewind the conversation and see where she inserted his name.

"You did. Is that why they're a bit funny with each other?"

Her lip curved up in a half smile. "You noticed that?"

I nodded.

"There's a lot more to it than unrequited lust, but that's when it came to a head. *But,* my point is that Cartwright men can't stand sharing anything they consider to be theirs. Just seeing you with that biker would have turned those blue eyes as green as green can be. And they aren't rational when they're like that."

"That's a bit hypocritical for men who make a living out of taking what isn't theirs."

She shrugged. "I didn't say it was logical."

"So, what you're saying is that I should just wait around until Kristian gets his head out of his arse and realises I didn't do anything his mind has conjured up?" I shook my head.

"That depends. Do you love him?"

Pressing my lips together, I knitted my brow. It wasn't something I liked to give a lot of thought to. We were mercurial. "Right now, all I want to do is hate him."

"That's not quite the same as *actually* hating him though, is it?"

"I don't know," I whispered, downing the last of my now cold toddy. The whiskey burned my throat.

"Maybe take the night to sleep on it. Things will seem a little clearer in the morning."

"You can't be alone. I was worried sick." Nate's voice bellowed from the other room. I sat up in bed, giving up on rest. I'd slept in fits and starts, exhaustion being the only thing keeping me lying down. But when he got home, Holland had obviously forgotten to text him about her whereabouts, and he'd started yelling.

I ran my hands over my face and through my hair as Holland argued back, telling him how she found me after Kristian accused me of cheating. "She needed someone to take care of her."

"And who was taking care of you? We aren't safe at the moment, duchess. I need to know where you are at all times. You're pregnant, for Christ's sake."

Not wanting to eavesdrop on their domestic situation any longer, I gathered up my things and stuffed my feet into my shoes before pushing open the window and climbing out. *Thank God the security here isn't as crazy as Jasmine's house.*

I left on foot, their arguing voices following me all the way to the road. As I headed toward town, the phone Breaker had given me started chirping in my bag. I pulled it out and flipped it open.

"Hello?"

"You were supposed to call me. Glad you're not dead in a ditch somewhere," he said.

"Hey. I got caught up and lost track of time."

"It's cool. I'm not your dad. Just wanted to check in. Everything OK? Your giant men welcome you home with open arms?"

I smiled but there wasn't any happiness to it. "Something like that," I lied.

"Something like that," he stated, saying each word slowly. "That doesn't sound good."

"Yeah. Well, I was thinking I might start working on my own again anyway."

"You need me to come get you?" The offer brought tears to my eyes. It would take him easily thirteen hours on his bike. *Why would he come here for me?*

I shook my head. "No. Thank you. I think I'm better off alone."

"That's bullshit and you know it. Tell me where you are. I'm leavin' now."

"No, Breaker. Honestly, I'm fine. I don't need anyone rescuing me. Turns out that doesn't work so well."

"Yeah. I'm still comin'. Either to get you or to knock some sense in the head of that fiancé of yours. Text me the address or I'll knock on every door in town lookin' for you. I'll see you tomorrow," he said. Then he disconnected.

Sighing, I closed my eyes and slid the phone back into my bag. "Just great," I said, knowing that the moment Breaker showed up in town, it would somehow get back to the Cartwrights. Then it wouldn't matter what I said anymore, Kristian would see it as proof. "Fucking men."

CHAPTER TWENTY-SEVEN
EIGHT HOURS

YOU NEVER REALISE how essential a little thing like your ID is until you're walking the streets at 10 PM trying to get a room to sleep in. It didn't matter that I had cash, and offered to pay double. Policy said they had to record ID. No one was willing to risk their job for some girl they didn't know.

That's okay. No one wants to take a risk on a girl they do know either.

After that, I went to a bar, deciding to drown my sorrows instead—they surprisingly did not ask for my ID. I figured that if I drank enough, it wouldn't matter where I slept.

"Mind if I sit?" a familiar voice sounded beside me. Dragging my eyes from their TV-staring daze, I turned to find Toby, looking as well put together as he always did in black pants and a button-up shirt. *Did he ever relax?*

"Oh, for fuck's sake. What is with you people? Do you have a sniffer dog on me or something?" I frowned when the memory of his incredibly inappropriate dog surfaced and changed my analogy. "Are you having me followed?" I didn't have my phone, the whole point of the Blackberry was that it was untraceable, and they had had no access to the phone Breaker gave me. They would have had to track me down the old-fashioned way.

"I got a call that you were here."

"So the answer is yes, you're having me followed, or at least watched." I rolled my eyes and turned away, sucking down the rest of my beer then signalling the bartender for new one.

He slid onto the barstool beside me and held up two fingers to the bartender. Two bottles of beer were set in front of us, and Toby handed him a twenty and told him to keep the change.

"I don't need your charity."

He gave me a very solemn smile. "Yes, you do." I hated that there was pity in his eyes. What I hated even more, was that he was right.

"Seriously, Toby, just leave me the fuck alone. I did fine without you Cartwrights in my life right up until a month ago. I'll do fine without you for the rest of it too. I don't want anything from you."

"I want you to tell me what happened to you up there."

I shook my head. "Ask your brother, Toby. He seems pretty set in his opinion."

"I want to hear it from you."

"Oh, I get it. You need to decide whether to get rid of me or not. I can't believe I forgot about the part where the only way you leave the family is in a body bag. How very blonde of me." I kept my voice low but his eyes still slid around to make sure no one was listening.

"That's not what I want," he said.

"Then what's the point of this?"

"Remember when I told you it's my job to look out for the others?"

I nodded, still frowning.

"Well, I take pride in that job. I thoroughly vet every person we work with, I analyse our marks, and perform risk assessments on every plan, right down to the finest details. It's rare that we have to cut and run, but occasionally something goes wrong. In this case, it started when you took the wrong car."

I rolled my eyes. "So, you think I planned this from the beginning too?" It was on the tip of my tongue to tell him it was Abbot who told me to take the stupid car, but I just shook my head and drank my beer. What the hell difference did it make, anyway? Another job I was a part of went sour. Of course they were going to blame me.

"What happened when the cop approached you?"

I sighed. "He asked me to get out of the car."

"Why didn't you?"

"Because I heard his radio confirm the car was stolen. He would have arrested me, and probably arrested Kristian too. I figured if they were busy coming after me then at least he could get away, and the rest of you could finish the job. I quickly called Kristian and told him to meet me at the hotel before the whole thing went down. But when I tried to text him to let him know I was okay, the phone spazzed out and sent the burn message. I thought they'd at least wait a fucking hour, or make sure I was caught before they cleaned out and ran." Pushing the beer away, I got up from my barstool. "I'm actually not thirsty anymore," I said, walking out of the bar and into the cool night air. I pulled the cardigan tighter around me.

"How did you get away?" Toby said, jogging to catch up.

"It wasn't the first time I've had to evade the cops. A bit of fancy driving then a dump and run."

"What did you leave in the car?"

I stopped. *So that's what he's worried about.* I pulled my bag under my arm and opened the pack, pulling out the walkie, the logbook, and the Blackberry. "I also wiped it for prints." I slapped the items into his hand. "Like I said, this wasn't my first getaway." Again, I turned to leave.

"Why were you with the Grim Order?"

Stopping again, I sighed so hard it made my chest hurt. "Pure fucking luck. I was running. The cops were coming. Breaker saw me and helped me hide." I turned around and faced him, those stupid tears burning behind my eyes again. I might have been a thief, but I've *never* been a cheat. "That's it. Then he helped me get home. Well, to the place I *thought* was my home. But, I guess we all make stupid assumptions sometimes, don't we? I assumed that when you all said 'welcome to the family' it actually meant that. Boy, do I have mud on my face now."

"Kristian said he saw you *together*."

"I don't know what he *thinks* he saw, but he didn't see that. The man did nothing more than give me a hug. Oh, and he kissed me on the cheek when I left, so if that's infidelity, then yeah, I'm guilty. Now, if you'll excuse me, I've got to go and find somewhere to waste the next eight hours."

"Why eight hours?"

"Because that's when my ride is coming."

"You're leaving town?"

"Of course. You, of all people, Toby, know I have

nothing left. No licence. No money. No clothes or a place to sleep. Thanks to my stupidity in trusting you guys, I have even less on me than when you took my fucking car. Or did you conveniently forget that part?"

"How is leaving town going to change that?"

"Because that same biker who saved my arse is the only person on this planet who seems to give a shit about me right now."

"Please don't get involved with the Grim Order, Ronnie. Surely you know how dangerous that is."

"Oh my God," I gasped, pressing my fingers against my eyes. "Just fuck off and let me survive. *Please*."

"Let me help you."

"No, Toby. *No*. I've had enough of your help. Just let me go." I pushed against his chest and turned away from him, walking as fast as I could in the opposite direction. I only got two steps before the chink of metal hit the foot-path in front of me. I looked down and spotted a set of keys then stooped to pick them up.

"There's an apartment on the Esplanade," he called after me. "Use it. And please reconsider leaving. I think we can sort this out—seems this is all just one big misun-derstanding."

"I don't give a fuck what it is. I don't want to be with some guy who doesn't trust me."

"He was jealous, Ronnie. He wasn't thinking right."

"That doesn't mean he needed to be an arsehole and attack my integrity."

Toby nodded. "I won't argue with you there. But he cares about you, Ronnie, more than he'd care to admit. If you saw him—saw the man I left to come find you—you'd think that too."

Letting out my breath, I looked at the keys in my hand, noting the address in blue ink on the tag. "Then maybe he should've asked the questions you did, instead of telling me what's what and fucking this whole thing to hell." I turned and left again. This time I wouldn't be turning back.

"Are you at least going to use the apartment?" he called after me

"It was nice knowing you, Toby."

"Use the apartment!"

CHAPTER TWENTY-EIGHT
THE ONE PERSON WHO
GIVES A DAMN

A THUMPING NOISE woke me out of the deepest sleep. I'd been dreaming about surfing and lying in the sun with Kristian by my side. We were laughing and having a great time until he said, "Race you?" Then we ran to the beach shack and he beat me by only a fraction of a second, locking me out. I beat on the door, screaming for him to let me in. But he wouldn't.

I sat up and rubbed my face as another round of banging assaulted the door.

God, that had better not be Toby. I groaned and dragged myself out of bed. I had gone to the apartment in the end, not because Toby told me to, but because I literally had no other options. Plus, I was too tired to walk anymore.

Grabbing the cardigan I borrowed from Holland, I wrapped myself up and went to the door. All I could see when I looked through the peephole was beard.

Breaker.

"How the hell did you get in here?" I asked, pulling open the door and squinting at him.

"Fuck. You look like shit. And you texted me the address."

"I know that. I meant the building. It has a security key." I purposely ignored the comment about my looks.

Half his mouth kicked up to side. "That was never gonna stop me."

I stepped back to let him inside and thumbed over my shoulder. "Just give me a minute to get my things and we can hit the road."

"Whoa, whoa," he said, catching me by the wrist before I got too far. Then he pulled me against his chest and held me real tight.

I tried not to cry. I really did. I even tried to push away, because comfort when I was hurting wasn't a normal thing for me. But he just held on, knowing what I needed better than I did. But it only reminded me of what I no longer had.

The tears pushed hard and fast at the backs of my eyes, flooding against the leather of his jacket and saturating my cheeks. My body felt so weak and incapable. I just wanted to stop hurting so bad.

"How about you tell me what happened? Start from the beginning and don't leave anythin' out."

FOR NEARLY TWO HOURS, I poured my heart and soul out to Breaker's sympathetic ears. Literally starting from the beginning of it all—childhood, right up until my pitiful now. I told him everything, only leaving out details that could compromise the Cartwright's operation because I wasn't about revenge…anymore. I'd lived that life and frankly, it got me nowhere.

"Babe," he said when I was finally done with my tale of woe. "You've lived a hard life. I'm not takin' a moment of that away from you."

"But?" I sniffed.

"But you're in love with the guy. I reckon you need to try and make him see things right." Love? I didn't know if that's what it was. *If it is love, I don't ever want to fall again.* All I knew was that this side of things hurt like a bitch.

"What? No. He should have trusted me, Breaker. He should have believed I'd do everything I could to get back to him. Fuck, I got into a car chase to save him. How could he not understand that?"

He wiped a hand over his beard and sat against the couch, his arm draped over the back of it. "I'm just try'na put it in perspective. If a girl I was crazy about turned up with some dude who seemed a little handsy with her, I might have a similar reaction."

"We didn't do anything wrong," I insisted.

He nodded. "I know that. And you know that. But he obviously saw somethin' we didn't."

Pressing my lips together, I frowned. "I don't care, Breaker. If you can know me for a few days and feel strongly enough about my character that you'd ride inter-state to come help me, why couldn't he feel strongly enough after a month that he'd give me the fucking benefit of the freaking doubt? We were *engaged.* I did everything I was supposed to do."

"Hearts don't make a whole lot of sense, babe."

"Mine is making plenty of sense. It's telling me it's broken and it can't live like this anymore. I don't care what his excuses are. He hurt me, Breaker. I *trusted him and he hurt me*. Do you understand that?"

He nodded slowly. "Yeah. I understand completely. You've gone through a lot of hurt in your life. It makes sense you wanna protect yourself against more."

Looking out the window, I shook my head. "I just…I want to go, Breaker. I want to leave this part of my life so far behind me that I struggle to remember what it was about. Can we do that?"

"Yeah, babe. We can do that."

I got up and collected my things. It took less than a couple of minutes.

"Where's the rest of your shit? That's less than what I sent you down here with. What are you even wearing?"

I pulled at the skirt of the dress Holland leant me. With the big brown cardigan over it, I looked super frumpy. "It's all gone," I said. "Let's just go."

Frowning, he took my bag from me and dug through it.

"Breaker!" I yelled.

"You have no ID. No change of clothes. The clothes you're wearing aren't even yours. Where the fuck is your shit?"

"It's with them," I said. "Can we just leave it? I can sort it all out later. I have some money. I'll be fine."

"No," he said. "We're going to get your stuff. They don't get to keep that too."

"Please, Breaker. Can we just leave?"

"You need your wallet, Ronnie."

"Surely you know someone who can make me a fake ID."

He gave me a look that said he thought I was being a child. "Ronnie."

I rolled my eyes. "Fine. My stuff is at the family house. That is, if he hasn't set it all on fire already."

CLIMBING on the back of his bike, I felt the familiar rumble of his Harley as it sparked to life and roared against the backdrop of the crashing sea. The waves were fierce today, and I wondered how big the surf would be at Bells. It was an instinct that came with growing up beside the sea. Realising that once I left, I may never surf these beaches again caused my insides to twist uncomfortably. I honestly never thought I'd leave this place.

"You know, it's not shit around here," Breaker said before he put his helmet on and took off towards the Cartwright house. Before we reached the end of the Esplanade, another two bikes merged in behind us, creating a V-shaped pattern. It kind of freaked me out a little at first, but then I realised it was for safety. They were travelling outside of their territory and there was safety in numbers. After realising that, it made me feel a little special. He'd made them come with him to take care of me. I didn't care what anyone said about bikers, Breaker was a true gentleman.

When we pulled into the driveway, I noticed the other two bikers drop off and wait by the curb while Breaker and I continued towards the house.

"You need to stay here," he said after he cut the engine and pulled his helmet from his head.

"Excuse me?" I said, fiddling with the strap of my helmet. "That is probably the worst idea I've ever heard."

"Actually, it's the best. You get to avoid the messy scene while I go and get your things. Sound good?" He didn't wait for my answer before he jumped off the bike and strode towards the house. I was about to jump off and chase after him but that little dog came running over and started jumping at my feet. Surprisingly, it made me smile.

"You really are a sick fuck, you know that, right?" I said, kneeling down to scratch him behind the ear. "Do they hate me in there?"

Rogue just panted and enjoyed the scratch.

"Thanks for the intel." I stood up and brushed my hands against the floral fabric of Holland's dress. As pitiful as my things were, I'd be glad to get them back.

Looking at the house, I watched as Breaker spoke to someone inside then stepped in. The shadows didn't give me the opportunity to see who he was talking to, but the fact Alesha came striding out told me it was probably Sam —maybe even Jasmine.

"I'm surprised you had the guts to come back here," she said, stopping a few feet away from me.

"I just want my stuff," I said, folding my arms across my middle.

"And then what? You're leaving?"

"What else would I do?"

She shrugged. "It's just as well, I guess. Kris can get on with his life, forget about you."

I looked away and shook my head. It was interesting how the claws came out and true colours were shown the moment a truce seemed broken. It made me realise that her kindness towards me was just an act.

"You'll be happy to know he doesn't give enough of a shit about me to be bothered I'm leaving. He made that very clear yesterday when he accused me of, well, everything."

"Do you blame him?"

I turned and met her eyes, locking for a beat before I responded. "Yeah. Actually, I do."

"You didn't see him the way I did. You broke him."

"I broke him? That's rich. I saved him. Saved the whole bloody lot of you. But I see how selflessness is rewarded. Forgive me if I go my own way now."

"Saved him? You took off at the first sign of a cop, burned the job, and went straight to a biker gang you were obviously very familiar with. What else were we supposed to think?"

"That I took off to keep the cops away. That I waited until they called off their search then headed straight back to the people I thought were my family. I'm so incredibly sorry that I was misled by *that*, Alesha. But you can be rest assured that you'll have all the Cartwright boys right at your feet the way you like them now I'm out of the way. I know how they revere you. You really must have missed that."

She shook her head. "Jealousy is very unbecoming."

I folded my arms across my chest. "I just call things as I see them. I wasn't taught to be anything other than what I am. And one thing I'm not, is a liar. You can believe what you want, Alesha. I honestly don't give a fuck."

She stood beside me, her arms folded across her chest, looking at the front wheel of the Harley. "What would you have me believe? You're here with him. Isn't that proof enough?"

I turned and met her eyes. "The only thing that's proof of is that one person in this world gives a fuck about me. Tell me, Alesha, what would you do if you were me? If you were cast aside by the Cartwrights and had nowhere in this world to go—no one to turn to—what would you do? Become another homeless statistic, or trust the one person who gives a damn to keep you off the street? How else should I be doing this? You seem so clear on what is right and wrong."

A quizzical look flashed across her face.

"You didn't know that about me, did you? I'm homeless, Alesha. Before I was taken by Kristian and Abbot, I was living in my car. Now, I have no car. I don't even have my things. That's why we're here."

"But why him? If you aren't together, why is he here speaking for you?"

"Because he's better than we are. I wanted to leave, but he wanted to try and straighten things out."

"Why would he do something like that?" *I have no clue. He shouldn't be bothering either. But he cares...*

"Because unlike you, maybe he actually sees some good in me."

CHAPTER TWENTY-NINE
I'M NOT A CARTWRIGHT

"VERONICA." Jasmine's voice sounded curt as she called me into the house. My instinct was not to go, but damn, if I didn't scurry in there like a little mouse. "Your things are upstairs," she said once I was standing in front of her in the foyer. "If you want, go get them and feel free to leave. But if you care about my son, and you still want to be a Cartwright, then fight like one, girl. Fight." *What the hell?*

Fight? She wanted me to stay? Didn't she believe what Kristian said about me? Why wasn't she demanding answers from me like everyone else?

"I believe you," she said, placing her hand on my shoulder and ushering me in.

Damn, if that didn't make me get all choked up. "Really?"

"Yes. Toby does too. Everyone else will agree once they quit judging and actually listen." She fixed her eyes over my shoulder to where Alesha stood with her arms folded.

"If you're cool with her then I am too," she said, dropping her arms with a sigh. "I hope we can put this behind us, Ronnie." Then she muttered something about how many times a person could fuck up. I kind of didn't blame her for thinking that, because that's exactly what I was wondering in that moment too.

Jasmine smiled. "I'm proud of the work you did up there."

"Even the part where I sent out the burn message?"

One side of her mouth quirked up. "Well, we could've done without that part. Holland explained what happened. All in all, you didn't panic, and I don't believe you had any plans to steal the job and take it to the Grim Order. If that were the case, the job would be done already, right?"

"I don't know," I gasped, forcing myself to meet her gaze. "I just feel that maybe this is too much for me. I'm not a liar, Jasmine. I'm not. Or a cheat. I can't stick around and fight for a guy who didn't fight for me. I think I need to walk away."

"I hope it doesn't come to that, Veronica. I see *so* much potential in you, but I understand." Gently, she cupped the side of my face. "He's upstairs."

I nodded then moved past her. I kind of wanted to thank her for feeling confident enough in my loyalty not to order my death, but didn't want to push my luck. There was still a chance she could change her mind.

There was also a chance she was lulling me into a false sense of security just to trap me in the house. *Shit*, come to think of it, where was Breaker? Had they dispatched of him and I was next?

When I reached the top of the stairs without anyone throwing a bag over my head and beating me up, I figured that was my imagination running wild. Breaker was probably in the office talking shit over with Toby or someone. No drama there.

But there was definitely drama here. When I entered the room Kristian and I had shared, I needed to close my eyes. I didn't know if I could look at him without breaking down and screaming the one word that captured everything I'd been feeling. *Why?*

"Ronnie?" His voice was rough, croaky, and broken.

Forcing my eyes to the bed, Kristian lay tangled in a pale blue sheet, the tan muscles of his back rippling as he twisted to look at me. It hurt just seeing him. *Fuck. I think I really did end up falling for him. Stupid girl.*

Kristian looked at me as though he thought I might be a dream.

"Come back to bed. I can't sleep anymore without you. I can't…" Deep breathing turned into a gentle snore as he wrapped his arm around the pillow at his side. The glint of my ring on his pinky caught the light. He was still asleep. If the stench of whiskey was anything to go by, he was probably still drunk too.

"Jesus. Why did you have to be such a stubborn fuck?" I gasped, pressing my hand against my chest. It felt like every wish I'd ever made existed within the sparkle of those diamonds around his pinky. It was so bright and so painful.

If he woke right now and told me he was wrong, would I be able to forgive him?

I didn't know. Maybe.

But the urge to leave, the anger over his words, they felt stronger than any hope I had for my future as a Cartwright. I didn't want to be here because I was a good thief. I wanted to be here because I was loved, trusted… wanted. Kristian's accusations had shot that to hell.

Moving around the room, I collected my meagre possessions, stuffing them in my bag as I stole glances at my sleeping giant.

Why'd you have to make me love you?

It was the first time I'd acknowledged that word in what I felt for him. Even in the privacy of my mind I'd been careful not to label my feelings for him. But in the pain of his rejection, I didn't have the energy to protect myself.

Crouching down beside the bed, I pulled my charging cord from the socket and wrapped it around my hand.

"I ruined us, didn't I?"

Lifting my gaze, we locked eyes on each other. My chest jolted and my emotions surged. I frowned, trying to push them back down. "I hate you again if that's what you're asking." Stuffing the cord in my bag, I zipped it closed and stood. There were so many things I wanted to say to him, but I was too proud to tell him I needed him, that I wanted desperately for him to call me 'doll' and take me surfing again, anything to make it like it was before. Except it wasn't like it was before.

"I don't hate you."

"That just makes it worse, really." I hooked both of my bags over my arm. "You know, your mother thinks I should stay and fight with you, or maybe *for* you. I don't really know…"

"It doesn't look like you plan on doing that." His gaze lowered to my packed bags.

"No. I'm not. Because as far as I'm concerned, a man

who's willing to believe the worst of me when I've been nothing but loyal, isn't worth fighting for."

He pulled back slightly, his jaw ticking like I'd actually slapped him.

"So yes, Kristian, you ruined us. You took something that was perfect and twisted it into a massive mistake. I wish I'd never stolen your stupid Ute. But mostly, I wish I'd never met you, because now I have to live with this hurt for the rest of my life."

"Doll," he started, and I held up my hand. Despite wanting to hear that, the reality felt icky. I just needed to leave.

"I'm going now."

"Where?"

"That really isn't your concern. I don't belong to you anymore." *Fuck that hurts to say.*

Taking a deep breath, I forced my feet to walk away from him. It was probably the hardest thing I'd ever done. It would have been easy to stay, to let him make his excuses and to forgive him, just like I had before with the other men in my life. I'd always dated arseholes. I'd been pushed around both physically and mentally—willing to put up with anything—all because I was *so desperate* to have someone care for me. But the thing living in my car had taught me was that in the end, the one person who needed to love you was yourself. When you're all alone, it's hard to escape your own mind. You analyse everything you did and regret everything you didn't. In those quiet nights when I was too full of regret to sleep, I'd made a promise to myself that I would never let a man push me around again. I'd rather be alone. I'd rather be homeless. At least then I'd know what to expect.

When I got downstairs, all I wanted to do was get the hell out of there. But the wind dropped out of my sails when I heard laughter coming from the back room followed by the deep rumble of Breaker's voice. *At least someone is having a nice time.*

"They're in there," Abbot said from the couch. He had his arms folded and his knee bouncing as he looked at the closed door of the office.

"I'm ready to go," I said, walking towards the room and lifting my hand to knock on the door.

"I wouldn't do that if I were you."

I froze with my fist in the air. "Why? What are they doing?" I frowned when I heard Jasmine laugh again. Actually, she giggled. Jasmine *giggled*. I lowered my hand back to my side.

Abbot shook his head. "I have *never* heard her do that."

Lowering my bags, I leaned against the wall, pressing my lips together, waiting. I really wanted to get out of there. A dramatic exit wasn't so dramatic when you then had to stand around with your thumb up your arse. It was like a little kid deciding to run away but only making it to the front gate because they didn't know how to cross the street on their own.

Breaker's voice caught my attention, a light-hearted tone to it. When Jasmine responded, it had the same teasing quality. Were they...*flirting*? She said something else then suddenly the furniture scraped against the floor and there was a crash. For a second I thought they were fighting—Abbot obviously did too, because he leapt to his feet and rushed for the door only stopping when we heard the telltale *thump, thump, thump.*

"Oh my God," I said, jumping back, my eyes wide as I put my hand over my mouth.

"Are they…" Abbot recoiled in horror.

Thump, thump, thump.

"Holy shit," he said. "They are. They're fucking." He jumped back like the door just burst into flames. "They're in there fucking." He looked at me. "I don't know whether to cheer or be sick. This is fucking *weird*. I need air."

I did too. Breaker certainly didn't waste any time finding himself a willing woman. I supposed there was one rumour about bikers that was true—they fucked around.

Once outside, Abbot set to pacing back and forth beside the pool, raking his fingers through his hair and muttering nonsensically.

"That's an interesting development," I said as I took a seat on one of the pool loungers, figuring I was going to be there awhile. Breaker didn't seem like a quick-fuck guy.

When Abbot stopped pacing long enough to light a cigarette, he looked over at the house then lifted his eyes to the second storey before returning them to me.

"If he's in there fucking my mother, I'm thinking he didn't fuck you."

I shook my head, already tired of answering that question.

He nodded and blew smoke out in a stream. "I knew it. We all told him he was being a dick by the way."

"Alesha seemed to see things Kristian's way."

He shrugged. "Well, me, Toby, Holland and Nate did."

"Nate did?"

He nodded. "Came here late last night giving him an earful after you took off from their place. Kris was pretty drunk and belligerent by then. But I know we got through to him. He wanted to go find you, but he wasn't in the state. Toby went instead."

"Well, he found me," I said, squinting against the sun.

"Did you talk things out with Kris?"

"He knows he fucked up, and that I don't forgive him."

He frowned, looking at me like a puzzle he couldn't figure out. "So, that's it, you're done, leaving?"

I shrugged. "I've got my pride."

"Fuck your pride. You had a misunderstanding. So what? Doesn't mean you just cut and run. Get up there and talk it out, scream it out. Hell, fuck it out. We can have the house thumping in stereo."

"Firstly, that's just gross. Secondly, he should have *trusted* me, Abbot. He asked me to marry him. I know there were no declarations of love or any sappy shit like that, but I thought we were solid. I had started believing in *us*. And I've never felt that way before. He shouldn't have doubted me. I'd done nothing to deserve *that*. I'm a lot of shitty things, but I'm not a cheat."

"And you know what? All of those shitty things you are, we are too. And it's those shitty things that do make us doubt each other and jump to conclusions and fuck things up, because we're *all* afraid of getting hurt. We live a life full of secrets and risk, and sometimes emotions get high. Us brothers have gotten into fist fights over the stupidest stuff and decided we never wanted to speak to each other again. But then we calm down, and we get over it because that's what family does. They fight and they make up, and they do it over and over again. I get that you don't understand that because you never had a proper family of your own, but you need to understand it now. Stay. Fight for what's yours. Cartwrights take what they want; they don't apologise for it, and they don't run away."

"You're missing that one very important thing. I'm *not* a Cartwright."

"Not yet. But you will be. *If* you stick around."

I closed my eyes and let my breath out carefully. "It's that easy, huh?" All I had to do was stay, fight, and get over it. But what if I couldn't? What if I was so hurt and angry that I couldn't be here anymore?

"It's up to you how easy it is. Just know we're with you. We want you *both* happy, and seriously, having a badarse on our team who can fishtail a Land Rover into traffic without tipping or losing control is someone I wouldn't mind keeping around."

Somehow, I managed to crack a smile. "That *was* pretty awesome."

He nodded. "And the drive back really sucked without you. I have an oversupply of smokes because you haven't been around to help me..." He grinned. "Listen, I know I was a total dick in the beginning, and it might have only been a short time, but you've etched your place in this family. You belong here, and you and my jackass of a twin belong together. He's never even cared about a girl enough to fight with me or get jealous of another guy before, so please, try and give *him* the benefit of the doubt. If you leave him, I'll have to watch him mope for the rest of our lives, and we don't look good when we mope. Plus, the mopey face will make him a really shitty wingman. I'll never get laid again. So think of me too."

With a chuckle, I shook my head. "Well, in that case I better get back up there."

"No need," Abbot said, flicking his finished cigarette into a planter. "He's standing right behind you."

Sucking in my breath, I turned around to find Kristian standing under the shade of the house, his hands shoved in his pockets, looking like a gorgeous mess.

"How long has he been there?"

Abbot shrugged. "The entire time." With a smile, he began to walk towards the house. "I'll leave you to it," he said, slapping his twin on the shoulder hard enough to jostle him forward.

Swinging my legs to the side of the lounger, I turned my body to face Kristian. "I thought maybe we could go for a drive," he said, nodding toward the front of the house.

"I don't know," I said. "I'm supposed to leave with that biker I'm supposedly whoring with."

"Is that who Jasmine's fucking?"

I nodded, and he shook his head like he needed to shake his thoughts away.

"Do you think we could get out of here and talk?" he asked, his hands still in the pockets of his jeans as he stepped a little closer.

"I don't know what to say to you."

"Then we won't talk. We'll just drive. Please."

"What about my ride?"

"I think he's already found a way to pass the time."

With a sigh then a nod, I gathered my things, not wanting to be parted from them again, and followed him to where his Ute was parked in the driveway.

"Your door is fixed," I commented, noticing the scratches were all gone.

"Yeah. Jazz had it done while we were in Sydney.

Maybe you won't scratch it up again?" He gave me one of his beautiful boyish smiles.

"I can't promise anything. But I'll try."

He nodded. "That's all I ask," he said, opening the door to get inside.

A nervous pressure tightened my lungs as he closed me in. It wasn't that I was afraid to be alone with him. It was that I was afraid of forgiving him and giving him the chance to hurt me all over again. What was the saying? Once bitten, twice shy? Most people never changed, they were what they were. I'd had enough experience with bad relationships to know that the same shit rolled around time and time again. The only difference was the smell.

For two and a half hours, we drove. Nothing was said besides him asking if I wanted music (I said yes) and me asking where we were going (he said somewhere quiet).

When we finally stopped, we were just outside Healesville. He turned off the asphalt and onto a narrow dirt road that lead to a clearing with some of those squat-log fences in it. Lush-looking trees from the outskirts of the forest surrounded us.

"Exactly what kind of talking are we going to be doing in a place like this?" I asked when he parked the car.

He opened his door and jumped out. "The talk-until-you-forgive-me kind."

Getting out, I slung my bags over my shoulder and looked at all the green. I'd never seen anything like it. The rich fragrant smell of the damp earth filled my nostrils, and the air felt cleansing in my lungs. Birds chirped, and I could hear the croaking of frogs. This was a part of Australia I'd been missing all my life. It was so peaceful.

"This doesn't feel like the place for speaking," I said. "It feels like a place for listening."

He reached out to take my bags, but I refused his help. A couple of hours in a car with him hadn't changed much about the way I felt or my lack of desire to fight. I simply wanted quiet, which was the only reason I followed when he walked. The lure of the forest gave me a sense of escape.

"This way," he said, leading me to a wooden pathway that looked a lot like a plank bridge. It wound down through the forest for at least eight hundred metres and ended when it wrapped around a fairy-tale cabin that literally hung off the edge of a cliff. I felt like I was standing in a dream.

"What is this place?" I asked, trying to wrap my head around the fact that such a place existed. I stepped carefully onto the balcony and bounced, checking the structures stability.

"It's not going anywhere," Kristian said, striding onto the wooden planks with confidence as he inserted the key in the door. "This is my favourite place to come when I need some time to think. It's also off the grid, so it's a good place if you ever need to hide."

Cautiously, I stepped inside and dropped my bags on the floor, still not trusting that we weren't going to go down in a landslide or something. When I reached the opposite side of the building without a death-defying drop, my worries were replaced with awe. *That view.*

Have you ever felt as though you were standing at the edge of the world? I thought I had, growing up in a coastal town with plenty of cliffs to tease the edge of, I felt like I'd stood with Mother Nature at the boundary of her creation.

But that was nothing compared to this place, the tops of trees, the mist rising into the sky, the quiet, the noise, the abundance of life hidden from view but right in front of my eyes. This wasn't the edge of creation. This felt more like the beginning of it.

"What do you think?" Kristian asked, standing just behind me.

"It's beautiful," I said, meaning it. I could already tell that my soul would find peace here, one way or another.

"Hungry?" he asked, and I nodded. I hadn't eaten all day.

Moving into the well-appointed kitchen, he opened the cupboards and looked inside. They were well stocked with long-life items, telling me this place was exactly what he said it was. Although, it could also be an apocalypse cabin, I supposed. He pulled out two cans of Irish stew then emptied them into a saucepan. While that heated on the stove, he shook out some flour and opened a long-life milk, mixing a basic damper with a final pinch of salt. Flattening them out, he cooked them in a frying pan then served it all up at the rustic wooden table in what looked like hand-sculpted bowls.

"I want to apologise to you for the way I treated you yesterday. There was no excuse," he said, pressing a torn piece of the damper into the beefy gravy.

"Apologise? Is that even something you do?"

"Not typically. But in this case, I think it's necessary."

"Well, I don't want your apology. People say sorry all the time, and it doesn't mean a damn thing." I sliced a cube of potato into increasingly tiny pieces with the side of my spoon.

"It does when you realise how very wrong you were. I

know this can't excuse my reaction, but seeing you with him, looking so…familiar…I jumped to conclusions."

"Well, he's obviously a very *familiar* person. He's probably still back there fucking your mother as we speak."

He winced. "I'd really rather not think about that."

"Why not? She's got needs like the rest of us."

"This is seriously the first time we've ever been aware of those *needs*."

Bouncing one shoulder, I chewed on a mouthful of stew then swallowed before I spoke. "Breaker is a pretty charming guy."

"Did he try anything with you?"

I swung my eyes in his direction and held his gaze in place. "No. He doesn't touch taken women. I made it *very* clear that the only thing I was worried about was getting back to my fiancé. I talked about you so much that I must have seemed pathetic." I shook my head and looked away, focusing on my bowl of food. "I feel pathetic now."

"You shouldn't," he said, reaching across the table to take my hand.

I pulled away. "But I do." We ate the rest of the meal in silence.

LIFE WAS BUILT FROM MOMENTS. The overall picture being formed by the tiniest of things. A step left instead of right. The decision to stay or to go. A yes or a no. A pause, a breath, a smile. A kind word when needed. A single moment of hurt. The realisation that dreams didn't come true and people weren't perfect...

"How could you believe I was a cheating whore who sold you out? Within *one* hour, I went from a member of your team—your family—to an unwanted piece of shit." I was lying on the couch while he built a fire, adding the kindling a little bit at a time to help feed the flame.

Picking up a pre-cut piece of wood, he played with the soft fray at the edge with the tip of his finger. "I don't know," he said. "I guess I was freaking out. Everyone was telling me to leave because the burn message came through, then Randy called and said the cars were no good. We *needed* to dump and run. I was fighting with them all, telling them you'd be back. We'd staked out the police station and tuned into their radio, so we knew the search for you had been scaled back. They didn't have anything but a description of you, and they weren't looking for us, so we could afford to wait. We had a van by that point, so we checked out and waited down the road a bit. Then, this couple turns up on a Harley and Sam made a comment about sweetbutts. Is that what the bikers girls are called?" I shrugged because I didn't know. "Anyway, it was a lewd comment and we all laughed. Then the girl gets off the bike and I think, I know that body. Then she took the helmet off and I *knew* it was you. You were smiling like you were having the greatest time. 'She probably hitch-hiked,' Abbot said. But Sam said that would have been too risky, that you must know him. Then you went into reception, and Leesh asked, 'Why would she bring him here, to us?' and the doubt that had already started, grew into this tightness in my chest. Then you stepped outside and it was like you were arguing with him. He grabbed you and held you, and it looked *intimate*. Leesh put her hand on my arm and said we should go. But I wouldn't, I needed to know who this guy was and why you were with him. So I jacked another car and followed you to his house, camped out for a few days, and watched you through the window, saw you coming and going. You smiled with him, held so tight to him on that bike, leaned into him whenever he put his arm around you. I felt like a fool after three days of it, so I came home. I didn't think you'd be coming back."

"Why?"

"What?"

"If you knew where I was and you thought I'd moved on with Breaker, why didn't you confront me, ask me what was going on? Abbot said that Cartwrights don't back down and they go after what they want. So, if you truly wanted me, why didn't you fight for me? I had no way of contacting you, Kristian. I had nothing. I thought you'd abandoned me. Just left me in Sydney with nothing but the clothes—"

"Because of your smile."

"My smile?"

He nodded. "When I saw you with him you were smiling. I'm not such an arsehole that I'd drag you away from someone who makes you happy."

Tears welled in the corner of my eyes and I dabbed at them while laughing. "You are such a fucking idiot. I wasn't smiling because of *him*. I was smiling because I loved riding on the bike."

"The bike."

I sat up. "*Yes*. Have you ever been on a Harley? Those things are almost as fun as surfing."

"The bike," he said again.

I nodded. "The bike, you fucked-up piece of shit." I spoke through tears as I pressed the heels of my hands against my eyes.

"Fuck. I couldn't see straight. And by the time I did, I'd already attacked you."

"I trusted you, you know," I whispered. "I've never trusted anyone, but you gave me…you gave me hope that I could actually be more than an obligation to someone. You made me feel wanted, and then you threw me away. Do you understand that? Do you have any clue how that made me feel? I came to you with nothing. You gave me everything then boom, one doubt, one moment, and it was gone." Even saying that made me feel so vulnerable again. I hated it.

"It doesn't have to be gone. We can go back to what we were. I can promise to never be an arse again."

"That would be impossible," I said.

And he smiled before saying, "Probably."

Then we sat in the quiet and thought. I revisited his words and tried to make peace with his reasons. I put myself in his shoes and imagined how I'd feel in the same situation—if I'd been scared he was in trouble then he turned up looking cosy with some girl, I'd probably assume the worst too. I knew I would.

There was always that problem with assuming; it made an 'ass' out of 'u' and 'me'. And boy, did I feel like one now. If he'd just approached me, if I'd seen him and approached him... All of this could have been avoided.

"DO YOU STILL HATE ME?" Kristian whispered early the next morning. We were lying in the giant king-sized bed, facing each other on our sides. Birds provided the background music and a parrot added a little noise, making the moment feel less like a Disney movie and more like reality.

"No," I whispered back, my hand tucked under my pillow. We weren't touching, and I didn't wake to find him spooning me like he had that first night we were together. He'd offered to sleep on the couch, but I told him he could share the bed as long as he stayed on his side. I had to admit that I was a little disappointed when the sun woke me and he'd actually obeyed my request. My head could be pretty messed up a lot of the time.

"Do you like me yet?"

"No."

He smiled. "Well, not hating me is something. That's where we started, after all."

We'd stayed up till the early hours of the morning, talking until our voices went hoarse. I gave him a blow-by-blow detail of everything that had happened in Sydney, and told him everything about my life that I'd never told anyone. Breaker didn't hear about the abuse. The emotional abuse from my mother, the physical abuse from my first serious boyfriend, the long list of people who'd used me, who I'd allowed to use me because I hadn't felt I'd deserved much more than the crumbs I was given. Then I told him how the fight with him on the beach had caused my rock-bottom moment, landed me homeless, and made me swear I'd never let any man use me and cast me aside again.

He'd shed more than a few tears in my honour, telling me he couldn't even imagine the life I'd led. He promised to make every day together better than the last, it would be his life's mission to show me a better world.

I told him that was too much to promise, and that all I needed was a promise I never had to struggle like that again. He gave me that immediately.

Then we moved to his stories. He spoke of growing up without his father in the house, of memories of his mother being so beside herself with grief that Toby and Nate were the ones who took care of all the boys. Then he went on to detail how they were raised to be thieves and that he knew no other way to live. Jasmine had convinced—or possibly brainwashed—them all into believing that relationships would be their family's downfall. But recent years had shown her undergo a change of heart. She wanted grandchildren, a new line of Cartwrights to continue what she'd built. It sounded as though she was a bit of a mad woman, but the kind of crazy that worked. I was honestly impressed by everything she'd built after her husband went to prison. She had erected her own mountain to sit on top of. I understood the need to keep that kind of effort within the family, no matter how crazy it made you appear.

On top of that, he also walked me through every moment of our Sydney trip—how it felt to see me speed off with a cop hot on my tail. He'd been petrified and said that he only just found me and wasn't ready to lose me yet.

It had been one of those nights that we should have had before now—the airing of all our laundry, the trusting of secrets, the sharing of stories. But we'd both been too afraid, too caught up to risk letting our walls down too far, to let someone in so deep that they saw all the ickiness we tried to hide. But we saw it now.

In the cold light of the day, everything that we were was in the space between us, looking on with hopeful eyes and crossed fingers whispering, "Just make the fuck up already."

Taking a lungful of air through my nose, I reached out and ran my fingers down the side of his face, feeling the prickle of his whiskers on my fingertips. He closed his eyes and hummed. I missed that sound. I missed the way he moaned when we were connected.

"Put your hands on me," I whispered, inching a little closer as his hand slid over my hip then up my side, pushing my shirt a little and landing on my bare skin. I shivered in the most wonderful way. "Why does your touch have to feel like the reason?"

"The reason for what?"

"For everything." My voice was so small, I wasn't sure if he heard it until his gaze softened and he pulled me closer so I was flush against his body. Then he pressed his lips to my forehead and breathed me in.

"You're my reason too, Ronnie."

My breath shuddered as his hand curved along the side of my head and angled me towards his, my entire body rejoicing at the touch of his lips to mine, the tender exploration of his tongue. I sighed with relief, knowing he was the only man who could make me feel this way.

I love him.

"Don't call me Ronnie," I whispered. "Call me doll. I want to be your doll again."

"Doll," he said over and over between kisses.

"Just promise me one thing," I gasped, sliding my hands beneath his shirt, loving the return of his silky skin against my palms. *My God, he's a drug.*

"Anything. I'll do anything to make us right again."

"Ask me next time. If you think something is going on, just fucking ask me and I'll tell you."

He held himself above me and we locked eyes. "I promise," he whispered, returning his lips to my mouth the moment I nodded in reply.

When his lips moved to my neck, I pressed myself against him, wanting to be closer, wanting this whole ordeal to be over and done with so we could get back to being us.

"Fuck, doll, I missed you. I messed up so much, I'm sorry. I really am."

Tears pushed at my eyes as I nodded, accepting that as his truth. "I've never had a real family before, Kristian. Every moment we were apart, I was petrified I wouldn't get it back." My dam burst on the last word, spilling from my eyes.

"Oh, doll," he whispered. "I'm sorry. I'm so fucking sorry."

"Me too," I cried, hating that I was doing it all over again. But this time, he kissed the tears away.

"I will *never* doubt you again, understand me?" he said, his hands on either side of my head. "You will never lose me or my family. Hell, they stuck up for you and called *me* an arse. We're all here for you, and we're not going anywhere." He slid the ring off his pinky and returned it to my finger. "*I'm* not going anywhere. I promise you *on my life*."

"Oh, Kristian," I cried, looking at the ring back where it belonged and feeling so overwhelmed that all I could do was leak tears and snot.

Leaning down, he kissed the mess that I was. "Call me Kris. It's the name everyone I love gives me."

Sniffing, I stopped my blubbering and locked eyes with him. "Love?"

He nodded, his thumb brushing lightly next to my temple. "Yeah. I love you, doll."

"I love you too," I said in a rush, a little afraid of the words that needed to burst from my mouth.

With a chuckle, Kristian brushed his fingers through my hair and down the side of my face, so lovingly. "I'm going to marry you. And once we're married, there is nothing on this earth that's ever going to get in the way of us again. Does that work for you?"

Biting my lip as I smiled, I wrapped my hand around his wrist and nodded. "Where do I sign?"

CHAPTER THIRTY-ONE
LET ME BE YOUR FIRST

"HMM," I hummed and rolled my hips against the warm mouth waking me before it was even light enough to see. "Kris."

"Mmm?" he responded, without pausing, his tongue teasing my opening.

"I was sleeping." I smiled as I said it. We had spent the last few days making up for lost time, hiding out in the forest, just the two of us getting to know each other on a deeper level while making love repeatedly. This was why people in the old days had so many children—no television to distract them.

"You were?" He pulled back a little and blew cool air over my clit, making me squirm and reach for him. "I could have sworn you were awake and begging, 'Please, Kris, make me come with your mouth.'" He pitched his voice to mimic what I assumed was supposed to be me.

My fingers sliding into his hair, I let out a moan when his mouth returned to me, his tongue sliding around my swollen clit, as he sucked.

"That is so not what I sound like," I forced out, half laughing, half moaning as he slid his fingers inside me.

He lifted his head and met my eyes, smiling, my fingers trailing down to his stubbled cheeks from his movement. "That's exactly how you sound, doll. '*Fuck me. Oh yes. Like that.*'"

I gasped and dropped my head back against the pillow as those finger curls did some pretty amazing things to my insides. I couldn't argue while he was pressing all my favourite buttons.

"You taste like fucking heaven," he groaned, working me with his strong fingers before closing his mouth over my clit again.

"Oh God, yes. Just like that." My eyes rolled back as he added another finger and slid all three in and out of me, my orgasm hurtling to the surface, so desperate for release even though I'd lost count of how many times I'd screamed his name in this very bed.

Unable to hold off, I let out a low satisfied moan as my body spasmed then exploded all around his fingers. "Kris-tiiiiiian." It was impossible for me to shorten his name in the throes of ecstasy. Something about the lengthening of the syllables as my back arched off the bed really did it for me.

"Mornin', doll," he said with a self-satisfied smile as he continued to pump his fingers inside me, bringing me down gently.

I stretched my arms above my head and grinned in return. "OK. So maybe I do sound a little like that," I said, making him laugh before placing his hands either side of me and kissing me tenderly.

"I like it. Let's me know I'm doing a good job."

"How could you not? You have a magic touch."

He quirked a brow. "Do I now?"

Nodding, I ran my hands up his sides, making him shudder slightly and release a soft rumble.

"You know, you make some funny noises too."

"Nah," he said, brushing his nose against mine. "I sound completely normal."

Placing my palms against his chest, I pushed until he rolled onto his back and brought me with him. "I'll bet I can make you hiss between your teeth and say, *'Fuck'.*" I lowered my voice to a grunt for the last word, making him laugh.

"I don't do that."

"You do. And you go, *'Ohhh'* and *'Ahhh'.*"

"So, I'm a ghost?"

Grinning, I ran my fingertips down his chest as I slid my way down his body. "Would you like me to show you?"

"If you're about to do what I think you're doin' then I'll make any noise you want. I'll even squeal like a pig."

Wrapping my hand around his already hard shaft, I flicked my tongue over his salty tip, keeping my eyes on his. "Just the hissing and groaning will be sufficient."

He nodded. "OK. And, doll, just so we're clear, I am so fucking hard for you right now. I will pull your hair and come down your throat. I'm not even gonna try to stop myself."

I grinned. "Ohhh. Ahhh."

He chuckled. "Put my dick in your mouth."

With a chuckle of my own, I took his tip inside my mouth, running my tongue around the base of his head. I smiled to myself when he hissed and tensed his washboard abs. Then I drew him in deeper and hummed around his length, my hand fisting his base.

Sitting up a little, he watched me, leaning his weight onto one elbow. "Take it deeper," he murmured, his other hand sweeping across the back of my neck, wrapping the length of my hair around his fingers so he had complete control of my head. Had this been any other man, I would have been worried, but it was Kristian, and I trusted him not to go beyond my point of comfort. He was more about my pleasure than he ever was about his. "Deeper, doll."

Looking up at him, my mouth full of his cock and my heart filled with love, I relaxed my throat and took him as far as I could. His hips moved as he watched his dick disappear, in and out. His teeth clenched. "Fuck," he ground out, pushing a little farther than was comfortable. But not so far I couldn't take it. I loved the view, watching that strong body tense and fight the urge to come before he was ready. He was so in control, his hand guiding my head, his eyes drinking in every detail of the slick movement as I sucked and swallowed.

"I fucking love your mouth," he said. His lips parted, his eyes started to get that hazy quality that meant an orgasm wasn't far off.

I hummed and kept my eyes locked with his as I lowered my free hand between my thighs, wetting a finger with my juices before I slid it between his legs and pressed a finger against his arse. He flinched slightly, his eyes going wide, but then I pressed past that tight bud and he moaned in surprise just before I pushed against his G-spot and he practically squealed through his sudden release.

I swallowed quickly as his cock shot hot cum down my throat and he released his hold on me, gripping onto the sheets and losing complete control of himself. He came harder than I think he ever had in his life.

"Holy *fucking* hell," he yelled when I sat back and wiped my mouth, feeling mighty pleased with myself.

"You liked that?"

"Um, well, I didn't think I would, but yeah. Fucking *wow*."

He picked me up and tossed me back on the bed, quickly holding himself over me before his mouth covered mine, kissing me firm then soft. "My God, I want to fuck you so hard right now, but we're finally out of condoms."

I wrapped my legs around him, moving against the roll of his body, creating a delicious friction. "Then pull out before you finish. Or better yet," I said, twisting beneath him so my back was to his front. "Do it here." I pressed my arse against his already revived cock.

He gulped. "Are you serious?"

I nodded. "It's only fair, since I just surprised you in yours."

"Right now, it's the best fucking surprise I've ever been given in my life."

He slid back as I shifted onto my knees. "You haven't done this before?"

"Shockingly"—I watched him over my shoulder as he shook his head—"I have not. I never pushed for it because of my size, you know."

"Then let me be your first."

He placed his big hands on my hips and slid them all over my smooth skin. I moaned and moved against him. "I'm really nervous about this, doll," he admitted. "I'm worried I'm gonna hurt you."

"You won't," I gasped, reaching between us and taking

his cock in my hand. "First, you're gonna get nice and wet in here." I placed him at the entrance to my pussy and pushed back, taking him inside me as we both groaned, moving together and building our arousal, coating him in my slick juices. "And then"—I was struggling to speak. God, I loved having this man in my body—"you slide back here." I pulled forward, using my hand to guide his tip back, transferring my juices to my arse before I released my breath and pushed against him.

"Holy fuck, doll," he rasped as I took him inside, nice and slow. I moaned so hard, my entire body tingled with a whole different kind of pleasure. I used my own hand to rub at my clit, so wet and slick.

"Oh God, Kris," I hissed as he moved inside me. "I can't hold it. I need to come." I pressed my whole hand against my pussy. The ache and need that accompanied his back-door movement made me desperate for release.

"Fuck. Me too. This is so tight. I'm dying."

Just as I screamed out, my whole body tightening, he withdrew, his dick landing against my lower back, cum spurting over my skin.

"Holy bloody hell and heaven and every other fucking thing in between. That was…"

I turned to him and smiled, panting. "The dirtiest sex you've ever had?"

He laughed. "Uh, yeah. And the best." Grabbing some tissues, he cleaned off my back then scooped me into his arms. "Let me get you cleaned up."

"Sounds perfect to me," I whispered, placing my hand against the side of his face as he bowed his head to kiss me.

"Then we need to pack up and get out of here."

I pouted. "That doesn't sound so perfect."

"I know, but we can't hide here forever. If I'm going to make you my wife, there's a whole bunch of stuff we need to do."

"The trees can marry us."

He chuckled. "I love you, doll," he whispered, nudging his nose against mine.

"I love you too. And fine. We can leave so I can marry you."

"I knew you'd see it my way."

"I CHANGED MY MIND. I don't wanna go back to the real world," I whined, pouting and folding my arms across my chest as Kristian placed the last of our things next to the front door.

"Doll, it's been a week already. If we don't go back now, they'll come and drag us back. In fact, I'm surprised Toby hasn't been here bashing down the door already."

"What is his deal anyway? I think he's great, but he's always up in everybody's business."

"He feels responsible for us all. Nate likes to think he's the next in charge, but if you notice the way Jasmine always looks to Toby before she makes a decision, you'll know that's not true."

"Yeah. I had noticed that."

"Jazz has been grooming him to take over for years. She's kind of semi-retired as it is. More a figurehead these days than the leader. I reckon once this shit is over with Conway's crew, she'll back right off. Take some time to enjoy the fruits of her labour."

"How old is she?"

"Young. She's fifty-seven. Had Tobes when she was seventeen."

"Hmm, like my mum."

"Do you ever talk to her?"

I shook my head. "I burn all of my bridges for a reason, Kris. It's so I'm never tempted to go back."

"So no chance at a reconciliation?"

"None."

He nodded. "OK. Cartwright will be the only name that matters then."

"That sounds perfect."

"We should get going. We have to sign some paper-work to make that happen."

"Then in one calendar month I get to be your wife." I grinned.

He took my hand and pulled me towards him. "Exactly as it should be. Now, let's go."

I pouted again. I loved it here.

"I promise to bring you back here as often as I can. We can spend all our downtime here if you like."

Running my hands down the front of the T-shirt, I let out a happy sigh. "You're making a lot of promises this past week, mister."

Leaning down, he pressed his lips to my forehead. "And I intend to keep every single one of them, soon-to-be missus. But we really need to go, we fucked up the Sydney job, and we still have to plan the transport gig, so there's work to be done."

"OK," I said, pulling the cardigan Holland leant me a little tighter. I kind of hoped she didn't want it back when we returned, because I'd grown to really love it.

Kristian watched me do it, thoughtfulness to his expression. "And I also think I need to take you shopping for some new clothes. Personally, I prefer you naked. But I can't help but notice you have very few things."

"I travel pretty light."

"I know, but you don't need to anymore. I'm gonna give you everything you need, OK? It's my job to take care of you."

Closing my eyes against the emotion that hit me at his words, I rested my head against his chest as he wrapped me in his arms. I had always wanted to belong. Turned out, I really needed to belong to *somebody* too. Kristian Cartwright owned me, and I couldn't be happier.

"OK," I said. "We can go shopping."

"Think we can make a stop in the lingerie department? I still owe you for those sexy little lace things I tore." He wiggled his brows and I laughed before grabbing his hand.

"You think they'll notice if I model them for you in the change rooms?"

He gulped. "That should totally be the first place we go."

"I thought everyone was waiting for us."

He pulled me to the door. "They can wait a little longer."

"What the actual…" Kris's words trailed off as he slowed the Ute to a stop outside the Cartwright family home. Lined up out front were *five* Harley Davidsons. When he cut the engine, the thump of music bounced out of the house.

"They're having a party?" I asked, unclipping my seat-belt. "With bikers? In the middle of the day?" That seemed like everything I would *never* expect Jasmine to do.

But then, she had been fucking Breaker rather loudly when we left.

"Or something much worse." With his brow knitted, Kris leaned forward and opened the glovebox, twisting his hand inside to open another compartment that was hiding a handgun.

"What the fuck are you doing?" I hissed, lurching away from the evil thing. "You can't take that in there."

"What if she's in trouble? What if these guys have moved in and are taking over and we weren't here to stop it?"

I looked at him and flattened my lips into a thin line. "Are you seriously jumping to conclusions right now? Didn't doing exactly that almost break us up?"

"Yes, but—"

"But *nothing*. Breaker would never do something like that. He's not that kind of person."

"How do you know that?"

"Because I do!" Frustration and disappointment reared its ugly head. I didn't want to go through this again. I closed my eyes and took a calming breath. "Kristian, do you trust me?"

He nodded. "With my life."

"Then trust me on this. Put the gun back where it was. Your mother isn't in danger. If anything, she's probably the safest she's ever been right now."

The tension slowly lifted from his chest. "All right. I trust your judgement." He slid the gun back into its hidey-hole.

Letting out my breath, I smiled as I took his hand in mine. "Look at us," I said. "Learning from our mistakes already."

He pressed his lips to my knuckles and nodded. "Let's go see what the hell is going on."

I smoothed my hands over my new jeans and pulled my tie-front shirt down a little. It was the most fashionable I'd been in a long time. After signing our Notice of Intended Marriage form, Kris took me shopping and didn't act bored for a single moment while I tried on shoes and clothes. I'd felt like a princess getting spoilt by her prince. People always said that things were unimportant, but those people had probably never lived a life without. The first time you entered a store and knew you could have whatever you wanted without having to steal it was fucking amazing. The whole back of the Ute was full of my new wardrobe. I would never wear my old cut-offs again.

Holding hands, Kris and I walked to the front door, the sound of someone hooting before a splash met our ears just as we pushed it open.

"Are they having a pool party?" Kris asked as the sound repeated itself. There was laughter and chatter, then a gleeful squeal.

"I think that's exactly what's going on." I smiled, mainly because my suspicions had been right. "Told you there was nothing to worry about."

He looked at me like I might be crazy. "My *mother* is having a *pool party* with a bunch of bikers *during the day*."

I scrunched up my nose. "Good point."

Closing the front door behind us, we headed to the back of the house where people we'd never seen before stood around drinking and shooting pool. There were a few more outside near the pool, some guy with a long grey beard was barbecuing, it sounded like the soundtrack of Supernatural was blaring out of a Bluetooth stereo. I half expected to see Sam and Dean Winchester out there, but found a few Cartwrights instead.

Sam was in the pool with Alesha on his shoulders. She was wrestling with some random busty girl on Abbot's shoulders. Nate was holding a beer while talking to the grey beard at the barbecue, and Holland was by his side, smiling as she listened on. It was surreal to say the least.

The only ones I couldn't immediately see were Jasmine and Toby, but I found him in the farthest lounger by the pool, relaxing with a beer and his dog by his side. I found her when a giggle came out of the kitchen. She was sitting on the bench with Breaker caging her in while he spoke real close to her ear then fed her cake. I felt happiness for her. She had taken a shitty hand and made something for herself. She'd kept her family together throughout some hard fucking years. Abbot had said he'd never heard his mother...*happy* like she'd been the other day with Breaker. And Breaker was the sort of man who would focus his complete attention on the main woman in his life, and I felt that it was about time someone gave that to Jasmine. She hadn't doubted me, so I had nothing but appreciation and respect for her.

"I feel like Marty McFly," Kris said, standing really still with his eyes wide.

"The guy in Back to the Future?"

He grinned. "You know that one?"

I shrugged. "I had a TV. I've seen *some* movies."

But he was right; this did feel like an altered reality.

"Hey, look who it is!" Breaker grinned as he spotted us between a pause in feeding Jasmine. She turned around, all pink-cheeked and stunning, her eyes lighting up when she saw us.

"They're back!" She jumped off the bench and rushed over to us, wearing a bikini and a silky sarong that she'd tied around her waist. Whatever she was doing certainly agreed with her; she was glowing. I felt frumpy near this lithe goddess.

"Mum," Kris said in a cautious voice. He surprised me by not calling her Jazz. "What is happening?"

She smiled then embraced us one by one. "So much," she said. "Come upstairs. We'll talk there."

I waved to Breaker and he gave me a wink before we followed her. I was happy for him too. He was a good man who was honestly more like a father to me than anyone else had ever been. I guess that made me understand the closeness Kristian felt towards Alesha. It was affection, but it was familial as opposed to romantic.

Once upstairs, Jasmine led us to the sitting area and we arranged ourselves on a cream leather couch. Kris kept his fingers entwined in mine as he watched his mother expectantly.

"I see you two are together again," she said, her hands clasped in front of her as she angled her knees towards us.

"Nothing some time and a lot of talking couldn't fix," I said with a smile.

"And as long as I quit bein' a judgy arsehole, we should be good from now on," Kris added.

"Good. I was really happy when Abbot told me you left together and that Kristian had taken the keys to the safe house. It's a beautiful place to heal yourself. The wedding back on too?"

Kris nodded. "In a month. We signed the NOIM this morning. Got a celebrant booked and everything."

"That's fantastic. We'll help make your day so special," she said looking between us.

"Mum," Kristian said, pressing his thumb and forefinger against his eyes. "Please explain what the fuck is going on downstairs."

Calling her Mum was obviously reserved for very serious situations.

"We're free," she stated, eyes twinkling, cheeks pushed high.

"Free? From what exactly and how?" Kris asked.

"From Conway's demands. Breaker used his connections to make them see that the fire was an act of God, and therefore nobody's fault. We don't have to pay anymore."

"Considerin' we all know that fire was set on purpose, that must've been some intense convincing they did. What do they want in return for their *services*?"

"And what about Maree and Dazz?" I asked. They were expecting a job.

"They'll be well compensated. As for the Grim Order, they did it as a favour." She smiled and shook her head at the same time.

"Mother," Kristian warned. "All favours cost something. What do they want?"

She shrugged and spoke in an airy voice. "A favour in return. One day, they'll need help with something that requires our skill set and we'll help them. In the meantime, we're free. It's a good day, Kristian. You should be happy." She looked to me. "You should both be happy. Now we can plan your wedding and get back to business as normal."

Kristian shook his head. "This is insane. We're working to get out of Conway's debt for good, and instead of waiting for that to happen, you got us in debt to the Grim Order instead. What possessed you to OK that?"

Jasmine pressed her lips together and stood, her body language slipping into the authoritarian stance she normally held where it felt like she looked down her nose at you. "It's *one* job. I made the call because I knew it was what's best for this family. The others agreed to avoid pulling that dangerous transport job. I'm sorry you don't feel the same, but you weren't here to object, so Abbot voted for you."

Kristian lifted his hands in acquiescence. "OK. I'm just…I'm surprised."

She placed a hand on his shoulder and gave it a squeeze. "Relax, darling, it's a party. Get your bathers on and go have fun." She bounced her shoulders to the beat of the music and turned to go before remembering something. "Oh, and don't plan anymore getaways for a few weeks. We're still doing that job in Sydney. Word is, they just had two more couples cash out of life and join them. It's a big score, and now we get to keep it all to ourselves." She rubbed her hands together then told us she'd see us downstairs.

Kristian shook his head and slouched back against the leather. "What is happening?" he moaned, running a hand over his face.

Tucking my legs beneath me, I leaned my elbow on the back of the couch as I turned towards him. "Things are changing. I think they might be changing in a good way too. I mean, look how happy your mum is. The others agreed, and I trust Breaker not to fuck us over."

"They're the *Grim Order*. You know the shit they're into."

I ran my fingers through his hair, soothing him. "I know what the papers want us to know, and I know what I learned while I was in Sydney. They're not that different from us. They live by their own code and they're fiercely loyal. Breaker will be loyal to us. I know he will."

Letting out his breath, he turned to face me. "You are so fucking smart, doll. How do you do that? How do you read a situation the way you do? I feel lost just thinking about this."

I shrugged. "I don't know. Survival instincts, I guess. You bounce around as much as I have, you become adept at reading people."

"Come here," he said. So I did and he kissed me. "You think we should join this party?"

I nodded. "Yeah. Let's celebrate our freedom and look forward to being mega rich."

His eyes lit up as a grin spread across his face. "We get to keep Sydney. It's a big score."

"It's a very big score. We're going to have to mow a lot of lawns to clean it."

"Oh, doll. We have a fuck load of businesses to clean it through. Mowing is the least of it. Once we're married, you'll learn it all. It's an art."

I grinned. "I can't wait."

CHAPTER THIRTY-THREE
BAND OF THIEVES

"I HEAR the wedding's back on," Breaker said as he sat on the edge of the pool lounger I was occupying after eating some food and having a swim. The party atmosphere had us all relaxing and making the most of this beautiful day.

"I kind of made you come down here for nothing, huh?" He held out a pack of cigarettes and offered me one, but I shook my head. I hadn't felt like one in a while. He took one out and lit up. "Are you mad I'm staying?" He'd obviously made the most of the situation, but he originally came here on a rescue mission before I disappeared with Kristian for a week.

He shook his head and chuckled. "How could I be mad? Do you see all this? I'm havin' a blast. And I want you happy, babe. That was the whole point of this."

"I'm very happy."

"Good."

"Seems you're pretty happy, enjoying a particular someone the most," I said, nodding towards Jasmine who was animatedly talking to Sam and Alesha and one of the biker's girls. I didn't know her name yet.

Grinning, the light in his eyes danced as he nodded. "That was a surprise. She's really somethin'. The classiest and sexiest woman I've ever known," he said before adding. "No hard feelin's."

I laughed. "Never. I think it's wonderful seeing you both smiling so much. You think it's going somewhere?"

He shrugged. "Who knows? I'm fuckin' smitten. But it's new. And logistics are hard."

"You'll work it out if you want to."

He bobbed his head. "Indeed."

"Is it a little weird though?" I asked, watching Jasmine laugh when Abbot walked over and slung a big arm across her shoulders with Kristian flanking her on the other side. They made like they were about to pick her up and throw her in the pool.

"What? Fuckin' the soon-to-be-mother-in-law of the arse I was chasin'?"

Shaking my head, I laughed. "No. Dating someone with sons around your age."

He laughed. "Babe, how old do you think I am?"

"About thirty-five?"

This time, he threw his head back and laughed a great big belly laugh.

"I take it I'm wrong?"

Nodding, he wiped a tear from his eye. "I'm forty-eight."

"*Forty-eight?*" He kept nodding. "You dirty old man! You were twenty-*one* when I was born."

He shrugged. "It's just a number, babe. Don't get so

caught up on it. As long as both parties are over eighteen, it doesn't fuckin' matter."

"I suppose you're right," I said, studying his face with curious eyes. "I just can't believe you're fucking forty-eight."

"Want proof?" He pulled out his wallet and showed me his ID. "Just good genes, I guess. My mum was a stripper, you know. Great body. Worked the pole into her fifties. She was just as popular as the twenty-somethings."

After confirming his birth date, I handed him back his card. "Ever have kids of your own?"

"Nah. Being someone's daddy was never gonna work for me. I got the snip in my twenties to make sure they didn't slip through."

"So you're taking the fountain of youth with you?"

"I could be. Or maybe I'm a Highlander and this is all just a ruse to cover-up for my immortality."

"What?"

He chuckled and patted me on the knee. "It's before your time," he said, finishing his cigarette.

"I have to ask you something important."

"What's that?" He blew out his final lungful of smoke then put the butt out in the ashtray on the small table next to us.

"What are you going to make them—us—do?" I nodded toward the small group of Cartwrights still larking about.

Following my gaze, he shrugged. "So, do I get an invite to this wedding of yours?"

"That's not answering my question."

"Maybe your question doesn't have an answer yet."

"Sure it does. Your club has the vote on stuff like this, right? You had to sell it to them somehow."

He ran his hand through his beard and chuckled. "Tell you what, ask me to your wedding, and after we've all had our fun, we'll talk business."

"OK. After the wedding. But can you at least give me a hint?"

"Now, that would be cheatin'. But since it's you, I'll leave you with this—we won't be asking you to do somethin' you haven't thought of before."

"So, cars?" I tried, but his look gave nothing away.

"We should quit being so antisocial and join in with the rest of them. I want you to introduce me to this man of yours. I need to make sure he knows to treat you right."

With a laugh, I stood up with him. "So you don't want kids, but you're happy to act like my father?"

He pressed a kiss on the top of my head. "You were lost. I found you. You're family now."

When I looked up at him, my bottom lip wobbled. *Two families?* For a girl who never had one, suddenly I was in abundance.

"Ah fuck. You're not gonna cry on me again, are you?"

I shook my head. "No," I said, blinking rapidly as a single tear splashed down my cheek.

Breaker chuckled and pulled me into a hug. "You're a baby."

"This is your fault," I said. "You're the one being nice to me."

"So I should be mean?" I felt his chest bounce with laughter.

"No. Nice is good. I just need to get used to it."

"Tryin' to steal my girl?" Kristian's voice—filled with

jest—cut into our embrace. He was obviously past his jealousy over Breaker's and my closeness. *Thank God.*

Breaker released me but kept one arm around my shoulders. "Not anymore," he said, grinning at me then meeting Kristian's eyes. "You're a lucky man, Kris." He held out his hand, which Kristian shook.

"Incredibly," he agreed, his eyes happy as they met mine. "It's not every day you find a woman willing to put up with all your shit and love you for it."

"Ain't that the truth, mate." Breaker slid his arm from around me, seamlessly passing me to my fiancé. Kristian and I laced our fingers as I leaned into his side. There was so much happiness living inside my chest that I felt like I might burst.

"Listen, I want to thank you for what you did for Ronnie," Kristian said, his expression growing serious as he met Breaker's eyes. "I let her down and you stepped in when you didn't need to. You helped make things right. I know I've been a really shitty fiancé—a shitty person, actually—but I can admit when I'm wrong. And I was wrong about you."

"Ah shit," Breaker said. "That's real big of you. But I don't think you were wrong about me at all. I was totally after your woman. If I hadn't met Jasmine when I did, I'd have taken this pretty young thing home with me and ruined her for all other men. So, I reckon you should be thankin' your mum, not me."

Kristian's face was completely impassive while Breaker spoke. I wasn't sure if he was trying hard not to hit him, or if he was trying not to laugh.

Kristian cleared his throat. "I was actually talkin' about helping her evade the cops and get back to Melbourne. I bloody well knew you wanted to fuck her, mate. I saw the way you looked at her. Although, I respect you for not putting the moves on her. You could have really taken advantage and chose not to."

Breaker grinned. "Call me a fool, but I believe in honour among thieves. We don't steal each other's women."

"Not that he could of," I put in, feeling that my voice needed to be heard in amongst this testosterone fest. I was surprised they weren't bumping their chests together and swinging their dicks from side to side to see whose was biggest. I was pretty confident Kristian would win. "You guys seem to be forgetting my honour. I don't, nor have I ever, been a cheat. So how about we go and get a beer and let this all go? And, Breaker?"

"Yes, babe?" I looked at him and saw a man who was truly honourable, formidable, yet altruistic. It felt like he'd entered my life at the exact moment I needed someone like him. I'd never known a man I respected more.

"Will you give me away at our wedding?"

Kristian had a momentary look of confusion before he relaxed by my side and gave my hand a reassuring squeeze.

A massive smile spread across Breaker's face. "I would be fuckin' honoured," he said, looking between the two of us and just nodding happily. "This is so great." He hugged me then went to shake Kristian's hand but went in for a hug instead. "So great," he said again. Then he headed back to Jasmine, telling everyone he was giving away the bride. They cheered.

"He's interesting," Kristian said with a smile, watching

over the rest of the party as they congratulated Breaker on his new role.

"He sure is," I said through a laugh. "Did you know he is *forty-eight*?"

"Serious?"

I nodded. "Forty–fucking–eight."

"Goin' after a twenty-seven-year-old." Kristian chuckled. "Good on him for tryin'."

"He was never going to win against you. As far as I was concerned, it was you or no one. That's how deeply I love you."

"Ah, shit. Now you're gonna make me cry."

Placing my hands on his chest, I lifted up on my toes. "Don't cry. Just kiss me, you fool," I whispered.

"I love you, doll," he whispered as he wrapped his arms around me and did just that.

LATER THAT NIGHT, when the party had calmed down and only the mess remained, the Cartwrights sat around in the living room, eating home-delivered pizza and relaxing. Breaker had left earlier with his men and their *guests*, telling Jasmine he'd be back later in the night after he finished up some business.

That just left the five brothers, two sisters-in-law to be, one mother-in-law to be, and me.

"What are your plans for the wedding?" Alesha asked, picking off a slice of pepperoni and popping it in her mouth. We'd had an individual talk earlier in the night where she admitted she jumped to conclusions out of protectiveness for Kristian.

"Why are you so protective over him, anyway," I'd asked, and she'd shrugged before explaining.

"Because he was the first person other than Sam to treat me like I was a member of this family. Before becoming a Cartwright, I never felt like I was wanted anywhere. I was always in the way. But he went out of his way to include me. Taught me to surf. So, he means a lot. All the brothers mean a lot. They're a special bunch."

That short explanation had really opened my eyes. Now I understood that she'd been a lot like me—lost then found by this band of thieves who were the most loyal and loving group. I made a promise to myself that I'd spend more time getting to know her. There was no space for any sort of animosity in our group. Especially petty stuff like jealousy.

"What do you reckon, doll?" Kristian looked toward me in expectation. I'd obviously missed what he'd said.

"About?"

He laughed. "Getting married on the beach where you stole my car keys. If it wasn't for that, we never would have met."

I nodded enthusiastically. "A wedding on the beach. I think that sounds perfect."

CHAPTER THIRTY-FOUR
SOPPY AS FUCK

"AND IF WE do your hair like this, the makeup will make you look like a sea goddess," Alesha said as she brushed pearlescent highlighter on my cheekbone. There was only one week until the wedding and we were at the beach shack, doing a trial run of hair and make-up. Before she was a Cartwright, Alesha was a make-up artist, so we were utilising her skills, and my God, if I didn't look amazing once she'd finished with me. Kristian was going to get a boner in public over this.

"I love it," I breathed, turning my head in the mirror so I could see the light reflecting off my dewy glow.

"I am so jealous of how stunning you are," Holland said, playing with the ribbon on the silk flower crown I would wear instead of a veil. The wedding was very boho chic: loose flowing dress, hair out and wavy, no shoes, or excess jewellery. It was going to be simple and perfect, just like Kristian and me. We had been planning to marry as soon as the twenty-one day cooling-off period had lapsed on our Intended Marriage notice, but planning needed a little longer so we extended it to two months instead.

"I think you're more jealous of there being another wedding you can't drink at," Alesha teased.

"That is seriously the worst thing about pregnancy," Holland said. "All the alcohol bottles at the house think I've forgotten them. They don't want to talk to me anymore. It's quite sad really."

"I suppose you can make up for it after the baby is born," I said. She was now in her second trimester and starting to show a little. Although she kept complaining that she just looked fatter than she already was. I kept arguing it wasn't true, but that's just what girls did, I supposed. It was fun being a part of it. And it made me think about when Kristian and I might be ready for kids. Not right away, because we needed more time with each other first.

"See, that's the problem," she said, handing the flower crown to Alesha who placed it on top of my head. "Once I pop the baby out, I won't be able to drink because I'll be breastfeeding for a good six months to a year. So that's almost two whole years of no alcohol. I didn't think this through."

Alesha laughed. "Just think of the rewards, Holl. You'll have a little rug rat who'll love you unconditionally. Just like in *Dating the Enemy*, how the baby is the real true love."

"Oh, I love that movie. We're watching that tonight. Along with *Pretty Woman*," Holland said. For the last six weeks, we'd been watching every pop classic movie they could think of. I was now able to understand jokes about

Clueless, *Empire Records*, *Mallrats*, and *Chasing Amy* to name a few.

"We've already watched *Pretty Woman*," I said, which sent both of them into a quoting marathon that made me laugh. I could tell they'd known each other for a really long time, and I thought it was wonderful that best friends had married brothers. In the past, I'd always felt like a third wheel, or worse, an intrusion into any friendship groups. Yet with these women, somehow I fit in. I was included. How was it possible that one moment in time— one quick decision to grab of a set of keys—would open more than just a door to a Ute?

"Oh my God." Holland stopped all of a sudden, her eyes wide as she looked at me. "Are you crying?"

I was, but I shook my head. "No. There's just mascara in my eye," I said, blinking rapidly as I fanned my hands at my eyes. It was crazy that I was crying so much, but this was also new to me—having people around to care—I was struggling to control my emotions most days. It was getting to the point where I wanted to punch myself in the face for being a sissy.

"Oh, honey," Alesha said, giving me a hug before walking me over to the couch to sit. "What's going on? Are you worried about the guys? They'll be back soon. We already know the job was a success." With Holland pregnant and wedding preparations to attend to, we three stayed behind with Toby for our protection while Jasmine, Nate, Sam, Abbot, and Kristian went to Sydney to finish our job. They'd called early in the morning to say they were on their way back with a very heavy safe after a detour to pick up somebody to open it. We were about to be very wealthy people.

"No. They're fine. I know they're fine. I'm not even upset. I'm just happy. My world is so full, and I'm crying because I never expected it."

Holland knelt in front of me and looked closely at my face. "Are you pregnant?" she asked.

"What? No." I sat a little straighter, dabbing at my eyes with the tissue Alesha handed me. "Not that I know of."

"When was the last time you had your period?" Alesha asked, and I shook my head.

"It's pretty erratic. Maybe a bit before Sydney. But it's not unusual for it to be this long, and Kristian and I always use protection. Except…" I thought back to that time at the cabin when we'd run out. He'd gone in bare before transferring to my rear. "Can you get pregnant on precum?"

"Yes," they both said in unison.

"Oh."

"Are your boobs sore?" Holland asked. "Because mine got really sore." I pressed my hands against them. *Ow!*

"Yes. I don't know. I could be imagining it now."

"We need a test," Alesha said definitively. "I'll go get you one. Wait right there. I'll be back." Scrambling off the couch, she grabbed her bag and dashed out the door, leaving Holland and me alone.

"We might have cousins together," Holland said, biting her lip as she looked at me with a smile.

"Holy shit," I gasped. This was so not what I was expecting. "I can't be a mum yet."

"You'll be fine. We're here to help you. All of us. Did you know that Leesh and Sam are starting IVF after your wedding? If you're pregnant and IVF works for them, then we might all have cousins really close in age. Wouldn't that be exciting?"

"We just need Abbot and Toby to knock a couple of girls up then the Cartwright population will explode," I said, feeling a little ill despite trying to sound positive.

"That would be something." She chuckled. "We just need to be sensitive toward Leesh too. If it turns out you are pregnant, she'll act super happy for you because that's who she is. But behind it all, she'll hurt. She wants a baby too, but she can't do it on her own." Wow, I couldn't imagine how hard that must be for her. But I did know what it was like to feel bereft of something others took for granted.

"OK. So if it's positive, do I play it down?" I was so nervous, I didn't really know how I would play it regardless.

"Oh no, she'd hate that. I'm just saying be sensitive. Don't exclude her but don't brag—does that make sense?"

I nodded. "I think so."

Then I felt light-headed and she tried to keep me talking until Alesha got back. I think I was in shock a little, because I didn't know what to do when Alesha handed me the bag.

"Go pee on the stick," she said.

"Oh, yeah," I said, heading toward the bathroom and pulling the box from the bag. When I was done reading the instructions, it seemed I just peed on the little stick then waited a couple of minutes. Nervously, I did just that, putting the cap on the stick before I took it out to Holland and Alesha.

"What did it say?" Alesha asked anxiously.

I held it out. "I don't want to look."

Holland took it and held it so she and Alesha could see.

They looked at it, at each other, then at me. "Do you want the good news or the bad news?" Holland asked.

"The bad news?" I said, more as a question as nerves swirled in my stomach. Was it weird that I was afraid of them saying I *wasn't* pregnant? I hadn't wanted to be, but still...

"You need to quit drinking," she said.

"And smoking," Alesha added with a smile. "Because the good news—the great news—is that you're pregnant. Congratulations."

My hands shook. "What?" My breath caught in my chest.

Holland turned the stick to face me so I could see the two pink lines. "You and Kris are having a baby. Or babies. You never know since he's a twin, right."

"Oh my God." I sat down. Right where I was in the middle of the floor and took my flower crown off my head.

"Aren't you happy?" Alesha asked, crouching to sit in front of me. Holland joined her at my side.

"I...I'm shocked. I didn't expect this to happen so soon."

"I think babies like to follow their own schedule," Alesha said. "I remember my sister-in-law—the one married to my brother—couldn't get pregnant for ages for her first, but her second one wasn't even planned. I think fate likes to step in."

"A baby," I said, placing my hand against my stomach.

Holland and Alesha both nodded, smiling. "A baby."

"What're you all doin' on the floor like that? Calling the Watchtowers? Don't you need a fourth for that?" Abbot asked, dropping his bag as he walked in the house, Kristian following right behind him.

"What's wrong?" he asked immediately, his voice laced with concern as he rushed to my side. Alesha and Holland moved away, collecting their things and insisting that Abbot helped them take it to Alesha's van.

Once they were out of the house, I uncurled my hand from the test. "Oh shit." He dropped on the floor in front of me. For the next few minutes we just sat in silence, staring at it.

"If you don't want it, we can—"

"I do," he said, quickly cutting me off. "Do you?"

I nodded. "I think so."

"When did we—"

"The cabin."

His mouth formed an O. "But I didn't—"

"Seems you've got some pretty powerful precum."

"You can get pregnant from that?"

"Looks like it."

"Wow. I have super sperm."

"Maybe I have super eggs."

He grinned. "We're pregnant."

"We are." Tears fell down my cheeks. "At least I know why I keep crying so much," I said, wiping them away.

"You cry all the time, doll. You're soppy as fuck."

I pushed him on his shoulder. "So are you."

"Come here," he said, pulling me to his lap and giving me a tender kiss. "Are you OK?"

"Yeah. I'm OK. I'm shocked. But I want kids with you, so…"

"OK. Then there's something I want to do." Standing, he helped me up then led me outside to where Abbot was talking to Alesha and Holland…and Nate, and Sam, and Jasmine, and Toby, and some red-headed woman. They were all there and looked our way the moment the door opened.

Kristian grinned then threw his head back and yelled, "We're going to have a baby," at the top of his lungs. Then he picked me up and spun me around in a circle, laughing.

We're having a baby.

CHAPTER THIRTY-FIVE
FOR A GIRL LIKE ME

SINGLE MOMENTS. They made up the story of our lives and were the basis of our memories. A perfect moment could produce smiles for years to come, a disappointing moment, tears.

There had been many moments since becoming a part of Kristian's life that had done both. I'd shed tears during some of my darkest moments. But mostly, I'd smiled because I'd found the one thing I never imagined having—family. Now, I had something worth fighting for, something worth loving. And the feeling of being loved in return, well, it was better than the thrill of stealing a hot car and chucking the perfect doughy.

It was everything.

Kristian was everything.

He drove me nuts sometimes, he made me laugh other times. But most of all, he made me feel wanted.

Letting out my breath, I read over my vows one more time before folding them and sliding them in the hidden pocket of my dress. I'd put everything I felt into those words, and I hoped I could say it all without becoming a blubbering mess. These pregnancy hormones were really doing me in. I cried whenever I saw that commercial for fabric softener where the kid thanked his mum for making his towel all cuddly, but he couldn't say the word, and it was so darn cute. And that wasn't the only thing I cried about. Anything sentimental happened and I was a mess. Breaker showed up a while ago, all ready to walk me down the aisle—he looked so handsome in his shirt and pants— and he gave me a corsage that matched my flower crown. A *corsage*! I blubbered like I was just handed the Oscar and was giving my speech. Poor Alesha had to do my make-up all over again, so I was told to sit quietly, and no one was allowed to talk to me until it was time to go.

I would not cry again.

"Almost ready? The bikes are outside."

I nodded. Did I mention my ride to the wedding was on the back of a Harley? A small group of the Grim Order were escorting the bridal party to the beach. They had decked their bikes out with silk ribbons and they looked perfect.

Alesha picked up my flower crown and handed it to me. I was going to loop it over my arm until we arrived at the beach and I could remove my helmet.

"Thanks for doing all this," I said to her. "You've been amazing."

She squeezed my shoulder. "I'm looking forward to having another sister."

My eyes watered. *I am not going to cry*.

"Let's go make you a Cartwright."

When I got outside, Holland smiled and gushed about how wonderful I looked. She had been talking to a family friend called Sloane, a tall redhead staying at the Cartwright house because the safe they'd brought back from Sydney was old and complicated. She was some kick-arse lock specialist that was *somehow* connected to *someone* from Jasmine's old crew (the details obviously weren't shared with me). All I knew was that Jasmine and Abbot had taken a detour on the way back from Sydney and returned with Sloane. The first time I met her was when Kristian had taken me outside and yelled about my pregnancy. I wasn't sure how great she actually was at safe cracking because it was still closed, and our money was still trapped on the inside. But, whatever, it just meant that there was an extra bridesmaid to balance things out. From the way Jasmine insisted on including her in the wedding as Abbot's date, I had a feeling she also thought Sloane was the solution to Abbot's single status. But, I didn't know about that. Abbot seemed pretty intent of being wild and free. Jasmine would be better off pushing her on Toby if she wanted to see more of her sons happily married....

Besides being a little uptight, Sloane seemed OK. She was a bit of a tomboy and she made a to-do about the bridesmaid dresses, but I honestly wasn't too fussed. I just wanted to get married and focus on bringing this baby into the world. Everyone else could worry about Sloane.

"You're real pretty, Ronnie," she said with a smile, surprising me. "Best of luck today, hey." She punched me in the arm, and I tilted a little off balance.

"Thanks, Sloane," I said, reminding myself to always give her a wide berth if I didn't want a bruised arm in future.

"Absolutely stunning," Jasmine beamed, her hand resting against Breaker's chest. They had barely spent more than a few days apart since they got together a little over two months ago. Breaker was actually looking into transferring to the Melbourne charter so he could be close. He kept saying he needed to stick around because he was worried about retaliation from Conway, but there hadn't been a blip on the radar, so we were more than sure he was staying because of Jasmine. The man was head over heels, and so was she. I was a little worried about what they were going to ask the Cartwrights to do in return for all the protection though. I knew that Breaker saw Jasmine and me as family, which meant he saw all the Cartwrights as his family. We'd seemed to be accepted into his biker family too, which was fine personally, but business-wise, it could make things way more complicated than growing poppies ever would. But I supposed that was a worry for tomorrow. Today was all about my wedding.

"Pretty as a picture," Breaker agreed as I moved to stand with them.

"Quit being so complimentary." I laughed. "You'll all make me cry again."

The photographer moved around and took pictures of us together, me on my own, then all of us on the bikes. I smiled so much my cheeks hurt. Then we were on our way, flying down the streets with passengers of passing cars gawking at us like tourists.

"Nervous?" Breaker asked when we arrived in the car park above Winkipop.

"A little," I said, smiling as he helped me put the floral crown on my head.

"You'll do great. He's a lucky man." He kissed me on the cheek.

"I think I'm luckier. Look at all this." I gestured around

us, to my bridal party and those gathered on the beach. So many faces that had entered my life because of my connection with Kristian. I'd said in the beginning of our relationship that he took up all the space in the room, but his love took up all the space in the world. I was full because of him, and he had stopped searching because of me. We'd found what we were looking for.

After taking a few more photos, we gathered around the top of the wooden stairs that led to the beach. Bridesmaids went first, then Breaker and I followed, one step at a time.

In the distance, I could see my man, standing and watching my every move with his brothers standing to his side. They were all so handsome in their white shirts and sand-coloured pants—well, I assumed they were all handsome. The only man I could focus on was mine. Kristian's gaze locked with mine, a smile mirroring my own. *I can't wait to be his wife. And then I'll be the mother of his child. Incredible.*

My heart hammered in my chest, my smile so wide I could see the apple of my cheeks as we walked along the sand and up the aisle created between the fold-out chairs our guests sat on. But we could have been alone. The whole world fell away around us, and all that I could see was him, waiting eagerly.

"She's all yours, mate," Breaker said as he transferred my hand to Kristian's and took a seat in the front row.

"I think she always was," Kristian said, taking hold of both my hands and bringing them to his lips. "We're getting married, doll."

"Did you think this is what you'd be doing that day you chased me up those stairs after I stole your keys?"

He shook his head. "I had no clue. But, man, it's been a wild ride so far. Ready to turn this into our greatest adventure?"

I nodded. "I will literally follow you anywhere."

Placing his hands on either side of my face, he bent down and kissed me. "I love you so much."

"I love you too," I whispered, feeling so much calmer from his touch.

The celebrant cleared his throat. "Well, now that we've got the kiss out of the way, how about we move on to the vows?"

With a chuckle, we turned to face him, hands and hearts wrapped together as we delivered our vows.

Since that moment I took his car to the moment I got caught scratching it up, I'd never dreamed that a man I had such contempt for could be the salve my heart needed to feel whole again. But, he'd taken me into his life, and with every moment from that point on, he gave me light and love and purpose. Now, looking back, I was thankful for the shit that came before our story because without it, we wouldn't have found, or needed each other. I never wanted to be apart. I had love, and it came in so many different forms. A mother-like love in Jasmine, a father-like love in Breaker. *Brothers*—often pains in my arse more times than not, but my God, I loved them. I'd never known how much having an elder brother rocked until I met those crazy-arsed boys. *Sisters*. Two women so incredible that they'd not only taken me under their wing as big sisters, but they'd included me in their tight-knit friendship.

I had family.

With so many people in my corner, not only did I not

feel alone or unwanted anymore, I felt like I had purpose. Drive.

Worth.

And then there was the man in front of me. My extraordinary, sexy-as-fuck, soon-to-be husband. There were no words that would adequately express how much I loved that man. He gave me everything. Believed in me. Loved me. And I knew he'd keep loving me long after this day. Just like he'd love the baby in my belly, and any others we created in the future. Life was finally happening, and it was wonderful.

For a girl like me, it didn't get any better than that.

The end.

Next in the Cartwright Brothers Series, *Fool's Errand* featuring Sloane and Abbot. Keep reading for the cover reveal and blurb!

I'M a tomboy through and through. But when the man of my dreams walks through my door, I want to be all woman. Too bad I have no idea how….

SKIRTS AND DRESSES, makeup and perfume. Things I knew nothing about. With my red hair and lanky body that I hid in shapeless clothes, I was just one of the guys. The 'cool' girl they hung out with but never dated. Not that I had time for relationships. Ever since my grandad passed, I'd been working day and night to try and salvage his failing business. I had no idea how he'd kept it afloat for so many years. His books said he had an abundance of clients, but my phone was barely ringing. I was in danger of losing the locksmith business he'd spent his lifetime building.

Then he walked in.

I noticed his height first. Then his smile, his eyes, his body… Wow. I could barely think just looking at him and slipped on the grinder, sending a flash of sparks in the air. *I guess you can say sparks literally flew when we locked eyes.*

Except they didn't, well, not for him. He got right down to business. He wanted my grandfather for a job. When I said he wasn't available, he turned to leave.

Wait!

I couldn't let him leave. I *needed* the work, bonus points if it meant I got to spend more time around the Adonis in front of me.

To get the job, I may have oversold my qualifications. I also may have oversold my knowledge of my grandad's past.

You see, I only knew him as a locksmith. But it turned out, he used to be a cat burglar—the fastest safe cracker in the business. I guess that explained where the money came from. I was running a front without any cash to launder.

Now, I was following his footsteps, all while pretending I knew what I was doing. I really didn't. Thankfully Google did, and bonus, my dream guy, Abbot Cartwright was supervising my work. Downside to all this? I was pretty sure Abbot had figured out I lied my way into this job. If I didn't get this safe open soon, I stood to lose a lot more than my business, I stood to lose my life.

Suddenly, I wished I knew how to bat my eyes and play the damsel in distress to get him to take pity on me and maybe let me go. But that wasn't how the Cartwright family worked, and I already knew too much...

preorder now - **books2read.com/u/bOAyYA**

For more information on upcoming releases visit

www.lillianaanderson.com/preorders

ABOUT THE AUTHOR

Bestselling Author of the Beautiful Series, Drawn and 47 Things, Lilliana has always loved to read and write, considering it the best form of escapism that the world has to offer.

Australian born and bred, she writes New Adult Romance revolving around her authentically Aussie characters with all the quirks you'd expect from those born Down Under.

Lilliana feels that the world should see Australia for more than just it's outback and tries to show characters in a city and suburban setting.

When she isn't writing, she wears the hat of 'wife and mother' to her husband and five children.

Before Lilliana turned to writing, she worked in a variety of industries and studied humanities and communications before transferring to commerce/law at university.

Originally from Sydney's Western suburbs, she currently lives a fairly quiet life in suburban Melbourne.

For more information on Lilliana and her work:
www.lillianaanderson.com
info@lillianaanderson.com

To join her Facebook reader group and talk books
https://www.facebook.com/groups/438800699591852

facebook.com/LillianaAndersonAuthor

twitter.com/confidante_lili

instagram.com/lilliana_anderson

ACKNOWLEDGMENTS

AS ALWAYS, there are people to be thanked! Many sets of eyes go in to the creation of each of my books and I am very grateful to every person who takes time out of their lives to help me.

To **Tammie Lee, Cyndi Hart-Duplessis, Marissa Burns** and **Julie Chippendale,** thank you so much for beta reading and giving me excellent feedback to work with. I can't tell you how much I appreciate your sage advice. To my editor, **Marion Archer**, I thank you all for your keen editing eyes and funny comments. **Margaret Neal**, **Mel Williams** and **Lisa May**, thank you for helping to proof the final copy—hopefully we got them all!

To my team of sharers, you're all so wonderful. I don't ask you to do what you do, but you see something I post and share it far and wide. I'm eternally grateful. Thank you all so much. I love you all!

To every blogger and reviewer who has an ARC or has signed up to post about my book – I thank you too. You are the first step to announcing my work to the world. No author can do this without you xoxox

Also, a big thank you to my husband for putting up with my bitching and moaning and his unending support and encouragement.

Thank you to my kids for being so patient while I stare at a computer screen and finish typing out a thought. I love that you all come and sit with me while I work just to spend a bit of extra time with mummy!

And of course – thank you to all of my readers. You are the most important of all. Without you, I would be writing to the crickets.

Mwah! xoxox